Dasamuka

Junaedi Setiyono
Translated from the Indonesian by
Maya Denisa Saputra

Dalang Publishing

Dasamuka
Originally published as *Dasamuka* in 2017 by Penerbit Ombak, Yogyakarta, Indonesia
(ISBN 602-258-432-2)

Copyright © 2018 Junaedi Setiyono
Translation copyright © 2017 Maya Denisa Saputra

Cover design: Tasya P. Maulana
Book Production by Cypress House
Editor: Tara Austen Weaver
Indonesian literary advisor: Manneke Budiman

Dalang Publishing LLC

San Mateo, California

www.dalangpublishing.com

dalangpublishing@gmail.com

ISBN: 978-0-9836273-1-9

Names: Setiyono, Junaedi, 1965- author. | Saputra, Maya Denisa, translator.
Title: *Dasamuka* / Junaedi Setiyono; translated from the Indonesian by Maya Denisa Saputra.

Description: San Mateo, California: Dalang Publishing, [2017] | "Originally published as *Dasamuka* in 2017 by Penerbit Ombak, Yogyakarta, Indonesia (ISBN 602-258-432-2)" --Title page verso. | Includes glossary of terms. | Summary: A love story set in the intricate political world of Javanese royalty under Dutch and British colonial reign. A Scottish academic, journeying to the island of Java in 1811, is quickly drawn into the struggle of the Javanese people as they fight back against colonial powers and their own corrupt aristocracy. -- Publisher.

Identifiers: ISBN: 978-0-9836273-1-9 | LCCN: 2017939394

Subjects: LCSH: Java (Indonesia)--History--19th century--Fiction. | Indonesia--History--19th century-- Fiction. | Java (Indonesia)--Politics and government--History--19th century--Fiction. | Indonesia--Politics and government--History--19th century--Fiction. | Sultans--Java (Indonesia)--History--19th century--Fiction. | Java (Indonesia)--Kings and rulers--19th century--Fiction. | Imperialism--Java (Indonesia)--Fiction. | Imperialism--Indonesia--Fiction. | Netherlands--Colonies--Asia--Fiction. | Great Britain--Colonies--Asia--Fiction. | Romance fiction. | LCGFT: Historical fiction. | Political fiction. | Romance fiction. | BISAC: FICTION / Historical. | FICTION / Political. | FICTION / Cultural Heritage. | HISTORY / Asia / Southeast Asia.

Classification: LCC: PL5089.S4835 D3713 2017 | DDC: 899/.22133--dc23

Printed in the United States of America

Dasamuka

South China Sea

MALAYSIA
Kuala Lumpur

PULAU-PULAU
NATUNA
BESAR

BRUNEI

MALAYSIA

Strait of Malacca

SINGAPORE
Singapore

Equator

Kalimantan

Sumatra

Selat Karimata

Java Sea

Merak
Selat
Sunda

Jakarta

J a v a

Bali

INDIAN   OCEAN

PHILIPPINES

Sulu Sea

Celebes Sea

PACIFIC
OCEAN

Halmahera

Molucca Sea

Strait

KEPULAUAN
SULA

Sorong

Biak

Massar

Sulawesi
(Celebes)

Jayap

Buru

Ceram

Ambon

Papua

Banda
Sea

Banda
Islands

KEPULAUAN
ARU

umbawa

KEPULAUAN
TANIMBAR

Dili

Arafura Sea

Merauk

Flores

EAST
TIMOR

EAST TIMOR

Sumba

Kupang

Timor Sea

Darwin

AUSTRALIA

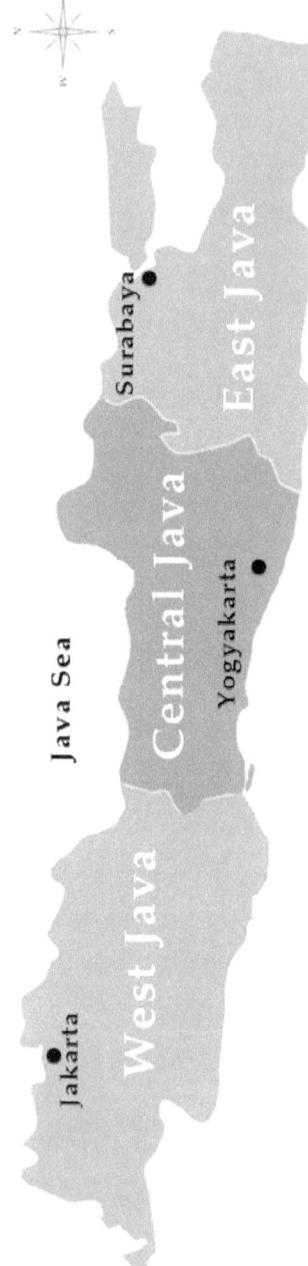

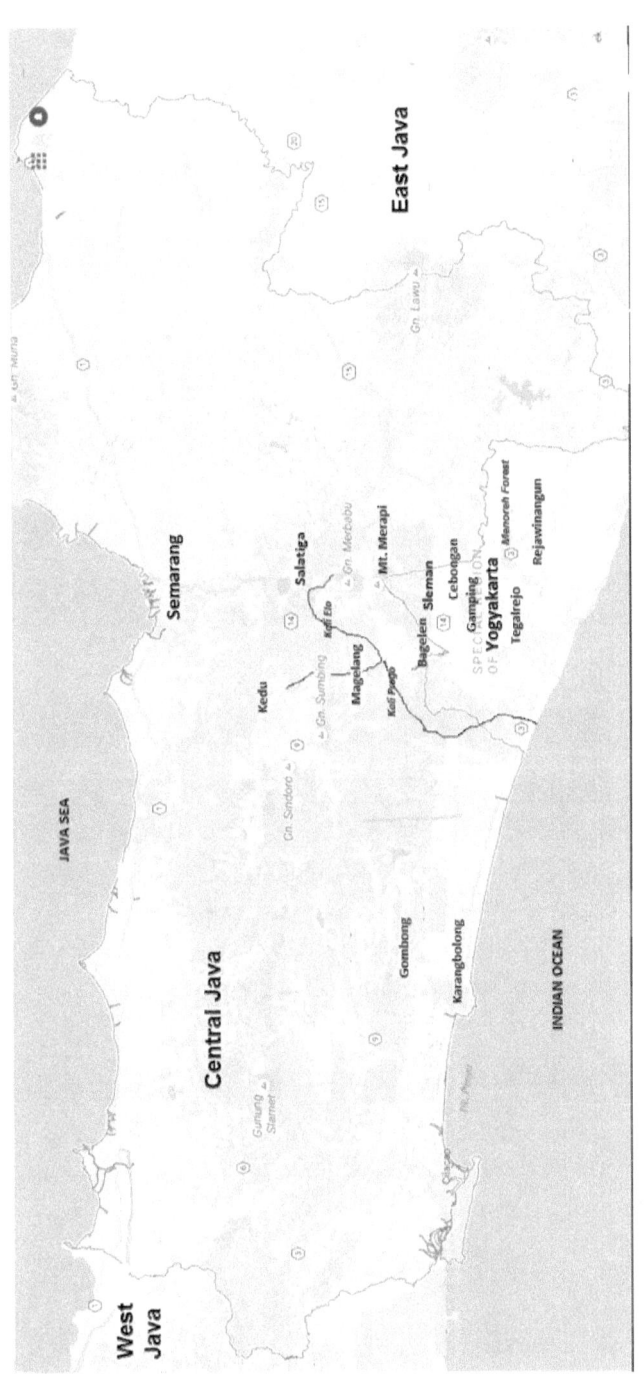

TRANSLATOR'S NOTE

I never imagined that I would be given the opportunity to translate a novel. Then, early last year, an email from Ms. Lian Gouw of Dalang Publishing arrived in my inbox with an offer to translate *Dasamuka*, a love story set in the intricate political world of Javanese royalty under Dutch and British colonial reign.

The story is narrated through the perspective of a Scottish scientist, instead of a native or Dutch character; yet, *Dasamuka* is a rich source of Javanese culture. As someone born and raised in Bali, an island geographically close and culturally related to Java, I found it relatively easy to grasp the depth of the unique Javanese philosophies and cultural aspects offered by the author.

While any attempt to bridge different cultures always poses a unique challenge, I hope my translation of *Dasamuka* has managed to accurately relay the author's blend of imagination and historical facts and rendered the main character—a charismatic, complex young Javanese man named Dasamuka—properly.

My deepest appreciation goes to Ms. Lian Gouw for the guidance and inspiring spirit that has sustained me throughout the translation process. I also thank Mr. Junaedi Setiyono, the author, who through this work has shed new light on many Javanese philosophies. His availability during the development of the translation was invaluable.

And last, but not least, I thank Dalang's editor Tara Weaver, whose deft yet sensitive editing skills assures the Western reader an entertaining, comprehensible transport into a different time and culture through story.

Maya Denisa Saputra

January 2017

Dasamuka

The knowledge seeker met him
who had been given mercy
and had been taught knowledge by God

They walked along together
until they met a child
and he killed the child right away

The knowledge seeker could not help asking:
"Why did you kill the child?
He did not bother anyone, did he?"

He withheld his answer
to reveal it at the proper time:
"His parents are pious folks
"he will cause them to become sacrilegious
"that is what I fear for them."

Adapted from the Holy Qur'an,
Sura XVIII: Kahf, verses 60-82.

Chapter 1

RADEN WAHYANA

On August 3, 1811, a fleet of one hundred English warships entered the Sunda Kelapa territorial waters under the command of Admiral Stopford. I was on board of the *HMS Harpy*. If the sailors on the ship decks were under command of a high-ranking navy official, I had come to the island of Java under the direction of a scientist and motivated by a death wish.

Conquering the Dutch military, who had settled in Batavia, was not as difficult as I had expected. The English troops proved to be far superior to the Dutch. Because I had no previous military training, my bravery at the front line was considered impressive. I owed my courage to the fact that I had come to Java running from the mockery of people I truly loved, and I wanted to die. I did not want to die by committing suicide, however. I wanted to die honorably, as a warrior.

After the British navy claimed the harbor, I set foot for the first time on the island of Java, which experienced sailors believed to be the most fertile island in the world. Unlike most crewmembers, I was neither perplexed nor surprised by the lush greenery.

Setting foot on Java's shore was like entering John Leyden's magical world. The renowned scientist, who had seeded my curiosity about this part of the world, had told me of the tall, slender coconut trees with their fan-shaped fronds. Swaying in the brisk sea breeze, the trees seem to offer a gracious welcome by providing relief from the blinding sun. Shorter trees with sprawling canopies made the coconut trees seem even taller.

As I ventured away from the ship, I noticed groups of dark-skinned men sitting under the trees. Most of them wore only a loincloth; their protruding collarbones and ribs were clear signs of serious malnutrition. Remembering Leyden's emphasis that Java was one of the most fertile places in the world, I figured they must be a part of the underprivileged that are found all over the world.

I wondered what the city would be like.

———•◆•———

I had met Leyden at the University of Edinburgh. The first time I heard him explain his research, my friends roared with laughter. They would realize too late that the man who appeared disheveled and sounded boring was a genius.

I did not know what exactly Leyden meant by "world view," but I was certain he would change my outlook on life. While the other students were busy covering their yawning mouths and wrinkling their foreheads, I raised my hand to ask a question.

"Isn't it a waste of energy, thought, and money to study an area notorious for its vicious mosquitoes, insects capable of taking the lives of a ship's entire crew?" I asked. My uncle had been residing in Java, and I had heard stories of the trials he had experienced, many of them having to do with local wildlife.

Leyden smiled. "The future of our world, young man, can be found on an island where trees grow as tall as the sky, an island where sunshine shows its optimal usefulness. The future of such a region is the future that belongs to all of us."

This exchange started our relationship. Perhaps Leyden took a liking to me because I was the only student who showed interest in the paper he had so carefully prepared. Whatever the reason, I considered myself fortunate to have made the acquaintance of John Casper Leyden, a preeminent scholar of Far East studies.

>———•———<

Leyden approached me one afternoon, as I sat alone beside a pile of books on a garden bench in front of the university's gate.

Only shortly before, I had sent a golden ring flying into the Water of Leith, the river that cleaved the city of Edinburgh. For a moment, the ring floated in the air. It did not last longer than a split second, yet the glitter burned an everlasting memory in my eyes. The token of my engagement to Ailsa now sank soundless into the calm, flowing water. If there were any sound, it would have come from my cracking chest, or perhaps from the muscle in my right arm, which trembled as I gripped the iron bridge rail.

I had wanted Ailsa to be honest with me. I had forced her to speak straight—not holding anything back, not covering anything up. But when she did, I was unable to listen to her frankness. I wanted to fling the cup in front of me at her, but my hands were paralyzed.

"I have thought it completely through," she said. "I have thought not only for days, but for weeks before deciding. I must marry him. *I must.* I hope you can understand." She looked me straight in the eyes.

I felt as if I were looking at the marble statue of a Greek goddess, a beauty so distant it made the time we had spent together feel far in the past.

I wanted to respond, but my tongue had turned stiff, and I was speechless. Chewing my lower lip, I touched my frozen face with equally cold hands.

Ever since my mother passed away, my father had tried to fill the void by living the life of a rake. As I grew older, we had several confrontations regarding his debauchery, but I never thought he would make Ailsa, my fiancée, the object of his lecherous behavior.

I rose, staggering, then left hurriedly, walking backward. When I ran into a chair behind me and knocked it over, I turned around and I ran, out of breath, along the banks of the Water of Leith. My only haven was the University of Edinburgh, where John Casper Leyden found me sitting by myself on a garden bench.

Without any hesitation, he took a seat next to me and patted my shoulder.

"I've struggled for quite some time to evoke students' interest in my paper about the Far East. Alas, until now, I haven't had a bit of success." Leyden had a concerned look, and his voice was hoarse.

"I'm sure that, in the next few years, many students will be interested in knowing more about what you call 'the emerald of the equator.'" I felt obligated to respond supportively.

"Please join our expedition—if you're interested," he said. "An organization is willing to facilitate students and scientists interested in Far Eastern affairs, especially the islands referred to as The Netherlands' East Indies, and the Royal navy will give us free transportation."

"I will join you, sir," I said, without a further word.

John Casper Leyden gave me a hard look.

"Just call me John." The scientist smiled, his eyes boring into mine. "I have no right to ask why you suddenly decided to join this expedition. The important thing is that, after arriving on Java, you'll proceed to write a complete description of *bronjong*— or is it *branjang*? Oh well, it is the Javanese way of punishing criminals that I explained in my paper." Leyden's thin hair blew about his head as he spoke.

I agreed immediately. I was sure Leyden was aware that my mind was unstable. He had previously suggested I join his expedition, but I had told him I could not consider it for another year or two, until I was married and able to provide my wife with a home to live in. My change of heart certainly raised questions, but he was sensitive enough to not inquire further.

I did not know if joining Leyden's expedition was the right decision. However, I was sure that if I did not leave quickly, I would be imprisoned for killing someone—or hospitalized for a failed attempt to commit suicide. Or I might be buried, after having been successful in my attempt.

I did not want to place myself into any of these situations, as each would prove my weakness. Those who considered me weak would certainly roar with laughter, and Ailsa and Jeremias would be among them. The thought of them together made me join the expedition.

I boarded one of the hundred warships that would journey to the island of Java. When we encountered violence, I ran amok, and fearlessly fought the Dutch soldiers who, to me, all represented Jeremias—the Dutchman who was my father and had betrayed me. My recklessness solicited admiration from a lot of British soldiers who valued their lives and had families they loved.

When an officer offered to enlist me with the British army on Java, I immediately accepted. I did explain, however, that I was a researcher for Doctor Leyden and had been assigned to work on Java. I was fortunate to be able to cite the University of Edinburgh as my alma mater. The soldiers respected Edinburgh academia like they respected their captain.

While the English prepared for further missions, I lived as a soldier on the British warship. The war had ended, and there were only minor battles still to be fought. The Dutch, who were believed to be very powerful in the Indian Archipelago, were as weak as a unit comprised of veterans. I wondered if this meant that the native kings and their armies were even weaker than the Dutch.

Before we were called to fight against the remaining stubborn Dutch troops in Semarang, to kill or to be killed, I received news that John Casper Leyden had passed away on August 28, and was buried in Batavia.

I heard from an officer that Leyden's death had been caused by Batavian fever, which he had contracted while digging, with great enthusiasm, into the holdings of a library that was supposed to have a valuable manuscript about the Far East World. It took only three days for the fever to take the doctor's life.

The death of the great scientist caused a commotion among the high-ranking officials, including the Governor General and Mrs. Raffles. The latter was deeply affected by the scientist's death. She wrote a beautiful poem that was engraved on John Casper Leyden's tombstone and made the governor jealous.

John Leyden's death forced me to decide between returning to Edinburgh or staying in Java. While contemplating my decision, I saw a war prisoner who resembled Jeremias stagger as he was pushed into a detention room. I decided to stay on in Java; I had no desire to encounter my father or my fiancée.

I told the officer who offered me passage back to Europe that I planned to see my uncle in Rejawinangun, an area in Central Java that was under the jurisdiction of the Yogyakarta Sultanate, then under the reign of Sultan Hamengkubuwono II.

My connection with a respected British scientist, as well as being a young Edinburgh academic, gave me enough credibility for the government to provide me with a horse-drawn carriage and a coachman who spoke a little Dutch. During the four-day journey to the Yogyakarta Sultanate, I learned from my coachman that most Javanese disliked Dutchmen. I, too, disliked all Dutchmen, but could not deny that my hatred for them stemmed from the mere existence of a certain Dutchman I was related to.

My uncle's residence, known by people living in the area as *loji Tuan Thomson*—Mr. Thomson's mansion—was located about three miles east of the *Keraton*, the sultan's royal palace. I had great difficulty finding the mansion, with its teak doors and a roof made of wooden shingles. If I had not mentioned John Leyden and the University of Edinburgh when asking for directions along the way, I am sure I would not have found it. Every British officer I met respected the two entities I mentioned. Even after his death, the famed scientist was still able to help me.

Uncle Thomson's mansion looked similar to those of the princes in the Yogyakarta Sultanate, and I noticed the house was filled with various kinds of tropical plants. The greenery did not grow only in the front yard; plants also thrived on the porch and in the vestibule. Dogs, cats, pigeons, peacocks, and turkeys were allowed to roam freely in a yard spacious enough for a dozen children to play hide-and-seek.

Upon my arrival, Harvey Thomson treated me more as a guest than a family member. I had expected this. Our kinship was established by records rather than personal interaction— Uncle Harvey had left Scotland for Java when I was only a child. It took a few days before he was able to relax in my presence.

One morning during breakfast, Uncle Harvey peered over the rim of his coffee cup. "At first I thought you had come here with the sole purpose of visiting your uncle," he said. He accentuated the words *sole purpose*, but indicated he was joking with a wink.

"I really did only come here to see you," I fibbed, afraid that telling the truth might make him feel unimportant.

"I heard that you came to Java to perform a duty for our kingdom. If nothing else, you came to assist someone who has a royal assignment." My uncle, the second husband of my mother's eldest sister, took a few sips of his coffee, then leaned back in his chair. He folded his hands behind the nape of his neck and gave me a hard look.

"It is more important to visit you, Uncle. Assisting Dr. Leyden was simply a means to bring me here." Perhaps I would not have said this if John Leyden had not perished from fever in Batavia.

"Didn't the British Empire sponsor your trip, and won't you have to account to them regarding the use of the funds?" Uncle Harvey asked. I could tell he was trying to find out why I was stranded on the other side of the world.

"The Edinburgh for Far East Club and the *London Times* sponsored me," I said, trying to set him straight. "The British Empire only provided passage on one of their ships. Like you, Uncle, I want to live on this island."

I would not have spoken these words, had my heart not been destroyed by Ailsa's marriage to my father, but my statement seemed to plunge my uncle into deep thoughts.

"Daisy will be coming home tomorrow," he finally said. "She's been in Buitenzorg for almost a week. Governor Raffles is landscaping the area surrounding the palace, and she's involved with starting a large botanical garden there." Uncle Harvey rested his hands on the arms of his chair. I kept silent, and my uncle continued talking about his daughter. "She's engrossed in tropical plants. That's probably why she doesn't want to go back to Scotland."

My mother had mentioned Daisy to me when I was much younger. From the tone of her voice, I knew she was very taken by her. Considering our ages and education, she figured Daisy and I would make a good couple. We were not blood related—she was a child from Uncle Thomson's previous marriage. At the time, I had not paid much attention to my mother's story, and Ailsa had erased what little interest I might have had in Daisy.

"Any educated person dreams of working in their field, Uncle. I'd like to get to work as soon as possible." I quickly tried to change the topic of conversation.

Uncle Harvey raised his eyebrows and smiled. "See, I am right! You came to Java for your work, not to see your uncle."

I grimaced. "Without my assignments to write reports for the club and the newspaper, it would be impossible to visit the territory of this sultanate for an extended time, let alone settle here."

"In that case, I will arrange for you to see Resident Crawfurd, tomorrow. It will be easier for you to do your work if he is well acquainted with you." With a nod, my uncle ended the conversation.

———•◦•———

It was easy for Harvey Thomson to connect me to the Resident of the Yogyakarta Sultanate. After I was introduced to John Crawfurd, it was not too difficult to sustain the relationship and nurture it into an even closer bond. As it turned out, Resident Crawfurd was a scientist who had also graduated from the University of Edinburgh. We had the same alma mater. Crawfurd was an academic, not a military man.

During a discussion of my plans, Crawfurd said, "We need to prove that the British are different from the Dutch. We certainly support your research regarding the bronjong. Your findings about Dr. Leyden's object of curiosity might very well prove to be valuable input for the manuscript of an agreement between the English government and the sultanate. This political document is currently being drafted." Crawfurd was clearly supportive.

"I want to start my research by learning the Javanese language first," I explained, following the advice of the late John Casper Leyden. "Can you recommend someone suitable to be my teacher?" Crawfurd's familiarity with the government community would enable him to point me in the right direction.

"I'll write you a letter of introduction and have an officer escort you to see Den Wahyana, an educated Javanese aristocrat. He's a reliable interpreter." Resident Crawfurd walked to his desk. I knew he was in the process of writing a book about the islands in the Indian Archipelago and their inhabitants; a pile of manuscript pages covered his desk.

"By the way," Crawfurd looked up from the letter he had just written, "you're staying with your uncle now, aren't you?"

Crawfurd had reminded me of an important thing: I needed to find my own place. "Yes," I said sheepishly, "I am. Hopefully, I'll find a place of my own soon."

Crawfurd rose and handed me the letter. "I believe there are a few empty houses in our government complex," he said. "Let's go take a look."

"Will I be allowed to live there without being a government employee?" I asked, as I followed him out the door.

Crawfurd threw me a scrutinizing look. "You can help me edit my manuscript," he said dryly.

The house was less than half a mile away from Crawfurd's office. "It's not exactly a *loji,* or a *puri*," Crawfurd turned the key and pushed the door open, "but it definitely is more than a *gubug*." He smiled.

He must have noticed my puzzled look and quickly explained, "A loji is a mansion—like your uncle and many of the Javanese royalty live in. A puri is the next step up. It's more castle-like; most princes and very wealthy noblemen live in puris. Now, a gubug is where you'd find the man off the streets. A gubug has no solid walls—the walls are woven bamboo mats, and the roof is made of rice- or coconut-leaf straw. It usually has a dirt floor."

I took a quick look around. The small brick house was furnished with the bare essentials and provided me with my immediate housing needs. Armed with the letter of recommendation, I was now set to embark on my adventure. I wanted to focus on my research of bronjong. I wanted to honor John Leyden's request to study and describe whatever bronjong or branjang was. Hopefully, it would also help me forget Ailsa.

After waiting for almost a week, I finally met Den Wahyana, the interpreter Crawfurd had recommended. The educated Javanese I met spoke Dutch well—and although I did not speak Dutch fluently, I could make myself understood. Thus, it did not bother me that Raden Wahyana had a much better command over Dutch than English.

I was impressed by the way this nobleman carried himself, as well as with the manner in which he spoke. Unlike most Javanese, including the aristocrats, he did not bow when standing before me. He didn't seem to have a problem looking me straight in the eyes.

"I am not an expert in English—I speak only a little, just enough to prevent me from being a rude guest." Den Wahyana spoke English with a Dutch accent.

"I speak just enough Dutch to keep me from being an inattentive host," I told him. Our conversation reminded me of

Jeremias Kappers, a Dutch scoundrel who was my father and I felt a knot forming in my stomach.

"I can look for an interpreter who is better than me, a competent linguist," Den Wahyana offered.

"I don't need a linguist. You're good enough."

"In that case, we can learn together," Den Wahyana said tactfully.

"I speak a little Dutch," I repeated.

"All right then. We will combine Javanese-Dutch-English." Den Wahyana smiled. It was the first Javanese smile I'd seen that felt sincere. I responded with a laugh and hoped he thought my laugh to be truthful.

"Where do we start our lesson?"

"You definitely don't intend to understand immediately all the different phrases the Javanese use in their daily conversation, do you? This would be impossible." Den Wahyana gave me a quizzical look, then continued. "For the first lesson, let's look at how to approach Javanese people in a manner acceptable to them. It is important to use the proper polite expressions when first meeting a Javanese person."

Den Wahyana taught me that *Raden,* or *Den* for short, was used to refer to address both royal men and women. If one needed to be specific, a woman would be *Raden* or *Den Rara* before marriage and *Den Ayu* after marriage. Den Wahyana paused before continuing his explanation. "A man would be *Raden* or *Den Mas.* Ayu means beautiful in Javanese. And Mas comes from the word *emas,* meaning gold."

While I was still trying to digest his lesson, he introduced me to yet another form of address. "*Ki,*" Den Wahyana said, "is used for middle-aged men who are not of royal blood." *Nyi* is used for middle-aged women who are not of royal blood. *Kiai* is for addressing an Islamic religious teacher."

Den Wahyana was right: addressing an individual properly was an integral, and complicated, part of the language.

———•••———

I visited Den Wahyana almost daily to learn Javanese. He lived in Tegalrejo, a fertile and prosperous district near the city of Yogyakarta, owned by a prince. After I learned the Javanese way of expressing myself politely, the next lesson was dedicated to learning verbs.

By using a combination of Dutch and English as the medium of instruction, Den Wahyana's language lessons were like learning to walk on a creaking, swaying bamboo bridge. If I hadn't been trying to forget a woman by learning a language, I would have quickly lost my enthusiasm. Instead, the challenge spurred me on. It was, after all, not my main goal to learn Javanese quickly. I was trying to forget Ailsa and avoid Daisy.

———•••———

It turned out that my fear of having to face Daisy was unfounded.

The first time we met, she stood, bent at the waist, over the red flowering shrubs in the garden at my uncle's mansion. Her slender, athletic figure very much resembled Ailsa's. Compelled to approach her, I moved closer and heard her talking to the plants. It was evident she treated them as if they were humans whose well-being she was fully responsible for.

She straightened herself when I said hello and quickly threw me a penetrating look. After she returned my greeting, she simply returned her attention to the plants.

My subsequent visits convinced me that I had nothing to fear from encounters with Daisy. A dashing young man visited her regularly. I assumed their relationship was that of a young man and a young woman weaving a tapestry depicting that ceremony in the life of human beings: marriage.

Once, I came upon Daisy as she was absorbed in her greenery in the front garden. "It seems you're busier by the day," I said.

She looked up briefly and wiped the perspiration off her forehead. "I have to make sure the plants I'll take to Buitenzorg are healthy. I don't know how many days it'll take the carriage to arrive there during this rainy season."

Suddenly curious to find out more about her male visitor, I teased her, "It doesn't matter how many days you spend on the road, if you don't travel alone."

Daisy looked at me. A childlike innocence filled her hazel-colored eyes. "My father has been reluctant to travel any distance lately. Will you accompany me?"

"When the young man who often visits you finds out I'll be taking you instead of him, he'll definitely come after me."

"Pieter? The lieutenant?" Daisy laughed and shrugged her shoulders. "He's just a friend." I wasn't sure how sincere she was.

Chapter 2

Ki Sena

The Javanese language lessons that Den Wahyana taught were beginning to deviate from the agreed-on topic. One day, we found ourselves discussing the *Europesche ambtenaar,* the Western civil service official. The address referred to both his civil as well as his military background. Perhaps my language teacher was influenced by my story about Pieter, the lieutenant who frequently visited Uncle Harvey's house in Rejawinangun.

"After the British occupied Java last September," Den Wahyana explained, "the Dutch personnel who worked here were given a choice: either go home to The Netherlands or stay and work for the British government. Pieter and his friends chose the second option."

"Do you know why people like Pieter are disliked by most Javanese?"

Den Wahyana remained quiet for a while. Seemingly deep in thought, he rubbed his thighs. Then, as if he was reminded of something, Den Wahyana rose and started to pace.

"Pieter was one of those who hunted Raden Rangga and his followers." Den Wahyana paused before continuing. "I hope I'm not mistaken, but that's why he's hated by most Javanese here."

"They hunted a man? To be killed?"

"Yes, they did," Den Wahyana said. He looked away and then continued. "In the end, Raden Rangga died." Den Wahyana swallowed and a deep sadness overtook him. "He died the death of a Javanese hero."

Raden Rangga was a rebel from Madiun, a nearby city, where he functioned as the regent. He was respected by the Javanese and, consequently, hated by the Dutch. Den Wahyana spoke of the man with great reverence.

"Den Rangga was always struggling to fix things that, in his opinion, were wrong." Den Wahyana explained.

"Can you please tell me what exactly he struggled for? What was the quest that caused his death?" I had become interested in Den Wahyana's hero, the late Raden Rangga.

"I've a good idea." Den Wahyana smiled. "If you are really interested in the story of the rebellion that exploded last year, just before Governor Daendels exiled Sultan Hamengkubuwono II, I will take you to meet someone who knows exactly what happened. The man is one of the rebels. You will not only hear a great story, you will also learn something about the Javanese language and history that should not be forgotten." Den Wahyana's enthusiasm was contagious.

"Very well, I'll try to understand the story." My agreement was motivated by my adventurousness, not by being a scientist. While I was very proud of being an academic, my actions were propelled by feeling rather than thought.

I had to wait for several days before I was able to meet the man who would tell me about the famous rebel, Raden Rangga.

Ki Sena, one of Raden Rangga's commanders, was now jailed in the Yogyakarta Sultanate. He was not confined in a regular prison together with thieves, street robbers, bandits, and the like. His visitors had to pass through extremely strict security.

My meeting with Ki Sena was the result of Den Wahyana's hard work. Not only had Den Wahyana arranged for my escort, he had also convinced the prison authorities that I was merely a spirited scientist. I was beginning to wonder if Den Wahyana was really just an interpreter or if that role hid another identity.

———•◆•———

When Den Wahyana and I visited Ki Sena, we had to bend to enter his dismal prison cell. A ray of sunshine tumbled through two ventilation holes, each the size of a fist in diameter. In the dim light, I saw Ki Sena seated with his head bowed. He paid no more attention to Den Wahyana and me than he did to the scoop of corn and rice mixture placed on a teak leaf next to a coconut shell filled with water.

After a while, Ki Sena raised his head. He looked at us, one by one, then very slightly smiled at Den Wahyana.

Ki Sena had good posture, the look in his eyes was calm and composed. Even though he was thin and looked pale, I was sure that, under normal circumstances, he would have been fit and handsome. The way he looked warned me not to underestimate him. His calm, unhurried voice, forced me to listen carefully to every word he spoke.

Our conversation was an extremely interesting Javanese language lesson. In the language classes at the University of Edinburgh, this way of learning was called the authentic-naturalistic learning technique. It was frequently more successful than the mere use of textbooks in the classroom.

Ki Sena spoke in the Javanese language form called *krama* because Den Wahyana had greeted him and started the conversation in this second-to-the-most-polite form of speech. The fact that they spoke in krama implied they were not close. It was difficult for me to understand Ki Sena. Only after discussing his stories later with Den Wahyana, was I able to understand them fully.

Ki Sena said he had met Raden Rangga for the first time when he visited him in his loji. The meeting was the result of conflict between the then Dutch Governor General Daendels and the charismatic Raden Rangga. The new regulations the governor general had implemented impacted the protocol of the Dutch colonial government. No longer were Dutch emissaries required to take off their hats when approaching the sultan, or to partake in beetlenut chewing or the beverages he offered. Instead, the sultan had to rise whenever a Dutch official entered the courtroom and offer him a seat next to the throne.

Ki Sena admitted he had joined the rebellion spurred by a personal reason. He was married to Den Rara Ningsih, a noblewoman. Born a commoner, Ki Sena was scorned by her family and forced to crawl along the cold floor of the palaces that belonged to his wife's relatives.

Ki Sena resented the way his wife's relatives treated him, even after he and his wife had children. He felt more at ease among the people who opposed the Dutch government. The rebels, led by Raden Rangga, were more interested in talking about keeping the Javanese royalty from being morally corrupted by the Dutch than about how to protect the purity of their noble blood.

In his veins, said Ki Sena, flowed the blood of the Bagelen peasants, who lived in a coastal region, west of the palace, a region frequently ridiculed for the crudeness of its language.

The Bagelen fighter offered to protect Raden Rangga's teak forests from looting criminals hired by the Dutch government. Despite its implications, Ki Sena's new responsibility brought him peace. He began to feel like a complete man again.

As Ki Sena's story unfolded, it became clear that the rebellion was not only a result of Raden Rangga's fearless personality. His sense of independence was a great departure from the slavishness exhibited by most Javanese, and caused him to refuse to bow down before Governor General Daendels' stooges.

It all started, Ki Sena explained, when the reigning Sultan Hamengkubuwono II openly favored his nephew, Prince Natadiningrat, over the royal counselor, Patih Danureja. The latter had fallen too much under the influence of the Dutch government, and the sultan, who was a proud Javanese, resented this. He requested the Governor General to fire Counselor Danureja and replace him with Prince Natadiningrat. The Governor General, who benefited from the presence of Patih Danureja in the palace, refused. This incident created tension in the palace.

Meanwhile, in the area outside the jurisdiction of the Yogyakarta Keraton, the situation was tense because of the robberies and plundering by the robber band led by Ki Poleng. This situation was particularly bad in the areas near Madiun, where Raden Rangga officiated as the ruling regent. When neither the Javanese kings nor the Dutch government officials would take any action, Raden Rangga took matters in his own hands.

Ki Sena's eyes lit up as he came to this part of his story. In a short time, Raden Rangga defeated the robbers and apprehended the looters. He burned down the villages he suspected of functioning as the bandits' hiding places.

However, the way Raden Rangga eliminated the pillagers was considered too close to anarchy by Governor General Daendels, and he put Raden Rangga on trial.

Meanwhile, the sultan lost his patience waiting for a response from the Governor General in Batavia and fired Patih Danureja, replacing him with Prince Natadiningrat. The ramifications of this action were easy to predict. Governor General Daendels commanded the sultan to immediately recall his appointment of Prince Natadiningrat and reinstate Danureja.

To take control over the situation, Governor General Daendels—who was known better as *Tuan Guntur*, Mr. Thunder—commanded Raden Rangga to come to Buitenzorg to apologize for his action, which had undermined government authority.

Ki Sena sighed. He was clearly still emotionally affected by the events.

On November 28, 1810, at about 9 o'clock in the evening, Raden Rangga, instead of going to Buitenzorg, headed for Madiun with three hundred excellent soldiers.

When taking his leave from Prince Natadiningrat, Raden Rangga told him that he wanted to follow his beloved wife, who had passed away a few months previous, and return to *Gusti Allah*. Raden Rangga stated that the sultan was not in the least involved in his subversion. Raden Rangga took full responsibility and was prepared to suffer any and all of the consequences.

When Raden Rangga said goodbye to Prince Natadiningrat, he also wrote a letter to Sultan Hamengkubuwono II. In the letter, he asked for the old sultan's blessing to rebel against the Dutch authorities on Java. He intended to unite the Javanese people. If he succeeded, Sultan Hamengkubuwono II would benefit; if he failed, Raden Rangga would bear the consequences alone.

This was not the first letter Raden Rangga had sent to a sultan. He had written several times to the neighboring Sultan of Surakarta, asking to be acknowledged as a king. However, the sultan had handed his letters over to the Dutch government. After that, the war between the Sultan of Surakarta and Raden Rangga exploded.

Raden Rangga's attack was amazing. In a short time, some areas of the Surakarta Sultanate were conquered and occupied. Unfortunately, the glory of victory did not last long. Raden Rangga's image quickly changed from that of an admired conqueror to that of a reprimanded rebel when the Dutch Governor General, while vacationing in Buitenzorg, took notice of his success.

Daendels ordered Hamengkubuwono II to destroy Raden Rangga and his men.

The sultan crumbled under Daendels' pressure and turned against Rangga. Now, Raden Rangga and his troops were not only hunted by the Dutch, but also by the armies of the two sultanates.

Blocked by the troops of the Surakarta Sultanate, hunted by the armies of Sultan Hamengkubuwono II of the Yogyakarta Sultanate, and attacked by the Dutch forces, Raden Rangga's fate was sealed. On their second offensive expedition, the combined Dutch and palace forces succeeded in capturing Raden Rangga's headquarters. Even though Raden Rangga fought bravely, he was killed in the end.

Ki Sena's voice trembled with emotion. "He died with the dignity of a man, not as a stooge of the Dutch government or a beast of burden. He deserves to be remembered by the Javanese people for years to come."

When Ki Sena and Den Wahyana exchanged glances, I wondered if they were part of another brewing rebellion.

During the time Raden Rangga was under the siege of rifle barrels and cannon muzzles aimed at his heart and brain, his son stood boldly next to him. Someone as steadfast as Raden Rangga would never raise his hands or wave a white flag. Unwilling to kneel and surrender, the bullets tore through his body, but even then, he did not cry out in pain. His death was dignified. He gave his life for the truth he believed in.

The name of the child who grabbed his father's dead body was Bagus. Stained with the blood of the man who created him, Bagus raised his head to observe the faces of the soldiers who had cruelly destroyed his father. He memorized those white faces; they became his nightmares.

Cheers of victory, yells of satisfaction, and the image of the glittering guilders they would receive blinded the attackers to the small, sobbing figure prostrate next to Den Rangga's body on the floor flooded with blood. That small figure would continue his father's struggle and take revenge.

Ki Sena ended his story quietly, but I recognized something that I had never encountered in the stories of my homeland, which was a prosperous country that thrived under abundant blessings. Ki Sena's story gave voice to the oppressed as they struggled for their dignity as human beings.

For almost a week, my language lesson only dealt with words I did not understand in Ki Sena's story. And even after I understood the words, I still was unable to grasp the meaning of the entire story.

Den Wahyana explained patiently what I was unable to comprehend. It became obvious that, in order to learn a language, one had to be passionate about it. If I really wanted to know more about the Javanese people and their struggle, I had to master their language.

I wondered if my interest would automatically erase Ailsa from my memory. I also wondered if I was using the plight and struggle of the Javanese people as a way to fight back against her haunting presence in my mind.

My enthusiasm for learning Javanese intensified when Den Wahyana hinted that he knew of another rebel who had fought the Dutch. He assured me that, while his subject was not as great a warrior as Raden Rangga, this man's story was equally engaging.

That man was none other than Ki Sena.

————•————

Den Wahyana began his story by saying, "Ki Sena was Begawan Vishrava."

"Who is Begawan Vishrava?" I asked.

"Vishrava is a complex character in the *Ramayana*, a classical Hindu epic that the Javanese love," Den Wahyana said.

It was the first time I had heard of this famous tale.

In halting Dutch, English, and Javanese, Den Wahyana explained that Ki Sena was a father who had been asked by his son to request the hand of his beloved. However, Ki Sena did not give the girl to his son, he married her himself.

My heart suddenly racing, I leaned against the woven bamboo wall and thought of my own father, my fiancée, and of their marriage. I anxiously waited for the rest of the story.

Reja, Ki Sena's son, had fallen in love with a girl from Kedu and asked Ki Sena to propose to the girl on his behalf. The girl's parents were known as high-ranking aristocrats, and her father was also an honored member of the *Korps Suranatan*, the religious section of the Keraton.

Den Wahyana shook his head. As usual, he explained, troubles in the lives of the Javanese came from fighting the Dutch.

Ki Sena was actually not Reja's father, but his uncle. Ki Sena's brother had died on the battlefield of one of the many rebellions against the Dutch. Reja had been too young, at the time, to understand the particulars of his father's death. Reja's mother, Nyi Wuli, felt uncomfortable with her position as a widow of someone who had suffered defeat. People often considered the widow of a loser the wrongdoer. This meant she was open game to men. She could be taken as someone's next concubine, or treated as a prostitute who could be discarded at any time.

Nyi Wuli's relatives were deeply concerned and decided to ask Ki Sena, who was still a bachelor, but of marrying age, to marry his brother's widow and raise his nephew as his own.

Ki Sena felt indebted to his brother, who had bestowed him with many gifts. The most significant of these gifts were the spiritual and physical strengths his elder brother had taught him. Ki Sena therefore had no reason not to lighten Nyi Wuli's burden, and agreed to take her as his wife. Hence, Reja became his stepson.

The spiritual and physical skills Ki Sena had mastered enabled him to chase and apprehend the band of robbers that was under the leadership of Ki Poleng, who was notorious for his savageness. Thus Ki Sena won the trust of Hamengkubuwono II and was appointed as a *jagabaya* at the court of the Yogyakarta Sultanate. As a marshal, it was his job to train the soldiers of the sultanate. It was a job that not only gave rise to pride, but also provided for his family.

When Ki Sena thought his livelihood was established, he invited his younger sister, Semi, to live with him and Nyi Wuli.

Semi, who was infatuated with everything that had to do with the Keraton royalty, loved living with her elder brother, whose position was no different from that of an aristocrat. It would not be too difficult for Ki Sena to help his younger sister realize her dream to be an *abdi dalem*, a member of the Keraton's household staff.

The problems in Ki Sena's household began to emerge in the tenth year of his and Nyi Wuli's marriage. Reja, who at that time was a fifteen-year-old boy, started to be interested in girls. His aunt Semi, who was then only sixteen, was one of several girls Reja was attracted to.

This situation worried Ki Sena and Nyi Wuli. More than once, they had caught Reja spying on his aunt while she was bathing. Bitter quarrels frequently disrupted the household because of Reja's interest in Semi.

So when Reja asked Ki Sena to propose for him to the girl from Kedu who he had fallen in love with, Ki Sena thought that would be the best way to solve this problem.

As he prepared for his trip, Ki Sena called to his wife. "While I'm gone," he said, "don't leave Reja and Semi by themselves."

"I will make sure to keep Semi next to me in your absence," Nyi Wuli replied. "She'll assist me in the kitchen. Whether or not you succeed in carrying off the bride-to-be, we still need to be prepared to serve more food and drink than usual."

"You're right." Ki Sena rose to check his *kris*, a double-edged dagger, and his lance.

"I must apologize," Nyi Wuli said, suddenly.

"Why do you need to apologize? What's the matter?"

Nyi Wuli bowed and kept silent. Her hands nervously folded the *jarit* material she was helping her husband pack. The batik cloth, worn like a long skirt, would be used as one of several bridal gifts in the marriage proposal ceremony.

Although Reja was not Ki Sena's biological son, Ki Sena had taken him into his fold and treated the boy as if he were his own flesh and blood. However, Ki Sena felt that Reja did not give him the respect of a father. He had the nerve to harass Semi, who was Ki Sena's own younger sister and therefore Reja's aunt.

"Reja has already caused you so much trouble," Nyi Wuli said. "And you don't know much about the Suteja's palace, where Reja's object of desire is being protected, do you? Frankly speaking, I'm worried." She had finished packing the items Ki Sena was to present at the ceremony of the marriage proposal.

"Trust me. I'm well-prepared." Ki Sena finished packing the weapons he might need. As a soldier, he lived by one rule: If someone wants to live in peace, he has to be prepared to fight. Roaming highway robbers would definitely be attracted to a convoy of horse-drawn carriages transporting valuable items.

"I know who Raden Mas Suteja is." Nyi Wuli's lips trembled as she spoke the name of Reja's intended father-in-law.

"Well, I also have taken note of who he and his children are. Especially Raden Rara Ningsih, the girl our son is infatuated with." Ki Sena rose and took a seat next to his wife.

"Did you also ask about Den Mas Mangli, her elder brother?" Nyi Wuli tested her husband's knowledge about the well-respected family.

"Of course. He's probably the most dangerous one." Ki Sena gently caressed his wife's shoulders.

Den Mas Mangli was known to pose an imminent danger for the young men who proposed to Den Rara Ningsih. There were two requirements a suitor had to fulfill before he could propose to the maiden of the Suteja castle, and more than a dozen bachelors had encountered ill fate before they could carry the bride home.

Den Wahyana's story began to sound like a fairy tale to me, and I started to lose interest. But I knew Den Wahyana was telling me this story for a reason, and I forced myself to listen as my teacher continued.

First, Den Rara Ningsih required the man to be intelligent. He had to be able to answer her questions satisfactorily. Second, Den Rara Ningsih expected the man to be a valiant warrior: He had to be able to defend her against an ambush by Den Mas Mangli, when he tried to forcefully abduct his younger sister during the journey to the groom's house.

These were unusual requirements, indeed, but the people of the Suteja palace were notorious for their eccentricities.

Ki Sena was already aware of these matters. He not only knew how to answer Den Rara Ningsih's questions, but also how to combat Den Mas Mangli's attack. It was not without purpose that Ki Sena had made friends with some of the young noblemen within Suteja's extended family circle. They had briefed him regarding the family's peculiarities.

Ki Sena and his entourage of two horse-drawn carriages, loaded with cloth, carpets, tea, palm sugar, and other gifts for the bride, left Bagelen with seven horsemen who were to escort the party. They traveled to the Suteja palace at normal speed.

After a journey of almost thirty-one miles, the group arrived at a palace that stood proudly amidst a vast field of irrigated rice paddies in the Kedu region.

The reception they received was so simple, it could be regarded as not being welcoming at all. Perhaps the frequency of visitors like them had made the hosts of Suteja palace indifferent. Especially because Ki Sena's group, when compared to previous delegations, must have seemed quite plain.

Furthermore, there was little to discuss. The ceremonial meeting during which the guests would convey the intention of their visit did not please Ki Sena. In his opinion, the host's cold reception showed him as being uncooperative. On the other hand, Ki Sena understood: Among all the suitors, they were perhaps the only ones who were not aristocrats.

After some idle conversation with Ki Sena, Den Mas Suteja said, "Next on the agenda is visiting with my only daughter, who is spoiled and still very childish. This overindulgence will make her sulk if her questions are not answered properly." Den Mas Suteja turned and beckoned to his daughter, who sat some distance behind him. Then, facing Ki Sena again, he said, "My daughter is ready, please meet her."

After that, the energetic and still handsome sixty-year-old man left the reception hall, escorted by some of his close relatives.

A few minutes later, Ki Sena sat face to face with Den Rara Ningsih. Even though they sat about eighteen feet away from each other, and the foliage of a wongai plum tree cast shade on them, Ki Sena saw clearly the most beautiful girl he had ever laid eyes on.

"Are you ready to answer my questions?" Den Rara Ningsih, known as the flower from Kedu, had spent her childhood in her grandfather's palace in Tegalrejo, an area within the jurisdiction of the Yogyakarta Sultanate.

"Yes, Den Rara, go ahead. I will answer to the best of my abilities," Ki Sena responded calmly.

Den Rara Ningsih's voice was too soft for the ears of most men, but not for Ki Sena. He was thankful for being able to catch everything she said. He had heard rumors that, if the man was unable to hear Den Rara Ningsih's questions and asked her to repeat them, the lovely, captivating expression on her beautiful face would change completely into a somber, foreboding look. This was the first test the suitor had to pass.

"I only have two questions; they are in regards to place and time. Please answer as clearly and briefly as possible." Den Rara forced a smile, then said, "Tell me what you know that happened here, in the Yogyakarta Sultanate, when the parents of your great-grandparents were still alive." Den Rara paused before she continued, "And, according to you, what will happen here when the children of your great-grandchildren are born into this world?"

For a moment, Ki Sena thought seriously. He had managed to meet with the escorts of the last suitor who had failed to carry off Den Rara Ningsih. That suitor, too, had been presented with two questions, albeit different from the ones she posed right now. Ki Sena wondered if Den Rara had different questions for each suitor. He shifted in his seat, first to the left, then to the right. Anxiety made it hard to remain calmly seated.

"All right, I will try to tell what happened in this sultanate when the parents of my great-grandparents were still alive. That takes us back to the early 1700s. To me, the most interesting event was the unsuccessful rebellion of the first Prince Diponegoro, who was the son of Pakubuwono I, then Sultan of Kartasura. The prince rebelled against the Dutch soldiers to defend the honor of the Javanese people. The Dutch had trampled their dignity by interfering in the Keraton government." Ki Sena scanned Den Rara's face.

"Can you tell me in detail who the first Prince Diponegoro was?" Her expression and the tone of her voice indicated Den Rara Ningsih's interest.

Ki Sena, regaining his confidence, replied, "As I said, he was a son of Sultan Pakubuwono I, who at that time ruled over

Kartasura, the kingdom before the sultanates of Surakarta and Yogyakarta were formed.

"The first Prince Diponegoro was commanded by his father to help the Dutch soldiers squelch an ongoing rebellion, headed by a mercenary hired by some aristocrats who were unhappy with the colonial oppression."

"Are you saying that the king turned against his own people?" I blurted out, interrupting the store entirely. I still remembered Den Rangga's story. *What was wrong with these people?*

Den Wahyana sighed. "It surely gives that impression, doesn't it?" He was silent for a while, then resumed his story about Ki Sena's quest.

"As it turned out, Prince Diponegoro I did not work with the Dutch soldiers to halt the rebellion. Instead, he joined the fighters who opposed the Dutch.

"Prince Diponegoro I left the luxuries of the Keraton—wealth, a throne, and women—all things aristocrats desire. His decision caused him to live like a wanderer, moving from one battlefield to another in pursuit of the dream to free his country from the Dutch oppression.

"The ordinary people regarded him as the king of justice, the king without a palace, leader of the Javanese people." Ki Sena solemnly finished his account about the warrior who first caused the name Diponegoro to be noted in history.

"Well, I know the rest of that story," Den Rara quipped at Ki Sena's declaration and proudly continued, "The rebellion failed and was crushed by the Dutch soldiers. Now, Raden Mas Antawirya, the grandson of Sultan Hamengkubuwono II, our current sultan, has chosen the name of Diponegoro for himself." Den Rara Ningsih straightened herself and tilted her face. She was obviously pleased with herself. She said, "Well, now tell me what will be experienced by the children of your great-grandchildren in the future."

"The children of my great-grandchildren will be born in the next century, around the year 1920. The struggle initiated by Prince Diponegoro I, whom I mentioned just now, will have borne fruit ready to be harvested. Of course, this will only happen after the struggle has been continued by other Diponegoros whose number can be in the tens, even hundreds. At that time, no Dutch soldiers will be found on Java. They will have surrendered. Java, and its people will no longer be ruled by foreign powers." Ki Sena exuded pride and an enormous inner strength as he delivered his statement.

Den Rara prodded, "In the future, will princes who are not sons of queens, like our Prince Diponegoro II, be able to become kings?"

"One's bloodline is not very important." Ki Sena chose his words carefully as he continued, "A great prince is sometimes born by a mistress, isn't he? His mother might be an ordinary girl, coming from ordinary people, but the fact that she was chosen to be a mistress of royalty certainly proves her not to be just anyone. I don't think pedigree is very important. *Bibit-bebet-bobot*: birth-affiliations-accomplishments. A combination of these three elements makes a man who he is."

Ki Sena's explanation seemed to impress the beautiful girl. She nodded a few times before motioning with a wave of her hand that he was to join his group again, to wait for Raden Mas Suteja's decision regarding acceptance or rejection.

After a short wait, the host's spokesman entered the room. The man who introduced himself as the representative of Den Mas Suteja congratulated Ki Sena.

Den Rara Ningsih was willing to be carried off to her suitor's home, he said. He reminded Ki Sena to be very careful during his trip back; the bride should not be seized by anyone, and should not be brought back to the Suteja palace. If that happened, the wedding plans would be cancelled.

Again, I had to stop Den Wahyana as he was telling the story. It amazed me how the Javanese regarded women like property. Did this Den Rara Ningsih have any say at all in the matter of who she was to marry? But Den Wahyana just shrugged, and I turned my attention back to his story.

As soon as Ki Sena received the Suteja family's decision, he hurried to arrange the trip home. So far, everything had gone according to plan. He knew that the second test was no less challenging than the first one. While the first test was mental, the second would be physical. The first test was to answer complex questions, the second was to face the challenge to fight.

"We will split into three groups," Ki Sena said, preparing for the dangerous journey. "The carriage that will carry Den Rara Ningsih, I will drive myself, no guards needed. The other carriage will be driven by the coachman and escorted by three horsemen. The other horsemen will go straight home by the way we came." Ki Sena turned to the four strong, young riders and commanded, "It's your job to pave the way for the two carriages following you. Take care of any obstacles you encounter."

In accordance with the well-arranged plan, the four horsemen departed first. Next came the carriage that carried the bride's belongings, flanked by another three horsemen. Ki Sena's carriage with Den Rara Ningsih was last. Two horsemen, who were her relatives, as well as guards from the Suteja palace, escorted that carriage. They would return to Kedu as soon as the bride had arrived safely at the groom's home.

They passed the first nine miles without encountering any problems. As they rode around a bend, however, Ki Sena suddenly steered his carriage in a different direction than the carriage in front of him. He was sure Den Mas Mangli was waiting for them farther down the road to obstruct their passage. Den Mas Mangli was known around the Yogyakarta and Surakarta sultanates as a fighter whose muscles were as strong as wire. The outcome of their fight could be easily predicted.

After veering off course, Ki Sena had to pass over a road that was only seven feet wide and usually not traveled by carriage. Stones as big as a cow's head lay scattered across the road. As a consequence, they moved slowly. The two horsemen from the Suteja palace who were assigned to escort Den Rara Ningsih kept shouting their objections to the route that Ki Sena had chosen.

"We have to ask an elder who lives in a remote village at the foot of the Menoreh mountain range for his blessing," Ki Sena explained. "This rocky, narrow road is the only way to get there."

As they rode deeper into the forest, the road became as rough as a stony, dry, riverbed. They had to pass large protruding rocks and treacherous holes. Den Rara let out muffled screams, several times, as the carriage jolted her.

When at last they were forced to stop, Ki Sena explained to the horsemen what he planned to do next. "This is as far as the carriage can go. I'm asking you the favor of looking after the carriage and its contents. The carriage horses are exhausted. I'm afraid I have to borrow your two horses. One for Den Rara to ride, and the other to carry a sack of rice which I prepared for the *kakek panembahan,* the holy man I intend to visit. I entrust both my kris and lance to you. This is a friendly family meeting. I won't need any weapons."

Doubtful at first, the guards obeyed in the end. Den Rara Ningsih also consented.

The road descended as Ki Sena and Den Rara Ningsih continued their trip. They moved slowly along the steep grade, until they arrived at the edge of a wide, calm river.

"I must apologize for this extremely difficult trip, Den Rara." Ki Sena helped her dismount and tethered the horses to a nearby tree. "We have to ride a raft down the river," he said and waved at a man who was tying down his raft.

"I trust you completely with the responsibility to take me to your home safely," Den Rara responded. She had quietly observed how the man who would be her protector in the future had avoided Den Mas Mangli. And when the well-built man managed to leave the two Suteja guards in the middle of the forest, she admired his tactics even more. Ki Sena was obviously trying to escape the dangerous net her brother had cast. Hopefully, this time her brother would not overtake the bridal party, as he had in the past.

"We had better moor and build a camp on the riverbank. It's too dangerous to travel at night," Ki Sena said to Den Rara, while handing the raft owner some money.

After they both stepped ashore, Ki Sena immediately began unloading sacks containing simple camping tools and some dried foods.

When Den Rara noticed that Ki Sena's supplies did not include rice, she casually said, "You seem to have changed your mind. Where's the rice? Don't we need the old man's blessing anymore?"

"There's no rice because there's no old man to see," Ki Sena smiled. "The most important thing is to avoid the eagle's attack."

"The eagle's name must be Den Mas Mangli," said Den Rara. "The groom has the right to do everything he deems necessary in order to carry off his bride." She threw Ki Sena a meaningful glance.

Ki Sena realized that a mistake had been made. He immediately explained, "I'm the *father* of the groom. You are for my son, Den Rara. Alas, did I not explain this to you?"

Den Rara Ningsih's eyes widened, and she stared at Ki Sena.

Ki Sena worried. He knew this misunderstanding could ruin the collaboration he needed to fend off an attack. What could he do if Den Rara became angry and refused to walk? The thought overwhelmed Ki Sena. He decided to find clarity by soaking in a nearby pond and left hurriedly.

Den Rara Ningsih watched Ki Sena disappear between the shrubberies. Slowly, his words began to sink in. The man she had begun to admire would not be her husband. She had to admit that Ki Sena's calm maturity impressed her. Despite the fact that he was an older man, she was attracted to him. But he was not her future husband, the man who would accompany her during her lifetime.

She suddenly felt embarrassed for having exposed her feelings toward him. None of the previous suitors had been capable of avoiding Den Mas Mangli's attack. Usually, her brother would ambush the home-going bridal party before they had traveled less than ten miles. It never took him long to slay the guards. Den Rara Ningsih had become used to the bloody spectacle.

However, this time, the situation was different. Den Rara Ningsih was unable to deny her admiration of Ki Sena. He was truly intelligent and had a broad knowledge. He had answered her questions well. Ki Sena's answers were even better formulated than Den Mas Suteja's, her father.

Also, so far, Ki Sena had succeeded in tricking her brother and the Suteja guards, who were her own relatives. And what attracted her more than anything were the man's eyes. The expression in those eyes was clear. When he looked at her, she did not catch any lust or flirtation, like she had seen in the eyes of all the other men who had visited the Suteja palace. The lust had made her feel as if she was being swallowed.

Ki Sena's eyes promised a peaceful life. She would find peace under his protection. But it was not he who wanted to marry her, it was his son. Den Rara wondered what Ki Sena's son would look like. By asking his father to risk his life to carry her off, it was almost certain his son was a coward.

Den Rara Ningsih became nervous and broke out in perspiration. She rose from her carpet and started to walk in the direction Ki Sena had headed. Perking her ears, she heard water splashing and walked toward the sound.

When the sound of splashing water became louder, Den Rara walked slower. A gentle male voice softly sang a *macapat*. Ki Sena, usually terse and firm, was singing a love song.

Den Rara Ningsih could not keep her heart from pounding. She eased toward the sound. Hidden behind the brush, she parted some branches and foliage. The clear visual made her legs tremble.

Ki Sena sat on a boulder at the base of a small waterfall, without any clothes on, rubbing his chest.

Den Rara Ningsih bent and carefully sat down. She was torn between fear, curiosity, and attraction to the bathing man. She rose and once again pushed aside the leaves in front of her.

Ki Sena's muscles moved as he rubbed himself to the rhythm of his song. He had a habit of singing when he bathed.

When Ki Sena rose from his sitting position and stood erect, Den Rara Ningsih gasped. Now she could see all of him. He had trained his body rigorously for years. His muscles were the result of disciplined physical exercise and flexed with even the slightest movement.

Den Rara Ningsih carefully rose, then walked backward. After she was far enough away from the pond, she started calling Ki Sena. She wanted to alert him of her presence, and stepped intentionally on dried twigs and stomped her feet as she walked back toward the pond.

As soon as Ki Sena heard approaching footsteps, he quickly plunged into the water and stood submerged up to his neck.

"I am afraid of being alone. You left me and went quite far away," Den Rara Ningsih said. Her voice trembled as she was gasping for breath.

"Before coming here, I checked the surroundings of our camp," said Ki Sena. "It's safe. Nothing will harm you." He kept his body immersed in the pond and glanced at his clothes hanging off the branch of a *duwet*, a Java plum tree. He regretted not having anticipated the possibility of being caught while bathing in the nude.

"I just better wait for you here. I don't want to be alone."

"Go back, please. I'll catch up with you soon."

"No, I don't want to. I'll wait for you here."

There was nothing Ki Sena could do, other than remain in the water. He was too embarrassed to tell Den Rara that he was naked. He was certain that, before long, the girl would get cold and leave.

"It's not good for your health to sit there." Ki Sena tried to sway her.

Den Rara shook her head firmly.

The moon climbed higher in the sky, and the night deepened. Still, there was no sign that Den Rara would go back to their camp. Trying to guess her intentions, Ki Sena reluctantly looked at the beautiful face and attractive figure right in front of him.

Den Rara, yawning, covered her mouth with both hands, elbows pointed upward. As she brought her hands up and stretched toward the sky, she looked ravishing. Lit by the full moon, the sight was captivating and became even more tantalizing when she leaned her head against the big rock she was seated on. The way she tilted her chin and lifted her breasts was seductive. When the girl raised one of her legs, a slim, tight calf and a sliver of white thigh shimmered in the moonlight.

Ki Sena stood in awe. Strangely, he enjoyed the torment. Because the marriage to his brother's widow had been arranged, this was the first time he had experienced the ecstasy of being seduced by a woman.

Den Rara called out, "Ki Sena, you're right. It is getting colder here. I'm sure it'll be warmer in the pond. Anyway, I won't be able to sleep without taking a bath." Den Rara started taking off her clothes. She dropped her garments one by one.

Ki Sena stood gaping, not saying a word. The moon, now a full round in the sky, revealed the secrets of the woman's body.

Ki Sena heard the splashing as she entered the pond. Then her warm body came near, within his reach. "I am sorry," he murmured and added, "I am just a man."

No more words were needed. A body intoxicated with an ancient instinct was far more powerful.

Smiling, Den Wahyana paused his story for a moment. I couldn't help but feel like he was laughing at me, but how could he know my secrets? Because I couldn't walk away, I began to pace the room. Den Wahyana gave me a scrutinizing look before he continued the story again.

In the early morning, a *trucukan* flew over the camp. Flying low, the yellow-vented bulbul spread it wings and sang a staccato song: *cok cok cok cok....*

To Den Mas Mangli, who felt defeated, the bird's singing seemed to be mocking him. He had stood for a while in front of Ki Sena's simple camp. The two relatives Ki Sena had left in the forest stood next to him, arms akimbo. Everyone waited anxiously. Their drawn faces reflected extreme annoyance and fatigue.

After waiting in vain for someone to appear, Den Mas Mangli decided to check Ki Sena's camp. He approached the tent with the stealth of a wild cat spying a mouse in the rice field. When there was no sign of anyone coming out of the tent, he ripped the flap open.

The scene before him made him reel backwards, and he drove his fist with brute force into the trunk of the tree next to him.

In the tent, Ki Sena and Den Rara Ningsih slept in each other's arms. The peaceful and satisfied expression on Den Rara's beautiful face told Den Mas Mangli the obvious. He no longer had the right to obstruct their wishes. Everything had already happened.

The marriage between two individuals who were born with very different bloodlines had been consummated. There was nothing he could do now.

Den Wahyana took a deep breath after finishing his tale.

My fate was similar to Reja's—my father, just like Ki Sena, had married my fiancée. Still, I considered my situation worse. Ki Sena was Reja's stepfather, while I was conceived from my father's seed.

Curious about Nyi Wuli and Reja's reaction to this turn of events, I asked Den Wahyana, "What happened when Ki Sena arrived home with Den Rara?"

Den Wahyana broke into a broad smile and dismissed my concerns with a hand wave. He chuckled, "Reja was obviously shocked and upset, but he quickly realized that, while he was much younger than Ki Sena, he was no match for his stepfather's mature composure."

"What about his wife, Nyi Wuli?" I simply could not imagine a similar situation in Scotland.

"Oh, Nyi Wuli?" Den Wahyana shrugged his shoulders. "After she saw how beautiful Den Rara was, she knew she could not compete against the girl's youth and beauty. Like a good Javanese woman, she understood her husband's desire and quietly moved into the position of first wife and made room for the newcomer."

Chapter 3

PIETER

Different kinds of hibiscus surrounded the terrace of Uncle Harvey's mansion. Relaxing in one of the rattan chairs, I was enjoying the vibrant colors when someone on horseback approached the gate. Since he did not seem to have any intention to move on, I decided to meet him.

The rider, despite his adult attire, was a youth, a child. From the way he scoured the area, I assumed he was looking for someone. I asked, "Who are you looking for?"

"Someone who looks like you, sir," the boy answered politely in Dutch. He was Javanese and very young, yet he spoke Dutch. He had to be someone of importance.

"There's another person who lives here and looks like me," I said. I was sure that he referred to another Caucasian, and that left only Uncle Harvey.

"He doesn't live here. He only comes to visit. Thank you," he said politely, then turned his horse and spurred it into a gallop.

Rubbing my chin, I watched him disappear into the distance. He was so small that the horse looked like it was running wildly by itself. I wondered who this lad could be. Despite his youth, he was a competent rider and spoke Dutch.

After that, I often saw the boy around the plantation and noticed that everyone treated him respectfully. One of the workers of my uncle's maintenance shop told me that the boy was Bagus, son of Raden Rangga, the famous rebel.

———•••———

Trying to guess the relationship between Daisy, Pieter, and me must have puzzled Uncle Harvey. Like any good father, he wanted his daughter to settle down in harmonious matrimony, and he often prodded me to gain insight into the situation.

I agreed with his assumption that Pieter and Daisy were a good match. One afternoon, she told me that Pieter had offered to accompany her when she had to look for a particular plant in the jungle.

Because Uncle Harvey had asked me to find out about the nature of Daisy and Pieter's relationship, I asked, "You two ever talk about love or marriage?"

"Why sure—you can't blame him for trying, can you?" Daisy laughed.

"Did you give him any hope?" I felt indebted to Uncle Harvey and wanted to give him the information he was looking for.

"No, I did not. Hey—am I under police interrogation?" Daisy tried to make light of the matter.

"You consider me your elder brother, don't you?" I tried to defuse the tension as well.

"No, I don't." Daisy threw me a teasing smile. "You're just like Pieter: a man who's after me."

I forced a laugh and Daisy joined me, thus ending our conversation.

I could not blame Uncle Harvey for assuming I had come to Java with Daisy on my mind. I had not told him anything about my father's betrayal, and had no intention of telling him about it in the future, either. No one needed to know that I had come to Java to flee from Jeremias Kappers and Ailsa Chambers.

The fact that I had graduated from the University of Edinburgh, known as one of the greatest universities in the world, was the only thing that kept me going during those days. I considered myself an intellectual, and therefore I should not allow my feelings to destroy me. After all, I had been educated that practicing common sense led to a better life.

I had to maintain a good relationship with the organization that had sponsored the late Dr. Leyden. Its headquarters in Edinburgh had funded my research. However, after Dr. Leyden's passing, I was doubtful whether the organization would continue their support. I expressed my anxiety in a letter.

Their response assured me that my funding would continue. However, they now required that my article prove the intricate connection between science and the business world. My honorarium depended on the clarity of my explanation.

I was not too worried about this. I still had enough savings. I could also—and sometimes was forced to—stay and eat in my uncle's house in Rejawinangun. I was physically content and did not feel like an unfortunate fugitive stranded far away from home.

A short time after I arrived in Yogyakarta, a Javanese office clerk delivered a job offer from John Crawfurd. The new Resident of Yogyakarta needed an Englishman who had a working knowledge of the Javanese language and was familiar with the Javanese psyche.

The man had to be able to sift through the complicated ways in which Javanese expressed themselves and know which of the winding, flowery statements to pay attention to and which to ignore. Crawfurd's need was closely related to the bitter feud between Sultan Hamengkubuwono II and his son, Sultan Hamengkubuwono III, which was created by interference from the colonial governments.

Years of Dutch colonialization had transformed the sultans from kings who reigned over their territories with wisdom and justice for their people, into puppets of the Dutch authorities. The English simply followed suit.

My job required seeking out the individual who opposed the colonial government, so he could be replaced with someone more cooperative.

It was common for the colonial government to replace a king who did not succumb to colonial power with another king who would. These tactics had brought about the removal and exile of Sultan Hamengkubuwono II to Penang on June 28, 1812.

The colonial powers had effectively destroyed the essence of the Javanese king. To the colonial authorities, the Javanese kings were no more than pieces in the chess game soldiers played in the military barracks.

In addition, not much was left of the once-opulent Keraton after General Robert Gillespie and his men stormed and plundered the palace on June 21, 1812. My article recounting the event satisfied the curiosity of my Edinburgh sponsors about the faraway lands, apparently waiting for the British to conquer and leach dry. However, I was still faced with the question: *What linked science to trade?*

I noticed that the Javanese people, especially the aristocrats, shunned hard work. Their mindset and subsequent behavior were not conducive to participation in determining the progress of human civilization of the world. The Chinese were much more practical—second only to the Europeans, who, of course, played a major role in this process.

The Javanese aristocrats exhausted themselves dealing with matters regarding *wisma, curiga, kukila, turangga,* and *wanita*: mansions, weaponry, prized fowl, horses, and women. They couldn't care less about affairs concerning their country and its people.

Except for a rebel like Raden Rangga, the Javanese were not equipped to think about the advancement of human civilization. The average Javanese merely wanted to live peacefully and prosperously, removed from danger. They were content to live and die without any participation in determining their destiny, without having played any significant role in the progress of mankind.

I was able to report to the Edinburgh for Far East Club on General Robert Gillespie's assault on the Keraton accurately, because I stood in the front yard of the palace that June day when Gillespie, with the blessing of Governor Raffles, plundered the sultan's palace.

After taking over the Keraton with no significant resistance, the British troops soon turned into a pack of hungry tigers that had succeeded in capturing an unlucky animal. The palace guards, household, and personnel fled to safety, like a herd of ambushed buffaloes. Within minutes, the scene became a beastly performance of greed.

While Resident Crawfurd shook his head, a Javanese nobleman, who stood nearby, grimly stated that the English had proven themselves to be nothing more than wild beasts. When I asked some other bystanders who the Javanese nobleman was, they told me he was the grandson of Sultan Hamengkubuwono II, Prince Diponegoro II.

As an educated Englishman, I was shamed and appalled by my countrymen's behavior. I feverishly recorded the screams of victory, mingled with the cries for help, the glimmer of swords, and the color of blood on the pavement.

I tried to describe the fever of victory that drove the raging Englishmen, and the deep sadness that emanated from the confused, overpowered Javanese. I tried to list the numerous valuables Gillespie's men loaded into the carts that would head for Batavia after they were done. I wanted to observe and record the Keraton robbery by the English army till the very end, when my attention was suddenly drawn by a woman howling for help.

A group of uniformed men headed for the outer Keraton walls. In their midst, they dragged a young, disheveled native woman along. Trying to fasten her loose hair, she tugged on her torn clothes to cover her exposed body.

Would, in this part of the world, robbery automatically be followed by rape? The scene assaulted my smug sense of white male superiority. *This was unacceptable behavior for members of a society that claimed to be leaders of human civilization.*

"Let her go!" I yelled, walking toward the woman. "You're British soldiers, not a gang of criminals!"

"Go away! Mind your own business!" One of the men scoffed.

From the way they talked and behaved, I figured they belonged to Europe's bottom layer of society. They probably would not be able to find any employment in Europe.

"I can identify each one of you," I threatened. "You'll be thrown in prison as soon as I report you."

One of the men peeled away from the crowd. Standing next to me, he said apologetically, "We're trying to make this woman talk. She must know where the queen's and mistresses' jewelry boxes are hidden."

From the way the soldier carried himself, I figured he had at least graduated from elementary school. I didn't really believe him, but said, "Go ahead, ask her. I'm sure you won't mind if I listen to your conversation."

My presence seemed to be intimidating enough to limit the mob's interrogations, and they soon ambled away.

The Javanese girl remained crouched against the wall. Her clothes were badly torn, and I was reluctant to approach her. "Go join the people outside the Keraton," I said in Javanese, pointing at the crowd that had watched the incident happen. "It's safer over there."

The girl stared at me. Fear and disbelief filling her dark, round eyes, she pressed herself closer against the wall.

I took her hand and helped her up.

She clumsily released her hand from my grip, then hurriedly tidied up her hair and clothes and quietly followed me.

"Thank you," she said, as we walked through the gate.

We stood for a moment, facing each other. I don't know why I could not make myself simply leave her.

"What's your name?" I asked, trying to release the tension.

"My name is Semi, sir," she answered with a tight voice, then joined the dispersing crowd.

———•———

The robbery of the Keraton by my countrymen shook my belief in the Caucasian race. I could no longer see how we could claim to be the God-appointed leaders of civilization. The beastly behavior of my fellow man would live in my memory, forever.

Despite the unrest of the Keraton invasion and robbery, I felt peaceful living among these people I had begun to like heartily. Cured from the wound inflicted by my father, my thoughts returned to John Leyden. If I wanted to perform my assignment from this great scientist, I would have to write about the Javanese world with its uniqueness. It was immaterial how much money I could earn writing for the Edinburgh Club or the *London Times*. I wanted to dedicate my hard work to John Casper Leyden.

Resident Crawfurd's appointing me as his editor for a manuscript that was to be published soon assured me of a steady income, and I could afford to concentrate on Leyden's Javanism expressed in the notion of bronjong. I knew now I had the right word; however, I was still in the dark regarding its meaning. I didn't even know if bronjong was a verb, noun, or adjective, or if it represented a creature. Den Wahyana was the most logical person to turn to for an explanation.

›———•••———‹

A few months after Gillespie stormed and robbed the Keraton for Governor Raffles, I visited Den Wahyana in his simple bamboo house in Tegalrejo and asked him what a bronjong could possibly be.

As usual, he contemplated my question before answering carefully. "Mr. Leyden just gave you a vague guideline." He paused, as if he wanted his words to sink in before he continued. "Usually, a bronjong is a bamboo cage, or basket, mostly used to transport fowl. At times, pigs and goats are kept confined in a bronjong at the markets. However, when an intellectual like Doctor Leyden mentions the bronjong as an object worthy of research, he must have had another type of bronjong in mind." Den Wahyana rubbed his hands and looked away.

"What about this other bronjong? What do you know about the bronjong Dr. Leyden referred to? Please tell me about it," I probed, impatiently.

"If you want to write about it, you had better see it yourself. I can take you to someone who can escort you to a bronjong event."

I was anxious to start my project. "An event? Where and when does it take place?"

Den Wahyana shook his head. "That is the problem," he said slowly. "Sometimes, it's held more than once in a month. However, during quiet times, years can go by without a bronjong event." Den Wahyana looked at me as if he was trying to figure out if I would have the patience to wait that long. After a while, he added, "Not too many things give reason to have a bronjong event."

Considering that I was still trying to figure out the real nature of Daisy's relationship with Pieter, and why Den Bagus was hanging around my uncle's mansion in Rejawinangun, along with my work on Resident Crawfurd's manuscript, I was not worried about getting bored while waiting.

Before leaving Tegalrejo to go home with the carriage I had borrowed from Uncle Harvey, I noticed Den Mas Bagus leaning against a tree near the carriage. Knowing that the lad had a limited knowledge of Dutch, and that I could carry on a conversation in Javanese, I approached him.

Den Mas Bagus responded in the usual, polite Javanese way.

This encounter led to the many meetings we had later on.

———◆———

One afternoon, Den Mas Bagus asked me to meet him at the house of a *demang*, a village elder, east of Rejawinangun. After he filled my teacup, Den Mas Bagus steered our conversation to Pieter and said, "If you don't mind, I would be much obliged if you could tell me what you know about Mr. Pieter."

I thanked him for the tea and said, "You must have an important reason to inquire about Mr. Pieter. Unfortunately, I can't tell you much. I only met him once, and at that time, we didn't have more than a brief conversation."

I took stock of my young host's appearance. He could not be more than eleven or twelve years old. I wondered if I was being fooled by his childlike build and the innocence in his eyes.

Den Bagus interrupted my thoughts. "You have certainly heard stories about a rebel named Raden Rangga, haven't you?" Our eyes locked for a moment, then Den Bagus said, "If you don't mind, I'd like you to ask Mr. Pieter about his involvement in the hunting and killing of Raden Rangga."

I swallowed. The lad seemed suddenly wrapped in a shroud of dark, immeasurable sadness. "I will try," I said, "but of course I can't promise that he will tell the truth." I purposely did not reveal that I knew Den Bagus was Den Rangga's son and that Pieter, indeed, was one of the soldiers who had first hunted, then murdered, his father.

"Shall we meet here again next week?" Den Mas Bagus asked. "Maybe you can bring me a story about Mr. Pieter."

"All right," I agreed and promised, "Whether or not I succeed, I will be here." I felt that Den Mas Bagus was not someone I could belittle. On the contrary, he deserved to be respected—especially for the way he conducted himself during our conversations.

"If you manage to make Mr. Pieter talk, I will take you to a bronjong event." Den Mas Bagus smiled. "You do want to see it, don't you?"

I was stunned. *How did Den Mas Bagus know that I was dying to find out what a bronjong event was all about?* I wondered if Den Wahyana had told him, and if Den Mas Bagus was the person Den Wahyana had chosen to take me to a bronjong.

"Well, thank you," I said, trying to hide my surprise.

I have to admit that I was careless when I met Pieter, as he arrived on horseback at the Rejawinangun mansion for his usual visit around twilight.

Unfortunately, I did not realize my carelessness until Daisy pointed it out to me the next day.

"What's your opinion of Pieter after you managed to have a conversation with him?" Daisy asked.

"Like I told you, he's an extremely serious young man," I answered slowly, looking for the right words to describe Pieter.

"Did his seriousness keep you from finding out what you wanted to know about him?" Daisy sounded worried.

"Are you implying that he is not serious?"

"To me, he is not serious but mysterious. He's definitely hiding something." Daisy threw me a quick glance, then burst out laughing. "Perhaps it's just me."

"Mysterious? Hmm…." The word reminded me of the palace robbery by the English troops. I had seen Pieter's tall, well-built figure as he enthusiastically loaded military carriages with the Keraton's valuables and mercilessly beat off one of the handmaids. I wasn't sure if he, in turn, had spotted me.

"Speaking of Pieter, do you have something interesting to tell about him?" Daisy cocked her head and tried to hold my eyes.

"Well…." Afraid she'd think I was spiteful and wanted to destroy their relationship, I refrained from telling her about the shameful Keraton robbery.

"Anything to tell?" Daisy pressed on.

"There is a Raden Mas who wants to know more about Pieter. That is why I'm trying to get acquainted with him." I was relieved to have found a good reason to explain to Daisy why I wanted to meet Pieter.

"I'm sure that you won't get what you want," Daisy laughed.

"That is why I need you to tell me about him."

"You talk in circles, like flying mahogany seeds," Daisy broke out into teasing laughter. "You want to know about Pieter because you think he's your opponent in vying over me—please, just admit it."

I joined her in laughter, but heard the discord in my voice. Then Daisy told me about Pieter.

It was hard to tell what her feelings were. From the way she told her story, she seemed totally disinterested and removed from whatever happened. But she did confirm that Pieter had participated in the manhunt and murder of Raden Rangga. This meant that Den Wahyana was correct, and I needed to relay this fact to Den Mas Bagus.

Later, when I recorded Daisy's story in my notebook, I had to go back to when the British troops took Java away from the Dutch, in 1811. When the British government offered Dutch employees and soldiers the choice of joining the British government instead of returning to The Netherlands, Pieter, who was a real opportunist, chose to work for the new government.

Daisy said that Pieter had only known Uncle Harvey for a short time. When Pieter was looking for a market for his loot, he found that Uncle Harvey was one of the biggest foreign investors on Java.

Pieter walked off with two important pieces of information from his first visit at Rejawinangun. While Harvey Thomson was not interested in any of the items he offered for sale, the older man did know people who would be interested, and he was willing to introduce Pieter to them. Also, Thomson had a daughter who was not only intelligent but also attractive.

Pieter's next visit was especially to offer his help to Daisy.

Daisy was a genuine plant lover. Her passion for tropical plants had caught the attention of the director at the Botanical Garden in Buitenzorg, and he had asked her to collect various kinds of tropical shrubs, especially from the genus of hibiscus, which grew in the forests of the Yogyakarta and Surakarta sultanates.

Daisy said that lately, Pieter had escalated his advances to her. However, since she was far more educated than Pieter, she managed to put him off easily.

My arrival might have bothered Pieter. Especially if he, like Uncle Harvey, assumed I had come to Java in search of a love affair.

I was certain that Pieter, who was a mercenary and military adventurer, was capable of doing anything to reach his goal. "From now on, you have to be careful when you're alone with Pieter in the middle of the jungle," I told Daisy.

"I am always with Jiya, my father's trusted houseboy, when I go to the jungle, and I also bring this with me." Daisy raised her hand. With her index finger pointed and her thumb up, her hand resembled a gun.

———•———

An insect called *garengpung* ruled the daylight hours in Rejawinangun. If the sun dominated this fertile area, flooding it with light, the cicada dominated it with its incessant buzzing noise. Wherever people in the Rejawinangun area were, the noise would fill their ears. The Javanese people were convinced that the arrival of the garengpung meant a prolonged dry season.

One afternoon, a few days after my conversation with Daisy about Pieter, it became unbearably hot at my house, and I decided to visit the Rejawinangun loji. Uncle Harvey was in his study, carefully examining his bookkeeping records.

"Daisy went out with Pieter, just now. She wanted to look for a certain plant in the Menoreh jungle." Uncle Harvey casually mentioned the name of a notoriously eerie area a short distance away from Rejawinangun.

"They went by themselves?"

"No, Jiya went with them." Uncle Harvey sent me a quizzical look. Perhaps he concluded from my question that I was jealous. In fact, I only worried about Daisy's safety. A palace robber would have no problem violating someone's daughter.

"All right, in that case, I'll go read on the verandah."

I had barely read a page from one of Daisy's books, a novel written by a Scotswoman named Mary Wollstonecraft, when Jiya came running up the steps of the verandah.

"What are you doing home?" I asked.

"Mr. Pieter left his hat and told me to get it." Jiya hurried into the house.

Daisy was alone with Pieter. I was certain Pieter had left his hat on purpose. Imagining what could be happening at that very moment, I jumped out of my chair.

"Jiya! Never mind Mr. Pieter's hat. Saddle me a horse!" I ran toward the stables.

With Jiya leading the way, we raced toward the southern edge of the jungle. When Jiya reined in his horse, I shouted, "Where are they?"

"At the foot of that hill, sir." Jiya pointed at a hill about half a mile away.

"Wait here for me. If I'm not back when the sun has moved to the west, you go home and tell Uncle Harvey," I commanded.

I left my horse tied to a sengon tree—I did not want Pieter to hear me coming. I wondered what I would do if something happened to Daisy. While I wanted to be prepared in the event something bad did happen, I did not want the embarrassment of looking like I had followed them.

When I heard a muffled scream, followed by loud laughter, I pushed aside the shrubbery and plunged in the direction of the sound.

I heard Pieter's voice first. "You don't believe that I can take you? I'll prove it here and now," he snarled.

I reached for the holster at my waist, but came up empty. In my hurry, I had forgotten my pistol.

"Damned beast! You had better kill me!" Daisy screamed between sobs.

Had she, too, left her gun?

"I won't. I've never fucked a dead body. I want you alive when I push my cock into your warm pussy. I'm sure you'll like it—and, later, you'll enjoy raising our child." Pieter's laughter was hoarse.

I edged closer until I could see Pieter standing, straddled over Daisy, who lay on her back, her khakis torn, her arms, chest, and parts of her thighs exposed.

Shocked and frightened, I jumped out of the shrubs. "You're a killer, a robber, and a rapist!" I yelled, pointing at Pieter.

Startled, Pieter stepped back. For a moment, he was stupefied, but he quickly regained self-control. He folded his arms and snarled, "You should've shot me. You'd become a hero, instantly. Or did you forget to bring your pistol?" Pieter threw me a pitying smile. "Or do you want to impress Daisy? Do you want to fight with your bare hands and bring me down?" His arms slightly bent, Pieter clenched his fists and lumbered toward me, breathing heavily.

I smelled his sweat as I realized that I faced a mercenary, a man of solid bones and iron strength; his sword and rifle were part of his body.

During the unequal fight, Pieter punched and kicked me, again and again. Between falling and rising, I saw Daisy getting up, staggering. I tried to keep Pieter's attention on me so Daisy could escape. Gathering all my strength, I swung at him.

Pieter retaliated with another series of kicks and punches, which sent me reeling. Gasping for air, I landed on the ground. When I lifted my head, Pieter was running after Daisy.

It didn't take long before he caught her. He ripped her blouse open and shoved her to the ground. Her white skin contrasted with the dark brown soil as she tried to scramble to her feet.

Pieter dropped his pants.

Gathering all my strength, I stumbled toward them. Then I heard Pieter scream. Suddenly, he dropped to the ground at Den Wahyana's feet. Each time Den Wahyana's foot slammed into his body, Pieter rolled, bawling, across the ground.

I rubbed my eyes in disbelief.

Den Wahyana bellowed, "You may want to know who I am. I was one of Raden Rangga's soldiers. Do you still remember Raden Rangga? He was the man you hunted as if he were a wild boar. You insulted and berated him as if he were a petty thief." Den Wahyana pressed his foot deeper into Pieter's chest.

Pieter, lying on his back, only groaned.

"Get up! Fight me!" Den Wahyana lifted his foot off Pieter's chest and nudged him in the side.

Unable to rise, Pieter turned his head. Blood seeped from both corners of his mouth.

"I must have kicked you too hard," Den Wahyana said dryly. "I didn't want to fight near a naked woman." Den Wahyana clapped, and Jiya emerged from the shrubbery.

Den Wahyana turned to him and said, "*Kang*, she is your employer, isn't she?" Den Wahyana took off his jarit and, throwing it at Jiya, said, "Here, cover her and guard her until she is conscious."

I rose and staggered toward Den Wahyana. My language teacher, now standing clad in trousers, was not at all surprised by my presence. He seemed to have known everything from the beginning.

"We'll just leave the scoundrel here. The elements will take care of him."

It was a while before Daisy regained consciousness. After she realized what had happened to her, she sent Jiya home to fetch a carriage along with a few handmaids and clothes.

I learned two new and important things from the incident: first, Den Wahyana was much more than an interpreter; and he and Den Mas Bagus had a unique relationship.

Later, Den Mas Bagus told me he had sent his father's former commander-in-chief to deal with Pieter. Fate had finally caught up with him.

Chapter 4

KIAI KASAN

After the Menoreh incident, I spent more time at Rejawinangun than in John Crawfurd's office. I told the Resident that I was having some personal problems and asked for an extension to deliver the edit of his manuscript.

Daisy and I did become closer, but our conversations were mostly about Mary Wollstonecraft's work and did not touch on any romantic notions. What made our relationship unique was that we were both conscious of the importance and possibility that a man and a woman could enjoy a close, platonic friendship.

I almost always had dinner at Rejawinangun on the weekends. After dinner, Uncle Harvey, Daisy, and I would engage in idle chitchat over coffee. After Uncle Harvey finished smoking his cigar, he'd excuse himself and leave Daisy and me alone.

Daisy usually led our conversations with talks about women's rights or her dreams about the botanical garden she was involved in.

One evening, when we sat on the verandah after dinner, Daisy mused, "Pieter's beastly conduct in the jungle makes me wonder about the importance of a woman's role in its most natural condition. In a lion family, the female provides the food, and thus she is the most important. All the male is expected to do is guard the den."

Daisy grimaced. "Regardless of the role of their reproductive organs, a woman's role compared to a man's in conserving and sustaining the human race is much more important."

I knew that Daisy supported Mary Wollstonecraft, who actively promoted women's equalization, socially as well as educationally. "I was always able to rely more on my mother than my father," I said. "That's why I support the notion of women's equality." I threw Daisy a sideways glance. "I wouldn't mind staying home to look after the children while my wife has gone to work to help earn a living."

Daisy seemed to take my jibe seriously. "Why sure, that would work well for you," she said enthusiastically. "As an author, you don't need any working space away from home. I'm pretty sure you want only one child and a good nanny to take care of it." Daisy paused, frowning. "You probably also expect your wife to be faithful." She hesitated before ending awkwardly, "I mean, she should only be physically intimate with you, her husband."

I suddenly wondered if Daisy supported polygamy. I didn't know much about women's issues and usually just tried to be a good listener. However, this time, it was strangely important to know where she stood on the matter.

"Do you think that's wrong?" I asked.

Daisy cocked her head and held my eyes while she answered, "Of course not."

"Good," I said. It was as if a heavy load had rolled off my chest.

"By the way, how far are you into writing about bronjong and branjang?" Daisy abruptly changed the topic of conversation.

"It isn't bronjong *and* branjang, it's either bronjong *or* branjang."

"What's the difference?"

"Dr. Leyden wasn't sure if it was bronjong or branjang. And before I managed to get a clarification from him, a deadly virus killed him in Batavia."

"Hmm...." Daisy sent me a quizzical look, then laughed. "Perhaps you can write about bronjong as well as about branjang to keep yourself from getting bored."

I chuckled at Daisy's sense of humor. "Sure," I said, joining Daisy's laughter. "I'll write about both."

I usually asked to be excused long before seven o'clock, but that evening, we talked till late into the night.

My mother had told me that Uncle Harvey's first wife had passed away when Daisy was less than a year old. He worried that his work on the plantation had caused him to fall short in performing his duties as a single parent.

It seemed he now hoped that I would help fill the void caused by his neglect. More than once, Uncle Harvey had asked me to spend the night at the Rejawinangun loji. However, unless Uncle Harvey saw Daisy's lack of interest in socializing—especially with the opposite sex—as a shortcoming, I could not see that she lacked anything. Despite her youth, she was a respected botanist, was well read, and stood her ground on women's rights. The more time I spent with her, the more I admired her.

———◆———

Before the Menoreh incident, I had regarded Den Wahyana as an educated aristocrat. He was a familiar face around the Keraton. After the Menoreh incident, however, I saw a difference between him and the other aristocrats I interacted with. It was clear that Den Wahyana was not an ordinary person. His identity was just as mysterious as Pieter's.

Den Wahyana was more agile than the other aristocrats. His dark, sun-bronzed skin attested to outdoor activities. The typical Javanese *surjan* clothes he usually wore could not disguise his athletic frame. He also seemed to be more alert than the others.

From carefully observing my teacher's social activities, I assumed he was involved in an underground political group formed by the religious leaders and aristocrats who opposed the colonial government as well as the puppet reign of the sultanate. I knew there was a group that met regularly under the leadership of Prince Diponegoro II and were referred to as the Tegalrejo Group.

Den Wahyana had also been a faithful follower of Raden Rangga, the defeated rebel. It was apparent that Den Wahyana had passed his loyalty on to Den Mas Bagus, Raden Rangga's son. I wondered why Den Wahyana kept his relationship with Ki Sena secret from everyone. They were supposed to have been chief commanders of Raden Rangga.

My meetings with Den Wahyana slowly changed from language lessons to meetings between two close friends.

Den Wahyana had revealed that he was someone who should be confined in a prison cell. Only the protection given by Prince Diponegoro II enabled him to breathe freely in the Yogyakarta Sultanate. I was sure the protection had not been granted without cause.

A few days after the Menoreh incident, Den Wahyana took me to the demang's house, where Den Mas Bagus was waiting to take me to a bronjong event.

"Don't you know the location?" I asked Den Wahyana.

"Yes, I do know the area, but I don't know when it will be held." Den Wahyana glanced at Den Mas Bagus, who nodded.

The three of us rode our horses through a heavily wooded area until we came to a clearing populated by a few hovels and one food vendor. A number of men wearing dark clothing were moving about and put me on guard. We left our horses in custody of the owner of the food stall and continued our journey on foot.

A foreboding starkness marked the area. Neither flowering shrubs nor bird cages brightened the drab settlement. The doors and windows of the huts we passed were all tightly shut. The farther we walked, the more men we met. Some of them were soldiers.

By now, I had lived for quite some time in the sultanate and recognized several guards from the Keraton.

After an hour walk into the interior, Den Mas Bagus said, "There's the bronjong you're looking for." He pointed at a bamboo cage that was a hundred times bigger than the bronjongs I had seen in the markets.

This bronjong was some six feet high and eighteen feet square. Poles the size of an adult's thigh staked the four corners. The walls were made of split bamboo, woven together and fastened to the corner posts with thick ropes.

"Why did they make such a large bronjong? Are they going to keep goats and pigs in it?"

"No," Den Mas Bagus came closer and said, "It's a fighting arena."

"Will they fight goats? Pigs?"

"It's for...."

A woman, appearing out of nowhere, interrupted Den Mas Bagus. "Mr. Willem, I hope you still remember me," she cried, dropping herself at my feet.

Startled, I stepped back, but the woman grabbed my legs. Sobbing, she pushed her head against my shins. It took a few moments before I realized it was Semi. I hadn't seen her since the day Gillespie ransacked the Keraton.

"You're Semi, aren't you? Of course I remember you!" I tried to step away, but Semi tightened her arms around my legs.

"I beg you to help my father. I swear, my father is not guilty," Semi sobbed. "Behead me if I turn out to be a liar!"

"First, you need to tell me clearly why your father is in this predicament." I gently pried myself loose.

"Your father is Kiai Kasan, right?" Den Wahyana said.

"Yes, you're correct, Den Mas. Please help my father. He's truly not guilty."

I turned to Den Wahyana, who stood some distance behind me. "You know Semi? She's Ki Sena's sister, isn't she?"

Den Wahyana glanced at Semi. "I heard that the prisoner who will be pitted against a tiger is Kiai Kasan. This woman is the daughter of the prisoner whose punishment is having to fight a tiger in this bronjong." Den Wahyana looked away and sighed, "I don't know much about Ki Sena's family...."

Knowing his close relationship with Ki Sena, this statement threw me, but the immediate situation demanded my full attention. *Would these people actually pit a man against a tiger in this cage?* "He will be pitted against a tiger?" I blurted. I could not believe that, in 1814, people would still engage in a cruel form of entertainment from ancient Roman times.

Den Wahyana nodded firmly.

I turned toward the woman, who had kept her head bowed. "Will your father have to fight a tiger in the bronjong?"

"You're correct, sir. Please help," she begged.

"Damn barbarians!"

Den Mas Bagus and Den Wahyana, ignoring my outburst, turned their heads.

"Meet me here tomorrow morning. Go home now," I said to Semi. She remained knelt before me.

People began to gather. Their curious stares made me uncomfortable, and I quickly said goodbye to Semi and walked away.

When I looked for my guides, they seemed to be keeping their distance. "Den Wahyana," I said, "I'd like to talk about this bronjong, about Kiai Kasan, about this barbaric performance."

We walked back to our horses along the same road we had come. Riding home at a leisurely pace, the reality of a man being pitted against a tiger riled me; but even more than that, Semi's worry about her father had me on edge. I asked Den Mas Bagus and Den Wahyana what I could do to help the woman.

"I'd actually suggest that you not involve yourself in the woman's problem," said Den Wahyana, who was riding next to me. He hesitated, "unless you're interested in her."

I did not understand the implication and tried to catch his eye, but he kept them focused on the road ahead of us.

"She is beautiful, indeed, and she is one of the handmaids in the Keraton. You can choose to take her as your *nyai*." Den Wahyana paused. "You will raise her social standing if you take her as your mistress, but I am afraid she is already married."

It began to dawn on me what he meant. I had already decided that, if I were to marry, I would not marry a European woman who would remind me of Ailsa. But for now, I chose to ignore Den Wahyana's statement that Semi was married.

Den Wahyana took my silence as an acceptance of his idea and conveyed his plan. "Don't take care of the matter yourself. You're a government employee who is close to the Resident—

your hands must remain clean. I will arrange for you to meet Dasamuka."

"Dasamuka? Who is he?"

"A man who is capable of helping you. I mean, of helping the girl."

I nodded. I really wanted to help the girl. I did not care whether or not her father was guilty; it was immaterial whether or not I would take her as my mistress.

———•••———

After returning home from the bronjong trip, I spent a long time thinking about it in my room. While we had not traveled far, the situation had been tense, and the experience gave me plenty to ponder.

I wondered if John Leyden had wanted me to write about the bronjong event, which turned out to be similar to an amphitheater where a gladiator fought against a tiger. It appeared that, in matters of judgment and punishment, the cruelty of the Javanese Sultanate today was no different from that of the Roman Empire.

My thoughts kept circling around the fact that, while Semi was a handmaid at the Keraton, her father was being subjected to savage punishment. *What had he done?*

I was also intrigued by this person Dasamuka. Den Wahyana believed Dasamuka would be able to save the prisoner from bronjong punishment. *Could that be true?*

I tossed and turned until, at last, the morning sun slipped through the transoms into my room. I opened the window and saw Den Wahyana waiting by the front door.

"I have been successful in bringing Dasamuka here. Can he see you now?" Den Wahyana called out.

"Of course." I rushed to let him in.

"Wait a minute. Let me get him." Den Wahyana hurried into the garden.

I almost dropped my pocket watch when I spotted the lad Den Wahyana brought along. In my mind, Dasamuka was an authoritative white-bearded, old man, or at least a mature middle-aged gentleman. Instead, it was a small boy who came to see me. Not an adult who was abnormally short or dwarfed, but a child.

I thought of Den Mas Bagus, who was also very young. I wondered if children matured faster on Java than in other places.

"Is this Dasamuka?" I asked.

Den Wahyana nodded.

I turned toward the handsome boy dressed in tidy, aristocratic clothes.

"Do you know what the bronjong punishment is?"

The small boy nodded firmly and said, "Yes, I do, sir. Leave the problem of the bronjong punishment to me. I will free Kiai Kasan. He will return to his home safely, healthy, and with nothing to worry about."

"What will you do?" I questioned his ability.

"I've already saved four prisoners from being fed to the tiger in the bronjong."

I looked at Den Wahyana, who nodded, endorsing Dasamuka's statement. Was my close friend being deceived by Dasamuka, I wondered, or did I trust the people around me too much? Was it possible that Den Wahyana and Dasamuka were conspiring to deceive me?

"If you don't believe me, find someone you trust. Ask him if he knows people who were about to undergo the bronjong punishment. Then visit the ex-prisoners and ask them whether or not it was Dasamuka who saved their lives." The young man exuded so much self-confidence, it came close to arrogance.

I kept silent for a moment. From the way Dasamuka carried himself, I had to believe him. And he had been brought to me by Den Wahyana, whom I trusted implicitly.

I worried that, in the time I spent looking for the individuals Dasamuka had saved, the hungry tiger would shred Kiai Kasan's body.

A vision of Semi flitted through my mind. I rubbed my eyes, but the image of her kneeling at my feet remained. I had to decide quickly; the faster I acted, the better the outcome would be.

"All right, I believe you, Dasamuka," I said. "This is a business deal. How much do you want me to pay for the task I have asked you to complete?"

"My fee won't be small, sir. But for now, I need only half of it." Dasamuka paused. "I'll take the other half after Kiai Kasan is home safe, surrounded by his family."

Dasamuka explained what he needed the money for and, upon Den Wahyana's whispered instructions, I gave him less than half the amount he requested. According to Den Wahyana, it was not wise to pay Dasamuka the full amount; it would make the youth feel that he had not charged me enough. Bargaining, on the other hand, would prove to Dasamuka that he had negotiated the best possible price for his services. And, judging by the gleam in Dasamuka's eyes when he received my money, Den Wahyana might have been right.

When I met Semi later that morning, she was not as nervous as she had been the day before and could engage in a normal conversation. I was able to convince her that her father would be safe. And when I told her that she looked beautiful that day, more beautiful than usual, she managed to smile.

I suddenly realized I needed to watch the fight, to enrich my articles. The altercation between a man and a beast had to be horrifying.

"Do you know when they will have the fight?" I asked.

"Yes, two days from today. Do you want to see it?" Semi's voice was filled with disgust. The corners of her mouth pulled slightly downward as she pressed her lips together.

"I just want to make sure that your father is really safe. I paid someone to save him and need to make sure he keeps his word."

"Oh… then I will try to come, also." Semi said, quietly.

———•——

Finally, the day when a man and a tiger were to fight each other in the bronjong arrived. I had told neither John Crawfurd nor Uncle Harvey about the event. I felt the matter was my personal business, something between Semi and me.

"Did you invite Den Mas Bagus to join us?" I asked Den Wahyana, who arrived alone at my house on horseback.

"He doesn't really care about bronjong," Den Wahyana answered. He's more interested in tracking the soldiers who killed his father."

We traveled on horseback on the same roads we had come the first time. Upon our arrival, Den Wahyana and I were greeted by a soldier and escorted to seats reserved for special guests. The soldier had probably been given orders by his superior, who might know us.

I was the only Caucasian. The other uniformed officials were Javanese. I declined their offer for preferred seating, being more comfortable among the common folks.

There were not many spectators, and I asked Den Wahyana for an explanation. He said that the public did not think the man who had been convicted was guilty, and people did not like to watch the killing of an innocent man. Den Wahyana assured me that people would flock to the stage if the bronjong held a well-known criminal.

The gamelan performance that preceded the fight wore on my patience. I could not keep from looking at my pocket watch.

Suddenly, the gamelan stopped playing and people stopped talking. A soldier walked onto the stage and spread out a document on the podium. He read out loud that the prisoner, Kiai Kasan from Bagelen, was convicted for hiding followers of the rebel Raden Rangga in his boarding school.

After the man left the stage, four soldiers escorted a prisoner to the only door of the bronjong.

The door was so low that the prisoner had to bend to get through the opening. When he straightened up, I could see him more clearly. The white-haired, bearded, old man walked across the cage, then turned to face the door and stood erect, calmly waiting.

Accompanied by agitating gamelan sounds, a four-wheeled, wooden cage holding a tiger was pushed against the bronjong door, and the cage door was removed. Using a long wooden stick, the handler then prodded the tiger, forcing it into the bronjong.

The tiger slowly entered the arena and took in his surroundings. For a moment, man and beast held each other at bay. There was no more than five feet of distance between them. The old man exuded no fear. It seemed that he positioned himself as a worthy opponent rather than defenseless prey. Man and beast eyed each other and started their ferocious battle in horrifying silence by establishing themselves.

The spectators, especially the low-ranking soldiers, became impatient. They shouted, to spur the tiger into action. When the tiger retained its composure, they tried to agitate it by throwing scattered pieces of wood and bamboo against the cage. Finally, the handler took a long spear and, thrusting it through the bronjong wall, he poked the tiger in his belly.

The tiger let out an earsplitting roar and lunged.

I automatically reached for my pistol in the holster hanging from my waist, to shoot the tiger in the head, but the cheering crowd reminded me that I was not in the jungle. Instead, I was in a primitive court where a tiger functioned as executioner. I steeled myself to witness what I expected to be a bloody scene.

Much to my surprise, the old man neither ran nor moved sideways away from the tiger. Instead, he lay himself on his back on the bronjong floor.

Accompanied by deafening cheering from a near-hysterical crowd, the tiger planted himself on top of the man. Everyone prepared for a bloody scene of the tiger tearing the man apart, when suddenly, the tiger slumped and fell onto his side, his head almost touching the old man's shoulders, blood gushing from his side.

The crowd held their breath and rose to stand in silent disbelief.

The old man slowly sat up. Leaning on his bloody spear, he rose to a standing position and waved at the now-roaring crowd. Despite his victory over the tiger, Kiai Kasan looked thin and weak.

I took a deep, relieved breath. There was no need to stay for the man's victory celebration, which undoubtedly would last a considerable amount of time. I pulled on Den Wahyana's arm. As we started to leave, I wondered who to pay tribute to: the old man or Dasamuka.

Riding home, I felt that someone was following us. I slowed my horse and turned in my saddle to see who it was. A small rider spurred his horse into a gallop, and Dasamuka soon joined us.

By the time I entered my front yard, Dasamuka had already dismounted and now walked toward me. I knew what he wanted and quickly handed him the money.

Dasamuka fingered the bills without counting them. He then tucked the money into the folds of his clothes, nodded, and said goodbye, breaking into a hearty smile before riding off.

———•—

That evening, I paced my bedroom floor for hours, contemplating the event that had disturbed me to no end. Several small, seemingly unrelated incidents came to mind and slowly began to form a whole, with the bronjong functioning as a spindle. I suddenly saw the impact the bronjong had on the everyday life of the average Javanese, how it was used to manipulate people's behavior.

I hurriedly walked toward my desk, pulled out pen and paper, and feverishly began to write.

My articles were aimed at the educated population in Europe. For the Edinburgh Club, I did not need to write stylistically. I could simply render the facts the way they were. It was different for the *London Times*. I needed to think about form in addition to content; hopefully my writing style would hold the reader's interest.

If I simplified the content, my writing would repeat Doctor Leyden's theory that the future of Europe was in the Far Eastern countries. And, by making the bronjong my topic, it would hopefully become the consideration for arranging and funding future expeditions.

Bronjong constituted the link that connected Raden Rangga's failed rebellion to Kiai Kasan, his sympathizer. Bronjong was the instrument the colonial government and the sultanate used to silence the unconventional voices that were growing in number.

It had been proven many times that the progress of human civilization was determined by rebels, individuals who were unconventional.

Raden Rangga and Kiai Kasan represented those rebels. Raden Rangga dared to challenge the colonial government, and Kiai Kasan, with the naiveté of a simple villager, tried to be helpful by housing Den Rangga's men. I wondered how many Ranggas and Kasans had already been silenced by the existence of bronjong.

My writings encouraged the developed countries in Europe to help the people in Asia, who were suppressed by their rulers, to become more independent. I emphasized that colonialism is different from imperialism. I closed my writing by concluding that the Javanese conscience needed to be awakened by a desire to become a nation that equaled the developed countries in Europe. It was rather provocative, but those were my thoughts after watching the bronjong performance.

I wasn't quite done yet, but I was getting tired. It had been a long day. Stretching, I yawned and was headed for bed, when I heard a woman's voice through the open window.

"*Kula nuwun....* Excuse me, please...."

The voice was familiar. *Semi? It couldn't be. Why would she come at this hour of the night?* I rushed to the front door.

When I opened the door, she was on my doorstep. The lurik kebaya and batik sarong she wore looked similar to the one she had been wearing before the bronjong, when she begged me on her knees to help her. Now she stood with her head lowered and her palms in front of her, a formal gesture the Javanese used as a greeting.

"*Kula nuwun, ndara Tuan,*" Semi repeated. "Excuse me, sir."

I opened the door wider. "Semi!" My heart was pounding, "Why are you here this late?"

Semi did not answer, but lowered her head even more.

"Please, come in."

Before I closed the door, I quickly looked around. Had I failed to notice a chaperone waiting outside the gate? Apparently Semi had come alone.

As she walked by, I smelled the fragrance of jasmine. Once she entered the living room, Semi immediately knelt down. "I'm sorry, Mr. Willem. I only wish to express my gratitude for the assistance you provided," she said in formal Javanese.

"Semi, it's only right that we help each other as human beings." I stood near the door I had just closed. I did not know what to do.

"I can't repay your kindness, sir," she answered even more softly, hanging her head low.

She came here alone, late at night, merely to thank me? I moved closer to the woman for whom I had gladly spent my savings.

"I want to repay your kindness, sir." Her voice was as soft as the whisper of tree leaves blown by the wind.

I took her by the arm to help her stand. We stood so close to each other that we were touching. When I put an arm around her waist, Semi's breathing became heavier and faster.

I led her to my bedroom, where I seated her on the edge of my bed and sat down next to her. Bending toward her, I brought my face close to hers.

Semi closed her eyes.

I noticed the fine down on her forehead, as I was about to kiss her. Her hair had come undone, and the flowers she had tucked in it fell on my hand as I caressed her slim neck. That's when a teardrop slipped from under her fluttering eyelids.

Semi burst into sobs, and I suddenly realized that my touch might have offended her. "I didn't mean to hurt you."

"No, sir. That wasn't it," Semi sighed. "I'm married, sir."

I wanted to respond to her last statement, but my tongue was frozen. Overcome by a sense of loss, I could only bow my head.

If Semi had not tearfully mentioned her marriage, I most definitely would have had her tonight. I simply would have had to. But the way she obviously valued her marriage was a huge hurdle. I would be no more than an animal if I gave in to my desire for her.

The wind moved the open window shutters in my bedroom. I rose and went to close them. When I turned around, Semi was gone.

I rushed outside and caught a glimpse of her walking away quickly, before she disappeared into the darkness of the night.

I stood in the doorway for a while, stunned, until the cool evening breeze gently calmed my pounding heart.

———•—•———

The day after saving Kiai Kasan from the bronjong punishment, I visited Den Wahyana at his home.

"It seems that you aren't bothered by the concept of bronjong punishment," I said, after making myself comfortable on the pandan mat in his living room. His stoic reaction to the uncivilized punishment still bothered me.

Den Wahyana didn't respond to my statement. Instead, he asked me to drink the warm tea without sugar and try a piece of the boiled taro a servant had brought from the back part of his home. After watching me partake in the offerings and taking a few sips of his tea, he began to speak.

"Javanese people place an enormous value on valor—they deeply respect an individual who possesses this trait. To me, valor means not only being brave, but also being sincere about not expecting anything in return for the good we do." He paused, as if looking for the right words to convey what was on his mind. "God's blessing should be the only motivation to do good."

"You still haven't told me how you can regard something as shocking as the bronjong punishment with such indifference." I could not keep the edge out of my voice.

"As far as I know, many prisoners choose to fight the tiger over an unknown time of imprisonment. The prisoner who dies in the bronjong would die in a fight against the king of the jungle and die honorably. If he manages to win the fight, the victory would be doubled. He would be freed by the sultan and reinstated respectfully in his neighborhood." Den Wahyana took another sip of his tea. He seemed to feel that he had addressed my concern adequately.

"When was the bronjong punishment implemented for the first time?" Frustrated, I stuck my hands in my pockets and began pacing the room.

Den Wahyana thought for a while, then answered matter-of-factly. "As far as I know, Sultan Hamengkubuwono I was the first sultan who convicted someone to be put into the bronjong. A rebel from the Gunung Kidul area was caught and put to fight a tiger. He died." Den Wahyana took a deep breath. "After more than a month in prison without good food and drink, the fight was by no means fair."

"Hmm." The whole idea of basically feeding a human being to a wild animal as a viable form of punishment in a court of law still did not sit well with me. "I still think that the bronjong punishment is barbaric and not acceptable in a civilized world."

"Yes, I agree with you. However, not all convicts are like Kiai Kasan. They could easily have been robbers who had killed many innocent people mercilessly." Den Wahyana rose. When our eyes met, he said, "I don't agree with the bronjong punishment. But right now, thinking of the immediate future of the Yogyakarta

Sultanate is more important than thinking of how to banish the bronjong punishment." He took another deep breath, then said quietly, "Only the sultan has the power to end the suffering of the Javanese people."

———•••———

Den Wahyana and Dasamuka appeared to have a close relationship, but it still took a month before I was told the details of Dasamuka's ploy to save Kiai Kasan.

Dasamuka had used my advance money to buy a goat and spear. Next, he bribed the tiger handler to feed the tiger the fat goat before it was let into the bronjong. Then Dasamuka bribed the guard to exchange the regular spear a prisoner was given for a special, longer lance that was much sharper, with a head that had been dipped in poison. While the method Dasamuka had employed seemed quite simple, it was not easy to move freely around the bronjong area, nor was it easy to strike up a friendship with tiger handlers and prison guards.

———•••———

Dasamuka crossed my path again when, a few months later, I accompanied John Crawfurd on a visit to Den Mas Suryanata, a highly regarded aristocrat who owned vast stretches of land in the Rejawinangun area, including the plantation Uncle Harvey had leased.

Den Mas Suryanata lived on a large estate in the northern part of the sultanate, and his stables were known for its great horses. The Resident was well liked for his friendliness with the aristocrats of the Yogyakarta Sultanate.

While Crawfurd was engaged in a conversation with Den Mas Suryanata, I noticed Dasamuka out of the corner of my eye.

"What's Dasamuka doing here?" I asked the guard.

After making sure no one was around to overhear us, he whispered, "Don't tell anyone, but he's been asked to find a new wife for Den Mas Suryanata." The guard smiled meaningfully.

I nodded. Den Wahyana had told me that Javanese aristocrats pursued five coveted items: women, weapons, mansions, prized fowl and horses. The most coveted, of course, were the women.

On my way home from the Suryanata mansion, I kept thinking about Dasamuka. The young boy was already confronting problems that should be handled by an adult. The business of saving someone's life or finding him a new wife were not issues a small boy should have to concern himself with.

———•———

My intention to keep track of Dasamuka was unfortunately interrupted when a courier from Kiai Kasan's family arrived at my house. The man very politely relayed the message from the highly respected family. On behalf of the family, he apologized for being tardy in thanking me for helping to save Kiai Kasan.

I responded to his apology by stating my desire to visit Kiai Kasan. I wanted to check on his condition after the horrible incident. The courier was happy for me to join him, and we soon rode our horses, side by side, to Kiai Kasan's boarding school in the Bagelen region.

Riding through the green, fertile land of the Bagelen territory, I noticed odd divisions. The borderlines of the Yogyakarta and Surakarta sultanates were extremely complicated—some Surakarta territories were inside the Yogyakarta jurisdiction. On the other hand, some Yogyakarta territories were inside the Surakarta jurisdiction. If such territories were mapped, the results would look quite disorderly, similar to a batik pattern painted by children. I was sure that such a volatile situation was intentionally created by the colonial government.

Kiai Kasan's boarding school fell under the jurisdiction of the Surakarta sultanate, even though it was located closer to the Yogyakarta Keraton than the Surakarta one.

When I arrived at his boarding school, Kiai Kasan lay on a wooden divan in his room. Other than looking a bit pale, he didn't seem any different from the time I first saw him at the bronjong. Even though he had won the fight, the tiger had hurt his chest.

"Thank you, sir. It's all I can say," Kiai Kasan wheezed.

"I tried to explain why I had involved myself in the incident, which was still being talked about by the people in the sultanate. "As human beings, we have a moral duty to help each other. The punishment was barbaric."

"I heard that Dasamuka was involved," Kiai Kasan whispered.

I did not want to take all the credit for saving Kiai Kasan's life. "Yes," I said. "He was the one who planned it all."

"Dasamuka is an extraordinary boy."

I had to agree with Kiai. "Especially considering how young he is, the boy is amazing."

"A young boy can have an extraordinary role," Kiai Kasan replied. "Being extraordinary, however, does not always mean being right."

I did not understand what he meant and kept silent while looking around his bedroom, which was narrow and dark compared to a European bedroom. My attention was drawn to a pile of old books with loose and dog-eared pages.

"Are you interested in theological issues?"

Kiai Kasan's question startled me. He had caught me taking stock of his bedroom; something I quickly realized was impolite.

"Not very much. I'm more interested in philosophy."

"Religion and philosophy do not oppose each other, though many people assume they do."

"I agree with you, Kiai. I am interested in philosophy, as it is my way to thank God for the gift which is only given to human beings: the ability to reason."

Kiai Kasan's statement reminded me of philosophy classes I had taken. The mystical experience of religion did not oppose the rational experience of philosophy. Neither could it be separated from the human philosophical aspiration to find the deepest and most thorough understanding of reality.

Kiai Kasan said, "Verse sixty-five of the Surah Al Kahf chapter in our Holy Book talks about a wisdom—a knowledge, if you will—far beyond our comprehension and ability to reason. Verse seventy-four says: *Then the two went forth until they met a lad whom he slew, whereupon Moses exclaimed: Why did you slay an innocent person who did not slay anyone? You have surely done a horrible thing.*" Kiai Kasan closed his eyes.

I noticed his eyelids flutter and watched the trembling of his beard. I wondered why he had recited the verse and what he was thinking, when he sat up and, looking me straight in the eye, asked, "What would you have done, if you were Moses?"

I resisted the urge to spontaneously respond, "Why the same, of course." Instead, I forced myself to think and tried hard to come up with any reason for someone to kill an innocent child.

"I probably would have asked the same question," I said finally. "I don't think anything could warrant the killing of a child."

Kiai Kasan shifted his gaze to something in the distance and softly said, "The one who decided this was one who was loved by God, a holy man. Thus, we can say that it is God Himself who decided that the child should die."

Noticing my confusion, Kiai Kasan continued.

"Verse eighty tells us that the child would lead his parents—who were righteous parents—to evil. In other words, if the child had not been killed, he would cause both his parents to be sent to hell. The child was destined to be bad."

I could not help myself and blurted out, "What? I think it's unfair for a child to be born merely to become a criminal and put to death."

"Well, that is the problem. Most people do not give God enough credit for His gift of reasoning and, rather than trying to work themselves out of a bad situation, they question His decisions and blame Him for any misfortune that befalls them. Under the disguise of accepting a misfortune as an act of His infinite wisdom, they don't do anything to try to get out of the situation.

"Many people erroneously refer to this attitude as *narima ing pandum*, which means accept what God gives us—while, in fact, what we Javanese refer to as *narima* is quite the opposite of this defeatist attitude. *Narima* to us is the ability to gracefully accept what *is*, after doing our very best to change it if it happens to be something bad."

Still riled by the idea of murdering a child, I rose and started pacing the room.

Kiai Kasan calmly continued, "Verse eighty-one says, '*and we desired that their Lord should grant them another in his place, a son more upright and more tender-hearted.*'" He paused for a moment, and gave me a look that made me return to my seat.

"Therefore, in essence, by killing the child, He saved the parents from suffering for their child's bad behavior and being sent to hell. He gave the parents a 'better' child to lessen their grief, and prevented the child from having to live a miserable life as a criminal." Kiai Kasan held my eyes. "Rather than questioning Him, Moses should have trusted God's infinite wisdom in the first place."

"Hmm...." I had lived long enough among the Javanese to hold back from airing my opinion. Instead, I said, "May I try to guess why, other than by destiny, the child was killed by someone whom God loved?"

"You may, of course. For a long time, I've wanted to hear an interpretation of the story from a different point of view. Coming from the hemisphere currently noted for its academia, your opinion will be very interesting."

"I apologize in advance if my explanation does not meet your expectations." I said.

"I imagine, both of this boy's parents unconsciously caused their beloved child to misbehave. Perhaps they loved him too much. Perhaps they spoiled the boy, and this caused the child to be demanding, selfish, and callous." I tried to explain my thoughts.

Kiai Kasan neither nodded nor shook his head. He seemed to be absorbed in his own thoughts.

I took a deep breath, "Human condition is the consequence of human action. It is not determined by destiny."

"Would our conversation apply to the Dasamuka who lives in this sultanate?" Kiai Kasan asked suddenly.

I was taken aback. *What prompted this question?*

Dasamuka, as far as I knew, had done only good things. He had shown me the way to the bronjong and saved Kiai Kasan's life. Why compare him to a spoiled child?

"I don't care to make that connection, Kiai."

Neither of us spoke, until the summons for the asar prayers broke the silence. Even though I did not understand the words, I knew the call brought people together for the afternoon prayer in the mosque or at home.

Kiai Kasan excused himself. He pulled himself up and, sitting cross-legged, softly recited some prayers.

Not wanting to disturb him, I left the room and sat down on the mat spread on the porch of his cool wooden house.

The problem of a child who was preordained to be evil and consequently killed still disturbed me. I pondered our conversation. As an academic, I was required to be skeptical, to doubt what was assumed to be final.

Spoiling was basically poisoning. If the parents had poisoned their child's mind, the potential that he'd produce evil definitely existed, and the holy man probably recognized this. Hence, he killed the child. That would be the logical way to give reason to the still unacceptable act of killing a child. I needed to find out why Kiai Kasan had mentioned Dasamuka.

When I knew that Kiai Kasan had finished his prayers, I peeked into his room. The old man was already lying down and snoring softly. After saying goodbye to his family members who were around, I rode my horse home.

The following day, the messenger of the Kiai Kasan family came to my house again. Noticing the man's sad face, I immediately asked about Kiai Kasan's health.

"Kiai Kasan passed away yesterday. He'll be buried today." The messenger's voice trembled. "After you left him yesterday, he asked for *degan*. A few minutes after drinking a small amount of the young coconut water, he started choking. Then, not long after that, he left all of us and returned to The Creator."

"When I was with him in his room, Kiai Kasan was not complaining about anything."

"The tiger had caused a deep internal wound, we're all certain of that. Such an injury would clearly endanger a man of his age."

"Does Dasamuka know?" I asked. Suddenly parts of my last conversation with Kiai Kasan jumped into my mind. *"A young boy can have an extraordinary role. However, being extraordinary does not always mean being right."*

"Dasamuka?"

"Never mind. My condolences." There was no reason to explain who Dasamuka was.

I remembered how hurried Dasamuka was to collect his payment immediately after Kiai Kasan won the fight. He must have known all along that, while Kiai Kasan's students carried their beloved teacher triumphantly on their shoulders home from the bronjong, the old man's life was in danger. *Had my conversation with Kiai been about Dasamuka?*

Chapter 5

KIAI BAKIR

My intention to track Dasamuka, the small boy who had aroused my curiosity, failed again when, the day after Kiai Kasan's passing, Jiya came to tell me that my presence was requested at Rejawinangun. When I arrived, Daisy was sitting on the terrace steps waiting for me.

She looked like a white orchid rising between the mossy blackish aerial roots of a giant banyan tree. Her natural beauty was striking.

"Where have you been? You must have a new girlfriend," she teased.

"Why would I need a new girlfriend? My old girlfriend always looks new. She'll never wear out." I countered.

"All right, how about this—will you accompany me to Buitenzorg?"

"I'd be happy to accompany my old girlfriend, who always looks as fresh as a daisy."

"We'll leave early tomorrow morning."

"What's the hurry? How about going the day after tomorrow?" I wanted to avoid having to cancel an appointment with Resident Crawfurd. I was supposed to go with him to a horse race and socialize with the aristocrats.

"Ahhh!" Daisy grimaced. "I caught you!" She pouted, "Your devotion is only skin deep."

"No, no. It's all right. I'll go with you." I hurried to rectify my reluctance, not wanting to have her mockery turn into true discontent.

——•—•——

This trip was one of many visits where I escorted Daisy to the Botanical Garden in Buitenzorg. During these long carriage rides over a wide dirt road and through vast stretches of bare land, we usually engaged in conversations about the theories and beliefs of John Casper Leyden and Mary Wollstonecraft, the two individuals who, separately, had impacted each of us the most.

Jolting out of her seat when we hit a deep pothole in the road, Daisy asked, "Have you read Mary's biography? She tried to jump off the Putney Bridge and had a child that was born out of wedlock."

"Really?" I steadied Daisy into her seat. While straightening up the stack of books in the corner next to her, I wondered if Daisy knew I too had contemplated suicide. I prodded, "If the existence of man and woman constitutes a binary opposition in which each person has its own characteristic, it means that these characteristics place a man and woman in an opposing situation. Does the theory of equality between genders acknowledge this?" We passed a ravine, and I noticed a guardrail built out of sturdy bamboo poles alongside the road.

"We don't object to the male's characteristic," Daisy said. "It's the male oppression that we challenge." She handed me a copy of *Maria, or The Wrongs of Woman.* "Here, read this."

"I certainly will; but for now, I'd like to hear what you have to say about the beliefs of the writer you so admire." I enjoyed our invigorating conversations about women's rights and morals. I didn't know many women who would have been able to defend their controversial beliefs the way Daisy did. I held the book for a moment before returning it to the pile beside her. I knew she would read it again and again and did not want her to be without a favorite title.

—————

Just as we had fallen into a routine to pass our traveling time, we had also established a routine to fill the time in Buitenzorg, where Daisy had to meet with the head botanist.

As soon as we arrived in Buitenzorg, I left Daisy at the caretaker's office and headed for the Tanah Abang cemetery in Batavia, where John Casper Leyden was buried.

I had never thought Leyden would die on Java, the island he frequently mentioned in his scientific lectures. I was still able to hear his coarse voice, which nonetheless sounded gentle and melodious to my ears. I was sure he would still be alive, if not for the time he spent searching the piles of dusty and moldy manuscripts stored in an old building in Batavia.

I obliged myself to pray at his grave. The elegant tomb was enhanced by an engraved poem written by Lady Olivia Mariamne Raffles, the governor's wife, who had recently passed away.

Trying to pray, I realized I was unable to recite prayers; I did not actually belong to any religion. The religious activities I performed were merely a ritual.

Junaedi Setiyono

I was certain that God, or whatever entity was being worshiped by the followers of various religions found around the world, had to be acknowledged as a respected presence. It was impossible that these religions made the same mistake by assuming the presence of a certain entity, when the entity was actually absent. I convinced myself that God was present, and asked Him to give John Casper Leyden the best possible place He had for him.

When I'd had conversations with Dr. Leyden, aside from discussions about the new world in the Far East countries, religion had been one of the most interesting topics. Our alma mater, the University of Edinburgh, indeed challenged the church doctrines that placated the common sense of human beings. The call to regard this virtue as God's gift to humans echoed throughout Edinburgh and caused the university to be referred to as "the lighthouse of the enlightenment age."

This influence was also felt on Java, at least when I was at the Botanical Garden in Buitenzorg, where scientists cared about the possible extinction of a plant species despite the fact that it grew abundantly. I was certain that scientists were far more aware of factual life than clergy. Factual life was the only bridge to eternity.

It would be wrong to think that the Edinburgh academia hated religion. The Edinburgh scientists just wanted religion to be regarded as a personal affair, rather than be institutionalized.

When I visited the Borobudur temple in Magelang, or the Roro Jonggrang temple in Prambanan, my mind was always pulled to the ancient Greek philosophers: Socrates, Plato, Aristotle, Archimedes, Pythagoras, and the like. The relationship between Javanese temples and ancient Greek philosophers was obvious. The ancient Greek philosopher spent most of his lifetime on sciences, while people of other countries spent their lifetime establishing buildings to worship. The works of ancient Greek philosophers not only existed, but had led the progress of human civilization, whereas buildings of worship built in the same time period were already crumbling. The practice of religion was closely related to the progress of human civilization, but if a church doctrine hampered human civilization, its teachings had to be re-evaluated.

———•••———

When I returned to Buitenzorg in the evening, Daisy had finished her job. She had seen to it that the plants she had brought to the Botanical Garden were properly labeled, and left detailed instructions for their care.

The plants she had brought on this trip belonged to the hibiscus family. Although the plants looked different, according to Daisy, who was an expert in identifying plants, they belonged to the same family. The specimen would become an integral part of the Botanical Garden.

The difference between my interest in plants and Daisy's was similar to the difference between the width of a blade of grass and the width of a banana tree leaf.

Our trip home to Rejawinangun was no different from all the others that had followed a visit to the Botanical Garden. However, this time we seemed to have exhausted the theories of John Leyden and Mary Wollstonecraft and had ran out of topics for conversation. The silence began to feel uncomfortable.

"Please don't forget to tell me a few days ahead of time when you need to go to Buitenzorg again," I said, in an attempt to start conversation.

"Are you sure you'll always be able to escort me? What would Resident Crawfurd think of that?"

"Don't worry. My employer is very understanding."

"Does he know how much time you spend at Rejawinangun?"

"Yes," I said with a smile. "I told him that Rejawinangun is the sanctuary of the maiden who has the key to my heart." I used my most dramatic tones, as if I were an actor on stage.

"I'm sure Crawfurd didn't believe you." Daisy pretended to be calm while biting her lip.

"Why wouldn't he believe me?"

"You're notorious for being unreliable, at least when you talk about marriage."

We fell silent again. In the silence, I tried to guess what Daisy was thinking and feeling. Glancing at her, I suspected she might be wondering how much truth there was in my dramatic performance.

Through the carriage windows, I watched the trees turn into shadows as darkness began to fall. The slow, rhythmic movement of the carriage, along with the swaying lantern light, began to shape the shadows, and suddenly Ailsa's silhouette appeared among the moving forms. I let out a deep sigh. *Why did she haunt me still?*

Daisy threw me a quizzical look. In the dim light, I saw her run her tongue across her lips. Perhaps she wanted to ask me something. Whatever it was, I would have no answer; I bowed my head to avoid the look in her eyes.

————•••————

There were times I liked to take a good look at my own face in the mirror. Now in my thirties, I was no longer a young man. The years I had spent in Java had leathered my skin, and I looked at least ten years older than my age. How true was the saying that time passed too fast, while life was so short. The saying concluded with stating, *hence, there's no time to waste.* I wondered what was considered a waste of time. Hopefully, my time in Java was not.

I found ways to satisfy my curiosity about Dasamuka's life, literally and figuratively. In Bagelen, the *pesantren*—the Islamic boarding school—that once belonged to Kiai Kasan was now run by his eldest son, Kiai Bakir.

After Kiai Kasan's passing, I occasionally visited the pesantren. I liked to wander in the area that had once played an important role in the history of the Mataram dynasty, but I had other motivations as well. I wanted to learn more about the teachings of Islam, a religion practiced by most Javanese, and I wanted to see Semi. I knew she had a family now, but I still hoped to see her.

My last memorable conversation with Kiai Bakir was when I told him that I believed in God.

He told me then that I only needed two more things in order to become a good human being who was loved by Him: to believe in Judgment Day, the day everyone will be held responsible for their actions, and to perform good deeds. I have no idea why his words brought me such joy—I, who had never practiced any faith.

While tethering my horse to the bamboo fence that surrounded the compound, I caught a glimpse of Dasamuka. He was leaving the pesantren and, judging by the direction he was coming from, I figured he had been in the main building where the headmaster lived. As usual, he moved with a spring in his steps.

"Dasamuka! Where are you going?" I greeted the handsome young man. Except for the intimidating look in his eyes, Dasamuka was indeed an attractive Javanese gentleman.

"I'm going to the Keraton. I'm meeting a prince." Dasamuka sauntered towards me. He seemed to be bothered by something.

From Den Wahyana, I had learned that a sultan's harem could produce as many as fifty children, and that all of them were referred to as princes and princesses. I took a wild guess, "The prince is Den Mas Suryanata, right?"

"Yes," he seemed perplexed at my accurate guess, and continued hesitantly, "about the horses and…"

"Women?" I finished for him.

Dasamuka did not answer. He only gave me a wan smile.

It was common for a prince to pursue women, I often heard about that. But this time, the rumor was louder. Perhaps this was caused by Den Mas Suryanata's latest indulgence.

He seemed to be bored of Javanese women and had turned his attention to the Chinese, Arabic, and Dutch women who were a common sight in the region of the sultanate. Like he had in the past, Den Mas Suryanata tasked Dasamuka with the job.

Perhaps Dasamuka had just received an order to find an Arabic woman, and his visit to the pesantren had something to do with it. If I were correct, Kiai Bakir would have opposed him.

"I'll tell you about it, but not now," Dasamuka said, walking towards his carriage. He must have been doing well to own a coach and be able to employ a coachman at such a young age. I was sure he could be no more than seventeen years old.

After Dasamuka left, I quickly headed to the house of the pesantren's headmaster. As always, I was well received. Kiai Bakir's hospitality made me feel very much at home.

According to Den Wahyana, I was slightly different from the typical British. I enjoyed talking for hours with Javanese nobilities, something that was not usually done. In this, he was correct. The British were a nation of workers. They were not used to passing the time with idle chitchat.

I did not blame other countries that perceived the British's businesslike manner as arrogant. Maybe I was influenced by Resident Crawfurd, who excelled in communicating with Javanese people from all social classes; I secretly wanted to be like him.

My conversations with Kiai Bakir never strayed too far from the two subjects we had a common interest in: religion and literature. But Java was an interesting place to be discussing religion and literature. I once read a book that claimed that all the religious and literary works that have been brought to the Indian Archipelago—especially to the island of Java—would experience more dynamic cultural developments there than in their place of origin. The academics of Edinburgh called it adaptation. The Javanese were acknowledged for their expertise in this matter.

"Many Javanese people think that Dasamuka was born evil. Do you think so, Kiai?" I had caught snippets of the tale around Dasamuka from conversations among the houseboys in the Karesidenan, the government complex where I both lived and worked.

"Dasamuka, the son of sage Vishrava in the Ramayana, the Hindu epic?"

"Surely not the one who just dropped by here?" I admitted not to know much about the legendary tale's character.

"Everyone is born without sins, even those born from an adulterous act. I believe that. Therefore, Dasamuka, as a newborn, was sinless. The changes in his character are caused by the events he comes across during his journey to adulthood."

"But isn't his birth alone already signifying the dawn of a dark age? Wasn't he born in the form of a pulsating clot of blood?" I had heard this part of the story from a member of the household staff in Rejawinangun.

"It is a symbol, sir. It's assumed that he was born out of wedlock. His birth was not favored by many. Neither would a disgusting lump of blood, would it?"

"Is it true that Dasamuka has a brother who is a handsome warrior?"

"Yes, the warrior's name is Vibisana. In my opinion, this has a symbolic aspect as well. The best kind of human is not one who never makes a mistake. The best kind of human is one who quickly realizes his faults and makes an attempt to atone for it. That warrior was born after sage Vishrava and his wife, Kaikeshi, realized their mistake and made amends."

"How about the Dasamuka who just came to see you?"

"Ah, him…. Yes, I still have the same opinion. All newborns are sinless. *When* and *where* they will go will mold them into *who* they become: Dasamuka or Vibisana."

"Would youngsters like Dasamuka, who become bad people due to lack of guidance, be at fault?"

"In my religion, there is a concept called *khusnul khotimah*, a good ending. If, according to God, Dasamuka's birth brings more good than harm to this world, he'll receive a *hidayah*—an enlightenment from Allah—and his death will be considered as khusnul khotimah. Surely, only the Almighty God can judge someone's good and bad deeds, and His view might be entirely different from that of humans."

We fell into silence, and I thought about Kiai Bakir's answer regarding Dasamuka.

I no longer felt the need to analyze his opinion on Dasamuka, the man who haunted my mind. I was more interested in the person who motivated me to travel all the way to Bagelen, a Javanese woman named Semi. Because she was a married woman, this was clearly an unwholesome thought.

"I haven't seen your sister Semi in quite a while."

"My sister?"

"The woman who approached me when Kiai Kasan was put in the bronjong to fight the tiger."

"Ah, my apology. Semi is my sister-in-law."

"So, she is your brother's wife?"

"Yes. I only have one brother, Ngusman. Semi is Ngusman's wife. Unfortunately, they're not home right now."

The mention of Semi's husband gently elbowed my heart. I had lost any hope of getting closer to Semi without feeling guilty. Strangely, I was eager to meet Ngusman, the lucky man who was her husband.

"Have you ever met Ngusman, sir?" Kiai Bakir asked me all of a sudden. I was sure he had noticed the look on my face when he mentioned his brother's name.

"Ngusman? I have not." I wasn't the type of person who could easily hide my feelings. My lips quivered when I uttered Semi's husband's name.

"He is rarely at home."

"When did Ngusman and Semi get married?"

"The wedding was actually held before Father was brought to trial by Den Mas Suryanata," Kiai Bakir answered wistfully. "It was kept secret due to our impossible circumstances during that time."

"Will you tell me more about the dispute?"

"If we trace it back, it all goes back to Semi," Kiai Bakir explained. "Den Mas Suryanata wanted to take Semi as one of his many concubines. Semi rejected his advances because she already had a suitor, Ngusman. Den Mas Suryanata then asked Father to foil their wedding. When Father wisely and politely objected, Den Mas Suryanata turned the disagreement into a dispute."

"So, denying Den Mas Suryanata the pleasure of courting Semi was the crime that put Kiai Kasan in the bronjong for punishment?"

"Den Mas Suryanata had been the prince who convinced the Keraton and the Dutch that Father's involvement in the rebellion of Raden Rangga was due to his naiveté and limited to providing them with shelter. But when Father refused to accommodate him in regards to Semi, Den Mas Suryanata crossed out the statement: *providing shelter upon lack of knowledge* and replaced it with: *providing shelter upon agreement with the purpose of their struggle.*"

In not stepping aside for royalty, Kiai Kasan had signed his own death warrant. No wonder Semi was so insistent in trying to help him; she had unwittingly played a role in bringing the charges against him.

———•—•—

I continued to meet with Kiai Bakir. Aside from learning more about Kiai Kasan and Den Mas Suryanata, I wanted to see Semi and meet her husband. I just wanted to see them together. I had no explanation for this irrational behavior and ascribed it to some malfunction of my nervous system. Most importantly, the thought of Semi kept Ailsa from appearing in my mind.

Alas, someone was watching Kiai Bakir and me. The people of the Keraton did not approve of my visits to Kiai Bakir's pesantren—I believe this had something to do with the bronjong punishment. Through Den Wahyana, they warned me to keep my distance from any group deemed dangerous by the palace.

"It was a pure coincidence that I became involved in their business," I protested to Den Wahyana. "You need to tell the palace that I am merely a writer who is writing about Javanese living in a pesantren."

"This is something serious," Den Wahyana warned me. "Den Mas Suryanata could not accept the fact that Semi had refused him; he wanted the extinction of Kiai Kasan's entire family. You have heard about the term *tumpes kelor*, right? It is when an entire family and their descendants are all killed." Den Wahyana was worried.

"Den Mas Suryanata? Isn't it the Keraton who is disturbed by my relationship with Kiai Bakir? Would that nobleman really kill everyone in Kiai Kasan's family only because of a woman named Semi?" I was at a loss for words.

"Pride." Den Wahyana sighed, then continued, "Javanese will rebel to the point of running amok when their pride is wounded. On the other hand, Javanese people will be forever indebted to someone who has taken care of them. They would willingly lay down their life for someone who has treated them well.

"Supposedly, you get yourself involved in a dispute with a Javanese man," Den Wahyana continued, "and challenge him to have a duel somewhere—the matter would come to an end when one of you dies. However, if you express your hatred in public, if you curse and defame him, the dispute will haunt you until you die. Den Mas Suryanata felt that Kiai Kasan had wounded his pride: his desire to take Semi as one of his concubines went up into smoke because of the kiai. He felt that people laughed at his failure."

Nevertheless, I thought Den Wahyana was wrong. It was not Kiai Kasan who had ruined Den Mas Suryanata's plan to take Semi as a concubine. I believed Kiai Kasan had a discussion with Semi about the matter, and it had been her decision; he was only Semi's messenger.

I had been educated to act with common sense. The warning against my visit was overly dramatic and seemed unreasonable. I found it difficult to understand Javanese pride, and so I continued to visit Kiai Bakir's pesantren.

———•—

During the reign of Sultan Hamengkubuwono III, there were three places I visited the most: my office in the Karesidenan compound, Uncle Harvey's loji in Rejawinangun, and the pesantren of Kiai Bakir in Bagelen. Those three places were more than enough to occupy all my time. The years passed by very quickly. Time had blurred the images of Ailsa and the city of Edinburgh in my mind.

During one of my meetings with Kiai Bakir, I met Semi's husband. I expected him to look like Kiai Bakir, whose appearance was a blend of a quick-witted merchant and a muscled farmer. However, Ngusman turned out to be a shy gentleman with a slight build.

During a discussion with my colleagues at the Karesidenan about the ideal figure for Javanese men, they stated that Arjuna, the famous archer in *Mahabharata*, another Hindu epic the Javanese cherished, was considered the *lelananging jagat*, the ideal male. Unlike Hercules or Samson, Arjuna was slim and slender.

Ngusman resembled Arjuna not only in build but also in his gracious mannerism. During a conversation, the gentle-mannered man mostly listened and only spoke when someone asked him a question. In Kiai Bakir's words, Ngusman was like a gamelan instrument: there would be no sound unless struck. But with the right questions, he filled in Semi's story about their first meeting a short time before the assault on the Keraton in June of 1812.

———•◆•———

Reja arrived long before Ngusman at a freshwater spring at the foot of a hill surrounded by shrubs and trees. Hiding in the lush foliage of a jambu tree, he startled when Ngusman approached and took up post below him.

"Do you think of yourself as Jaka Tarub, the lad who stole the nymph's clothes?" Ngusman could guess why Reja was up in the tree overlooking the pond.

"Damn it! Go away!" Reja shouted, annoyed.

Ngusman ignored him.

"I'll pierce your skull if you don't leave." Reja's finger pointed at Ngusman's forehead.

"Your finger looks hard and sharp." Ngusman sat down nonchalantly, stretching his legs and crossing his arms.

"Are you challenging me?" Reja jumped out of the tree like a mad monkey and kicked Ngusman in his jaw.

Caught by surprise while mindlessly chewing on a blade of wild grass, Ngusman jumped up and ran.

Reja did not waste any time chasing Ngusman, who snaked through the thickets. In a matter of seconds, the two had trampled the lush vegetation.

Reja, soaked in perspiration, soon realized Ngusman had tricked him. Panting, he pulled out his dagger and pointed it at Ngusman with a shaking hand. "You've worn out my patience. I'll kill you!"

Reja lunged forward, but quickly realized that he had wasted a lot of energy tearing through the bushes. He moved carefully now, from one clear spot to another, trying to get to Ngusman, who kept ducking behind shrubbery.

I chuckled when Ngusman told this part of the story. The two of them must have looked like a kitten trying to catch an old mouse between thorny shrubs. I listened to the rest of Ngusman's story, amused.

When Reja's legs gave way under him, Ngusman stepped into the open, holding a thorny branch.

When Reja tried to stab him with his kris, Ngusman hit the boy in the face. Reja screamed in pain and dropped his kris. When Ngusman raised his stick again, Reja jumped backward and ran.

Ngusman picked up the kris. The dagger had a beautiful hilt. He was sure the owner was someone other than the boisterous youth who had tried to hurt him. Its owner would definitely consider it a precious possession.

Ngusman started to run after Reja.

"Stop! Can I see it?" A gentle voice coming from his right stopped Ngusman in his tracks. He turned and gave the girl standing by the roadside, holding a laundry basket gracefully on her hip, a quick once over.

"Ah, so you're the nymph Nawangwulan that grumpy Jaka Tarub was after?" Ngusman plucked a few thorns off his clothes.

Semi blushed. Nawangwulan was a revered beauty amongst the Javanese girls.

"So, you know that bad-tempered man?" Ngusman handed Semi the bare kris.

I leaned forward, curious. During one of our lessons, Den Wahyana had told me that to receive a kris without its sheath from a man was deemed inappropriate for a Javanese woman. The kris was considered to have a phallic connotation. I was anxious to find out how Semi would react.

Ngusman smiled. He appeared to relish recalling the rest of the story.

Semi gulped when she saw the kris and stammered, "It's my brother's."

Ngusman's handing her the kris, as a Javanese expression of his attraction to her, flustered her even more. Blushing, she gestured him to place the kris on top of a flat rock.

Ngusman walked away, straightening his clothes that were still in disarray from the fight.

Semi seemed stunned by his nonchalant attitude. She only realized Ngusman was leaving after he had walked some feet away from her.

"Please, wait!"

Ngusman slowed, without turning, and continued to walk away after Semi called out, "Thank you."

Semi watched as Ngusman quickly disappeared into the distance. She knew that the purple headband Ngusman wore was only worn by members of a pesantren family.

Semi picked up her brother's kris. She knew there were not many villagers who wore that kind of headband. Neither were there many men who remained calm in her presence. Semi quietly made her way back to the spring and pretended to concern herself with the laundry she needed to take home.

Ngusman had made the right decision to leave quickly. Soon after he left, Reja returned with a gang of twelve men. Upon realizing that he was no longer around, they simply made a big ruckus.

The story was meaningful to me, for I would hate to see Semi give herself up to a loser like Reja. I believed that Ngusman would be able to make her happy. I, on the other hand, was no different from Reja. I would only bring more suffering into her life. At one time, I was sure that I would manage to make her my mistress. However, I now realized that someone with her dignity would definitely turn me down right away.

My visits to Kiai Bakir's pesantren continued to bother Den Mas Suryanata, and Den Wahyana's warning turned out to be valid.

I always rode my horse to visit Kiai Bakir's pesantren. But, returning home after one visit, I could tell I was being followed. When I reached the village's border, a large tree branch with its foliage still intact lay across the middle of the usually empty trail. Clearly, neither a storm nor termites had lain it there—the branch had been chopped by someone who wanted to have business with me. I stopped and dismounted, reaching for the gun at my waist.

"I know you're armed," a man said in informal Javanese, suddenly standing next to me.

I had no idea where he came from, but I noticed that he was an albino.

He continued, "You're now surrounded by people who carry even more weapons and are ready to break your skull and rip your body apart."

"What do you want?" I tried to cut the conversation short. I just wanted to leave this dangerous situation as soon as possible.

"I'm ordered to take your life, but I'm not a butcher. I like to warn you first."

"Don't beat around the bush. What do you want?"

"If I see you one more time around Kiai Bakir's pesantren, I will immediately have a hole dug by the roadside to dump your corpse."

"I'm a government employee. You'll be facing the soldiers who protect your country."

"We are felons, we are vagabonds, and we have no business with the government. The only ones who are afraid of the government are those whom they feed. We find our own food."

"I don't believe I'm surrounded by lowly creatures like you. I thought you were merely trying to rob me. Go ahead. I'm challenging you." I could not show my fear. A government official like me should never appear weak in the eyes of an *inlander*—the colonialist's term for local scum.

"Fine—have it your way. There's no need to mob you. I could kill you by myself, but I'll show you that my threats are not empty." He turned to his right and shouted, "C'mon out!"

Someone carrying a rifle did appear. I was sure there were only the two of them, and doubted the rifle was of any use. I could not allow myself to be fooled by these hoodlums.

"Let's fight like men: a fistfight with no weapons. If you go down, your thugs need to remove this log. If I lose, you can take everything I carry. Deal?" I was much more familiar with books than martial arts, but during my student years, I had often worked out at the school's gymnasium, and this hoodlum was much shorter than a European. He only reached my ears. Like typical Javanese men, he had bad posture.

The fight soon ensued. It took me only a few moments to realize I had underestimated this albino. While his physique barely made an impression on me, his agility did. Not a single punch I launched reached his body, let alone his face.

Soaked in my sweat, I continued the fight. When I let my guard down, an iron-like fist punched my ribs. I staggered and lost my balance.

My attacker moved aside and let me take a breath. It seemed he intended to torture me.

With a declining level of confidence, I forced myself to get up. This time, his punch landed on my jaw. I immediately thudded against the ground. He could have jumped and smashed my chest, but instead, he circled me. Perhaps he was blinded by my shiny government uniform.

"Who are you?" I started to feel desperate. My defeat by this strange-looking man had come too quickly.

"People call me Ki Bule," he answered coldly, without any trace of victory in his voice.

Before I could accept my defeat, I heard the pounding sound of horses' hooves approaching. A cloud of dust soon formed, and the criminals jumped onto their saddles and disappeared into thick bushes at the side of the trail.

I waited for the approaching horsemen.

Undoubtedly, they were the Keraton guards. Their spokesman was no other than Dasamuka, the young gentleman who was often on my mind.

"One of our scouts reported this holdup. I'm sorry we're late." Dasamuka dismounted his dappled gray stallion.

My face felt bruised. When I brought my hand up to feel my cheek, my shirtsleeve came away with blood on it.

"Thank you," I sighed. I could already guess what would happen next.

Dasamuka escorted me back to the Karesidenan building. After offering me some Javanese medications to treat my wounds, he politely informed me that I needed to reward the soldiers who had come to my rescue.

I paid him handsomely, not wanting to be bothered by the triviality. However, that night, I kept thinking about the holdup. I couldn't help but wonder if Dasamuka's appearance on the scene was a pure coincidence, or if he had a hand in it.

Before I was lulled to sleep, I arrived at a conclusion that hit me hard. I was convinced that Dasamuka had benefited from the incident in two ways: from the party who was concerned with my visits to Kiai Bakir's pesantren, and from the "gratitude money" I had paid him for saving my life.

I was convinced that Ki Bule was just an extension of Dasamuka, and the Keraton guards were rewarded by the person who had asked him to stop my visits. After all, hadn't it been Den Mas Suryanata, Dasamuka's patron, who had objected to my visits to Kiai Bakir?

Chapter 6

DEN MAS SURYANATA

While assisting Resident Crawfurd in his effort to document the island of Java and its people, I was reminded of Dr. Leyden. In compliance to his request, I had written some articles about the bronjong incident and sent them to the Edinburgh Club and the *London Times*. I also reported the matter to Resident Crawfurd, who discussed it with Governor General Raffles.

The issue of a forced fight between a human and wild animal seemed to bother the Governor General, and he issued a decree on the prohibition of pitting humans against tigers. The new law was published on October 2, 1813, and distributed in English and Javanese.

Secretly, I took pride in this. I felt that my articles about bronjong for the *London Times* had contributed to the treaty between the British government and the Yogyakarta Sultanate. The treaty asserted that it was unacceptable for one human being to violate another one's rights, regardless of circumstance.

However, after this small triumph, an old question started to poke at me again. *Was it bronjong or branjang? Or both?* Dr. Leyden seemed to have been unsure of exactly what it was he had heard. Perhaps I should listen to the high-spirited Daisy and try to write on both matters. I had already tackled the bronjong, but had no clue what branjang could be about.

———•—•———

"Do you know what a branjang is?" I asked Den Wahyana.

"Branjangan? It's a type of bird."

"Is it a special kind of bird?"

"Many would like to think of it that way."

"Can you explain further?"

"This type of bird is kept as a pet for its song. It loves to fly up and down while singing, and therefore needs a taller cage than most other birds."

"What does it look like? What's the color of its feathers?"

"It looks ordinary. A wren is more attractive."

"Other than being a certain kind of bird, what else could a branjang possibly be?"

Den Wahyana went silent for a while, then quietly said, "I can take you to meet Branjang in Puri Tegalrejo."

———•—•———

Maybe my fate was to be intertwined with Dasamuka's.

One night, I dreamed that my horse was whinnying and jumping around restlessly. I went to check on it and was surprised to find Dasamuka standing near my front door.

My horse was acting as if it had just encountered a tiger.

When Dasamuka walked slowly toward me, I began to shudder. *Could he be a wolf in human form, a devil disguised as a human?* I wanted to part his thick hair to see if there were three rows of the number six written on his scalp. In the book of Revelation, this mark is used to distinguish those who are an incarnation of the devil.

I gathered the courage to approach him and reached toward his head. But before I had a chance to part his hair, Dasamuka growled. The fierce sound immobilized me and, before I knew it, he had sunk his teeth into my chest. My blood splattered on the tiles and walls.

As I screamed for help, someone knocked on the door. When the knocking persisted and became louder, Dasamuka quickly let go. He jumped away and disappeared into nowhere.

I woke up with cold sweat around my neck. The knocks sounded louder and were real now. I looked at my watch; it was six o'clock in the morning. I jumped out of bed and went to open the door.

Den Wahyana said, "Good morning. I can take you to meet Branjang now, sir."

"Very well, let's go," I tried hard to hide the discomfort I felt about the awful nightmare.

Within the next hour, Den Wahyana and I rode our horses between yellowing rice fields. The crops of these fields did not belong to the farmers who planted them, nor to the nobility who had inherited the land for generations; the harvest from these fields and plantations would be taken by people like Uncle Harvey, who leased the land.

Javanese landowners did not manage their fields well. Most of them were noblemen, who would never dirty their hands with the mud of the fields. They were content with simply receiving rent money from the farmers. It seemed to me that the Javanese were typically lazy, except when it involved the pursuit of women.

I had taken the time to observe life in my surroundings.

The abundance of arable lands and sunshine all year long ironically kept the Javanese from living life more meaningfully. By employing their ability to reason and by working hard, they could have led a more dignified life.

However, those who were at the top of the social class, the aristocrats, preferred to be employees rather than make their own money. Those who were at the bottom of the social ladder would rather work as a coolie than work independently—as traders, for example.

My conclusion was that the Javanese were not confrontational and were adverse to risk. They preferred to live, as they would say, *adem-ayem-tentrem*—coolly, blissfully and tranquilly—in lieu of living a more passionate and turbulent life with greater opportunities.

I could not see anything wrong with the Javanese preference of lifestyle. There were many Javanese who were neither lazy nor cowardly, yet they treated their inherited wealth differently than a Westerner.

Den Wahyana told me that Javanese people lived by a concept they referred to as *sak madya*, or the middle path, and avoided extremes. They thought life was too short. Their expression for this concept was, *urip mung mampir ngombe*—meaning this life is only meant for taking a short sip of water. Thus, it was more important to them to prepare for an eternal afterlife, than to focus on enjoying this short and temporary one.

One should always be in control of life's passions and desires to be able to attain purification at the time of death, which was the only gateway to eternity.

Before long, we arrived at a mansion surrounded by the bamboo houses of servants. The princedom estate was quite far from the center of the Yogyakarta Sultanate.

"Isn't this Puri Tegalrejo?" I asked, after moving closer to the mansion that appeared stately in the shadow of a majestic banyan tree. I had often visited the Tegalrejo district, but I had been to the estate only once.

"You're correct. Have you been here before?"

I nodded. Resident Crawfurd thought the prince who lived here was the only suitable figure to be the next heir to the throne of the Yogyakarta Sultanate.

"Please wait here. I need to talk to the doorman of the house first. The rules here are slightly different from that of the Keraton." Den Wahyana walked his horse to a small bamboo house located relatively close to the main house.

When Den Wahyana returned, I had already dismounted from my horse.

"He's ready to meet you, sir," Den Wahyana said lightly.

"He? Is Branjang the name of a person?"

"Yes, and today he's not going anywhere. Let's go see him."

After making sure I was comfortably seated on an *ambin*—a bamboo cot lined with a woven pandan mat—Den Wahyana excused himself. He had already told me he had another engagement, later in the afternoon.

"Welcome, sir. How can I help you?" A slight man dressed like a member of the Keraton's household greeted me and sat down cross-legged across from me.

"I would like to meet Den Branjang," I answered him straightforwardly.

"You don't need to call me 'Den.' Just 'Branjang' is good enough. Yes, I'm the person you're looking for, sir."

I was stunned. I felt that this could not be the right person. Dr. Leyden could not possibly have asked me to write about this person. There was nothing special about him. He was an average Javanese—the type of man I could easily pass by in the street

111

tomorrow morning. I caught myself stereotyping the Javanese, and I stuttered, "Ah, I just wanted to meet you."

"Something is not quite right, sir. I'm certain that your visit to my humble shed is not just to meet me."

"Actually, I just wanted to meet you. Is there anything wrong with that? Perhaps you can share a story with me." I realized I needed to consider his feelings.

"I would be glad to share with you whatever I know. What or whose story would you like to hear, sir?"

"What do you know about Dasamuka? Can you tell me about him?" Not only had the lad been on my mind for some time, he had appeared in my nightmare as well.

Branjang gazed at me for a while, then bowed his head and started his story.

"All Javanese know the tale of Dasamuka. His father was the sage Vishrava, and his mother was a royal princess named Kaikeshi. The sage Vishrava first visited the princess to propose for his son, Kubera.

"Kaikeshi would only accept a man who could decipher the riddle of the *Sastra Jendra Hayuningrat,* a holy book bestowed by God containing the secret that would save the entire human race and this world. Sage Vishrava was the only one with that knowledge.

"When Sage Vishrava and Kaikeshi were left alone in a room inside the princess's quarters for the decipherment of the divine knowledge, they became attracted to each other. Their infatuation for each other started with the union of souls, and ended with the union of the body. That intercourse occurred in a consecrated room meant for the exchange of divine knowledge. Yes, they did it at the wrong time and place. They performed an act that was only appropriate for a legal husband and wife, not an unmarried woman and her future father-in-law.

"The unfortunate occurrence resulted in the pregnancy of Kaikeshi. When the child was due, a frightening creature came out of her womb—a pulsating blood lump, with two big ears and sharp nails. The blood lump split itself into three parts. The main part became Dasamuka, the ears became his brother named Kumbhakarna, and the nails became his sister named Shurpanakha. Each of the siblings took on the shape of a *raksasa*, a demon with sharp fangs and claw-like fingernails."

Branjang's story was affecting me badly. He had retold the story of Ailsa, my father, and their child. And I was the ill-fated Kubera.

Two individuals with such a big age difference was like a father having an incestuous relationship with his own daughter. I imagined the scene of Sage Vishrava and Kaikeshi having intercourse and broke into a cold sweat and started to feel ill. I remembered my nightmare about Dasamuka terrorizing my horse and started to tremble.

Branjang peered at me. His eyes were filled with concern. "Sir, you look pale. Are you sick? Please lie down here. I'll prepare a cup of hot water for you."

I tried to get rid of the image by blinking my eyes and then closing them tightly. When I opened my eyes again, I felt as if I was being thrown into the sky. I floated for a while before I dropped and smashed to the ground. Suddenly nauseated, I gasped for fresh air.

"I'm not feeling well," I stammered. "Can I rest here?" It was impossible for me to ride home in this condition.

"Of course, sir. Please wait here. I'll be right back." Branjang hurriedly left. He returned a few minutes later and helped me walk to a narrower and darker room adjacent to the one we had been in.

I lay down on a bed made from *pelupuh*, split and flattened bamboo. A cup of hot tea with brown sugar and a plate of *pisang raja* waited on the table next to me. Den Wahyana had once told me this variety of bananas was served to honor a guest.

I offered Branjang a couple of silver coins for taking care of me, but he politely refused. He told me that it was his responsibility to care for his guest. His tone was sincere.

I felt fortunate to have a host like Branjang and soon fell asleep.

I was awakened the next day by the creaking of a door as it opened. A man entered the room and walked toward me. In the dim light, I could not see his face, but I knew it was not Branjang. The night of rest had taken care of my headache and nausea, but when I rose, I was overcome by dizziness and forced to lie back down.

"How are you feeling, sir? Do you feel better now?" The ambin creaked and swayed as the stranger sat down beside me. His serene face gave him a sincere and pleasant attitude.

"Yes, I feel much better than yesterday." I tried to get up again and instinctively held on to the sturdy arm he offered. *Who is this? I know we've met before, but where?*

"You can stay here until you're fully recovered." Before I could say anything more, the man walked out of the door.

Exhausted, I lay back down. I had felt protected by his presence. It was strange to feel safe in a foreign place with strangers around me.

"Who is he?" I asked Branjang, when he came in with my breakfast, a plate of steamed rice and fried eggs.

"He is my master, the owner of this house and the surrounding rice fields," Branjang answered proudly.

"Only wealthy people and royalty can own such a large plot of fertile land as this."

"He's royalty, a prince," Branjang continued, "His name is Pangeran Diponegoro II."

"The son of Sultan Hamengkubuwono III?" I remembered the robbery of the Keraton's treasures, then realized that the man who had looked in on me was the same prince who had stood next to me while the palace of his ancestors was being pillaged

"Yes, but he was not born from the queen consort," Branjang explained.

I was not particularly interested in discussing the ancestry of Javanese royalties; it was too complex. Trying to get the conversation back on track, I asked, "Can you continue your story about Dasamuka?"

"Are you feeling better now, sir?"

"Well enough to listen to your story."

"Where did I end the story?"

"With Dasamuka's birth. You said that Dasamuka was a demonic giant, but why does he appear to me as a handsome and charismatic man?"

"Dasamuka is, indeed, a raksasa."

"Dasamuka whom I met here in the Yogyakarta Sultanate is not a raksasa. He's one of the most charming Javanese men I've ever met."

"Oh, I think we have a misunderstanding here. Dasamuka in my story is a character in a Hindu epic. The Dasamuka you talk about must be the one who's often seen with Den Wahyana," Branjang said while touching his head. "Den Wahyana who also lives within the vicinity of Puri Tegalrejo."

"Can you tell me more about the Dasamuka who is Den Wahyana's friend?"

"There are similarities between Dasamuka from the epic and Dasamuka who often comes to Tegalrejo. They're quite comparable to each other."

"Really? Tell me."

"The similarity is their parents. The story of his father, Ki Sena and his mother, Den Ayu Ningsih, is similar to that of the sage Vishrava and Kaikeshi. Ki Sena married his own son's bride-to-be."

I gasped, but before I could say anything, Branjang continued.

"I'm going to tell you the most recent story about him. It's about him and his lover, and links my master to him." Branjang then broke off. After giving me a serious once-over he said, "Please keep it to yourself. There are a lot of important people involved."

———•———

One fine morning, Dasamuka rode his horse to Puri Suryanata. The guards at the castle gate knew him well and allowed him to continue his ride deep into the castle compound. Dasamuka dismounted from his horse and, after briefly talking to another guard, walked his way to the *joglo*. The biggest building was a traditional Javanese house. The two banyan trees shading it added to the serene ambience of the estate.

Dasamuka climbed up the steps. He slowed down upon entering a verandah decorated with flowering anthurium placed inside earthen-colored pots. Cages holding turtledoves, singing and chirping happily in the early morning, hung from the ceiling.

Dasamuka walked into the next room, furnished with carved teakwood chairs. An abdi was tidying up a maroon rug.

"Can I see Den Mas Suryanata?" Dasamuka asked the house servant.

"Do you have an appointment, Den?"

"Of course."

"Please, have a seat. I'll be right back." The abdi quickly left the room.

Sitting cross-legged on the rug, Dasamuka enjoyed the turtledove's lilting songs that created the ambience of adem, ayem, and tentrem—cool, blissful, tranquility.

The Javanese aristocrats thought that songbirds, such as starlings and straw-headed bulbuls, made good pets for children, while turtledoves, spotted doves, and collared doves were pet birds of adults. Dasamuka no longer considered himself a young child and tried to enjoy the singing of the turtledoves.

"Dasamuka! Welcome!" A loud, albeit slightly shaken, voice interrupted Dasamuka's reverie.

He quickly rose and, joining both of his palms in front of his chest, greeted his host respectfully.

Den Mas Suryanata took a seat in one of the teakwood chairs and waved Dasamuka back to his seat.

"I am here, Den Mas." Dasamuka quietly studied the older man's face. Over time, he had learned to accurately read a person's motives and sense their disposition. He was a master in detecting pretense as well as the act of pretending. He could easily change his facial expressions as needed. Hence, his friends called him Dasamuka, meaning ten faces.

"You must know my reason for calling you here."

"Yes, I do, Den Mas. Is it regarding horses, birds, or women?"

"The latter. I'm infatuated with a girl."

"Is it just for pleasure or to become one of your wives?"

"She'll be my concubine."

"Who is she?"

"Rara Ireng from Puri Wibawa."

Dasamuka closed his eyes. He had heard rumors about the beautiful maiden of the Wibawa castle. This was the umpteenth time Den Mas Suryanata tasked him with procuring a woman. From his past experiences, he knew this time would be harder than before.

Arjun Singh, Rara Ireng's father, was a Bengali low-ranked infantry officer with the British government, and her mother was a blue-blooded raden ayu from the Yogyakarta Keraton. Political unrest caused by rebels had torn the family apart.

Arjun Singh had been arrested at his lavish house in Srondol, an upscale neighborhood in Semarang. While waiting for his trial, his family tried hard to visit and lift his spirits. His father-in-law spent large sums of money to negate or at least commute his sentence, all to no avail. The family had continued their efforts until the prison authorities denied them.

There were rumors about Arjun Singh's failed escape to Batavia. No one knew whether he was still alive and hiding somewhere, waiting for a chance to sail back to India. There was nothing certain about his current fate. He could be already buried. Even his wife had not heard from him. His only daughter, the beautiful Rara Ireng, was now being cared for by her grandfather, Raden Mas Wibawa.

"You must've heard about her," Den Mas Suryanata looked intently at Dasamuka.

"Yes, sir," Dasamuka answered, quickly. A few days prior, an opium trade government supervisor had told him the story of Arjun Singh. He never thought the piece of gossip would be so quickly of use to him.

"I want you to bring Rara Ireng here, prepared to be a bride, who will be willingly taken to the chamber I've arranged for her." Den Mas Suryanata paused and added, "You can do it in whichever way you want."

"This is not an easy job, Den Mas."

"If it were easy, I wouldn't have called you," Den Mas Suryanata smirked.

"I'll need some funds," Dasamuka said quietly.

"I'm prepared. I know the way you work."

The two of them looked at each other.

"It's a lot of money, Den Mas."

"Do you think I'm a pauper now?"

"All right, then. Give me a week. Yes, in a week's time you'll receive good news, Den Mas," Dasamuka promised.

Den Mas Suryanata did not respond. He merely gestured Dasamuka to wait while he left the room.

Den Mas Suryanata returned with two purses of money and threw the velvet moneybags at Dasamuka.

One of the bags fell to the ground and split a seam. The clattering of golden coins rolling across the tiled floor made Dasamuka smile as he managed to catch the other bag.

—•◆•—

As always, Dasamuka moved fast. His first step was to find out who was close kin to Den Mas Wibawa. He then could sort and select who he thought could be the most helpful to him. Based on past experience in the business of pursuing virgins, a poor relative who had wide connections proved to be the best candidate. Dasamuka would meet with more than a dozen individuals before making a final choice.

After long deliberations, Dasamuka chose Raden Ayu Larmi as his liaison. The middle-aged woman was related to Den Wibawa's family, while being one of Den Mangli's wives made her Dasamuka's aunt. She was the perfect choice.

Den Ayu Larmi enthusiastically offered to help her nephew. Among the family members of the Wibawa family, she was one of the less fortunate. Her husband was a victim of *malima*—the five bad habits known to the Javanese as: *main* (gambling), *mabok* (getting drunk), *madon* (prostitution), *madat* (taking drugs), and *maling* (stealing). As a result, he had put them deeply in debt.

After receiving enough funds, Dasamuka sent Den Ayu Larmi to Puri Wibawa to explore the possibilities of proposing to Rara Ireng. Clutching a golden chain necklace, Den Ayu Larmi went to see her cousin Den Mas Wibawa in a luxurious carriage.

She was greeted by the lord of the estate, and Den Ayu Larmi inquired about the health of her host and the situation at Puri Wibawa. Such inquiries were important. After the passing of Sultan Hamengkubuwono I in 1792, the Sultanate of Yogyakarta had not seen a day free from unsettling political intricacies.

Den Ayu Larmi then proceeded to steer the conversation to the heart of the matter. "Kang Mas, are you aware that you own a peacock that is the subject of most conversations among the aristocrats?"

"I haven't been keeping peacocks for quite some time; I might not be the person they are talking about." Den Mas Wibawa sipped his hot tea. He had lost interest in keeping peacocks, or anything that demanded much of his money and time. Due to the failed uprising by the Bengali infantry unit that had embroiled his son-in-law, he was no longer a prosperous man.

"Oh, they're talking about you, Kang Mas. The beautiful peacock is your granddaughter, Rara Ireng."

"Ah… her," Den Mas Wibawa sighed. "What do they say?"

"They all have been praising your granddaughter. They said she's as beautiful as Subhadra, Arjuna's wife."

Den Ayu Larmi knew Den Mas Wibawa was having trouble paying off his debts. It was public knowledge that his estate had deteriorated, and he'd had to dismiss most of the household servants. She smiled, "Kang Mas, there's someone who wishes to see the return of Puri Wibawa's glory. He would like to provide some assistance, if he's allowed to do so." Den Ayu Larmi chose her words and tone carefully, to avoid hurting Den Mas Wibawa's feelings.

Den Mas Wibawa sighed. He often recalled the days when he proudly invited the noblemen from the sultanates of Yogyakarta and Surakarta to parties that included Bengali officers, whose presence elevated the status of the princedom at that time.

"I'll just hand the matter over to you. I'm an old man now and have no energy left." Den Mas Wibawa leaned back in his chair.

"Sure, Kang Mas. I'll take care of everything. You just wait for the result that will bring happiness to your family."

Den Mas Wibawa reached for his teacup. The tea had turned cold, but the hope that he would regain the splendor of his loji slowly warmed the blood flowing through his veins.

Den Ayu Larmi rose. Smiling, she said, "I'll come back on the day after tomorrow to introduce you to the admirer of your granddaughter. He's a mature aristocrat who's prepared to make both his wife and his in-law's family happy."

Den Ayu Larmi immediately started preparations for the Javanese ceremony referred to as *nontoni*, a "sighting" ceremony that happens before the official proposal.

The future groom would visit his future bride to take a closer look at her. For couples who knew each other, this event was not as significant as for those whose marriages were being arranged by their family.

Den Mas Suryanata had not had a close look at the physical beauty of Rara Ireng. The first time he had seen her was at a party, hosted by one of the Keraton royalties, and he was unable to come too close. Rumors about her famed beauty reached him through the praises of his aides, people he deemed knowledgeable in assessing a woman's quality, and now he wanted to see this beauty himself.

At the nontoni ceremony, the future bride would join the party and serve the guests refreshments, along with the female servants of the house. Hence, the future groom and his family would be able to observe her closely.

In the days leading to the event, Dasamuka was the busiest person around. He had been put in charge of organizing the groom's entourage. Thus, he had to take care of every detail, starting from the simplest thing—such as the kind of chariot to be used—to very important matters, such as choosing the gifts they should bring, and the suitable elder to represent the groom's family.

The charisma of certain elders, and the value of those gifts, would contribute greatly to the success of the discussion between the two families that could lead to the arrangement of a suitable date for the wedding.

———•———

The nontoni event was a long-awaited festivity at Puri Wibawa. The usually quiet estate filled with happy chatters as the abdis arranged the eight guest chariots to line up and face the entrance of the mansion.

The passengers were mostly middle-aged gentlemen formally dressed in surjan. The traditional high-collared Javanese striped cotton shirt was worn over a jarit with a special pattern and completed with a dark-colored destar headband. Accompanying accessories displayed the importance of the event they were attending.

The courtyard of Puri Wibawa had been swept clean for the occasion, and the flowering hedge of red and white hibiscus had been pruned. Standing outside of the loji, one could see the rows of guests sitting cross-legged to listen to the *atur pambagya*, opening speech by the host, Raden Mas Wibawa.

"What a neat and breezy loji you have," Den Mas Suryanata complimented his host after his speech.

"The trees kept growing and were long unattended, and as a result, the air is cool here. We removed the furniture a long time ago, hence the neatness of this space." Den Mas Wibawa tried to hide his embarrassment. When the trees around a house grew too big and appeared untrimmed, and when the walls and floors of a house were void of decorations, it was a clear sign that the owner was in deep financial trouble.

There was something amiss about the house, indeed. Den Mas Wibawa could not stop apologizing for the vast differences between this event and the celebration he hosted ten years ago. He felt that his provisions for the party today were inadequate for his royal guests.

"Truly, I did not expect to be visited by this many important guests today. I feel much honored by your presence."

"We, too, want to apologize for our unannounced arrival. We must have caused you an inconvenience, sir."

"Please don't say that. Not at all. It's our pleasure to receive you and your entourage."

"It's an honor for us to be received by someone whose fame has been brought to our attention. We wish to acquaint ourselves with you, sir."

"Ah, you could not be more wrong about me, Den Mas. I'm only a humble nobleman who doesn't have much now. I no longer have anything to be proud of." Den Mas Wibawa always assumed that people—especially those who lived within the Yogyakarta area—were well aware of the financial disaster that caused him to live isolated in his loji.

Finally, the long-awaited part of the evening's celebration started. Rara Ireng, the future bride, and her female abdis entered with soundless steps to serve the food and drinks.

The guests were seated casually on a thick rug around four short, round tables.

The first table Rara Ireng served was her grandfather's. Walking in a squatting position, she and her abdis approached the table. When Rara Ireng started to take the plates of food from the trays carried by her abdis, the conversation died down immediately. The ensuing silence was broken only by the soft clinking of the china teacups that were passed and the small cough that escaped from Den Mas Suryanata's suddenly pounding chest.

Dasamuka leaned back for a better view of the girl, whose name was often on his lips lately but whom he had never met. This was a good opportunity not only to see her figure, but also to study her face.

Dasamuka usually used his sister, Danti, as the standard when judging a woman's beauty. True to her nickname, Rara Ireng's skin was not as fair as his sister's. The dark-skinned beauty seemed to be slightly taller than Danti; the height she inherited from her Bengali father made her look quite thin.

When Rara Ireng finally served the table he was seated at with younger gentlemen his age, Dasamuka decided that what distinguished Rara Ireng the most from Danti were her eyes. Rara Ireng's eyes were rounder than usual and accentuated by long, curly eyelashes. Rara Ireng's nose, too, was unusual. It was too high and pointy for Javanese standards.

While his sister Danti was much more beautiful, Dasamuka found it difficult to accept that idea as fact. It was like having to choose between a jasmine and frangipani flower—each of them had their own uniqueness and charm. This kind of comparison could only lead to endless debates.

Dasamuka's heartbeat quickened when Rara Ireng placed a plate of *nagasari*, a steamed banana and rice flour cake, in front of him. He took the opportunity to admire her beautiful face as it glowed under the light of the oil lamp.

Rara Ireng returned his look, and for a moment, their eyes locked.

Dasamuka knew that a Javanese noblewoman would not dare to do such a thing, especially during a formal event like nontoni. But Rara Ireng was not a pure-blooded Javanese; her father was Bengalese.

The usual party noise of conversation and clinking china and silverware soon filled the air. Meanwhile, the principals slowly narrowed their conversation to the party's objective. Dasamuka strained to eavesdrop.

"Can the proposed ceremony be conducted in a week's time? If that's considered too early, we can postpone it." Den Suryanata's voice was thick with suppressed anxiety.

"It's not like that. I need to discuss the matter with my granddaughter, Rara Ireng. She has yet to be informed about the reason of your visit. Right, Den Mas?"

"Yes, I only just now stated my intent clearly, and it would be inappropriate if I were to act like an immature teenager."

"I'll pass your intentions on to Rara Ireng and will get back to you as soon as she tells me her decision. We always have to be prepared for the worst possible case, don't we?"

Den Mas Suryanata nodded his head, slowly.

Rara Ireng surely was aware that, as one of Den Mas Suryanata's wives, she could pay off her grandfather's debts and even rebuild Puri Wibawa to its former glory, the way it had been when her father was still around.

Dasamuka, who usually was the center of attention among his peers for his interesting and peculiar stories, was quiet for the rest of the party. He ignored his friends' jokes about his silence being the result of having a diamond in his mouth and pondered the situation.

He had made a grave mistake in enabling a womanizer like Den Mas Suryanata, who still lusted after young virgins. He could not allow this old lecher to defile this beautiful young girl. But more than that: Dasamuka was surprised to discover that he wanted Rara Ireng for himself.

Chapter 7

RARA IRENG

If Dasamuka were to redeem his mistake, he needed to have a serious, genuine talk with Rara Ireng. For this matter, the assistance from his aunt Raden Ayu Larmi was crucial.

"Don't look for trouble," his aunt admonished him. "If you desire a woman, you should look in other places. There are still many, much prettier girls with better backgrounds," his aunt advised him when she realized Dasamuka's intentions.

"I won't ask her to run away with me, if she tells me she'll happily marry Den Mas Suryanata. I promise you that."

"What if she's unhappy or in agony because of it?"

"Then I'll surely do my best to help her."

"By asking her to run away and marry you, right?"

Dasamuka could not say anything more.

A long silence fell between the two who were still connected by family ties. Dasamuka had lost count of the times he'd had to find a woman for Den Mas Suryanata, to function either as his concubine or merely satisfy him with a quick affair. Until now, he'd never felt guilty about it. Most likely, his guilt was caused by his attraction to Rara Ireng. It also could be because he'd reached the marrying age.

"Auntie, please. Arrange for me to see her."

Raden Ayu Larmi not only cared about her nephew's feelings, she also disagreed with Den Mas Suryanata's inappropriate desire, as a man in his sixties, to bed a sixteen-year-old girl. She finally promised Dasamuka to arrange his meeting with Rara Ireng.

Raden Ayu Larmi started by contacting Den Mas Wibawa. Then, she proceeded to talk to Rara Ireng. This conversation resulted in a date to go shopping, in preparation for the proposal ceremony. Dasamuka would be their coachman.

The three of them would shop for the best jarit from Nyi Canting, the most famous batik maker in the sultanate at that time.

After they arrived at the residence of Nyi Canting, Dasamuka executed his plan. While Den Ayu Larmi rummaged through several jarits, Rara Ireng waited near a room used for batik making.

"Please excuse me, Den Rara," Dasamuka approached her carefully. "It seems we've met before." He had to calm his suddenly erratic breathing before continuing on. "Unfortunately, I can't remember when and where."

"But I do," Rara Ireng cocked her head and threw him a smile. "We met at Puri Wibawa, my grandfather's estate. You were among Den Suryanata's entourage."

Rara Ireng's smile lifted Dasamuka's spirit. He was convinced she reciprocated his interest, and the thought sparked his passion. He smiled back.

"We met long before that."

"Ah, really? Where?"

"Don't you remember, Den Rara?"

As Rara Ireng tried hard to remember, the lines of her face became sharper. Her nose and chin looked tapered. She finally said, "I'm sorry, I give up. I really don't remember. Please tell me when and where we met before."

"Ah, unfortunately, it's the same for me. I, too, can't remember where we first met," Dasamuka mused. He suddenly seemed much older.

For a while, they looked at each other silently.

Then Dasamuka continued laconically, "I can't remember, because it was just a dream."

Unexpectedly, Rara Ireng let out a loud giggle. She quickly covered her mouth with her hand, but both of her eyes were filled with laughter.

The two of them gazed at each other once again.

Rara Ireng gradually shifted her gaze towards the smoking peak of Mount Merapi, the most active volcano on Java. It was as if the mountain's heat had spread through her heart. Playing with fire was indeed a dangerous act. Still, it was only natural that coming face to face with such an attractive young man had ignited sparks.

"What kind of jarit did I wear in your dream?" Rara Ireng continued the flirtation.

"It was one with a *truntum* batik pattern, I can remember that clearly." Dasamuka referred to a pattern created a long time ago by a queen consort of Sultan Pakubuwono III and known for depicting eternal love.

"I'm surprised you can remember the kind of jarit I wore in your dream."

"There's no need to be surprised. In my dream, I gave you the jarit, and you immediately wore it."

Rara Ireng could not contain her giggles, and again, she swiftly brought her hand to her mouth. "You're a great storyteller, Dasamuka. That's your name, right? Dasamuka?"

"It's just a nickname, given as a tease. My real name is Danar." It was the first time Dasamuka had felt compelled to give an explanation of his name. It was the only time his nickname made him feel uncomfortable.

"Do you like being called Dasamuka?"

"Oftentimes, we can't avoid things from happening."

"I have a story about Dasamuka."

"When can I listen to your story? Your story must be different from the stories I've heard before."

"It's definitely different."

Their conversation was interrupted when Den Ayu Larmi came with samples of jarits in various batik patterns.

"Here," Den Ayu Larmi spread the jarits out on a wooden bench near Rara Ireng, "Pick three patterns you like the most, then we can take them home." There were a total of five, and Den Ayu Larmi would take the other two for herself. It all was a part of Dasamuka's plan; he had paid for all of it.

Rara Ireng picked up one jarit, then another. They looked equally beautiful, and she kept vacillating between them.

"If I may suggest, the far left one is the most suitable for Den Rara. It looks exactly like the jarit I gave you in my dream," Dasamuka said gently. He was clever enough to take advantage of Rara Ireng's confusion.

"Well then, I'll just follow your advice, *kakang,*" Rara Ireng held Dasamuka's gaze before she turned to Den Ayu Larmi. "Great-aunt, I'll just take this one." By calling him "kakang," the endearing form of "kang," brother, the usual way of addressing a male of the same age, Rara Ireng showed she reciprocated Danar's feelings.

"You can pick two more. Perhaps I can help you to choose."

"Yes, please, Great-aunt. However, I still think that the most beautiful one is the one chosen by Kakang Danar." Rara Ireng's eyes softened as she looked once again into Dasamuka's eyes.

Rara Ireng and Dasamuka were clearly attracted to each other. They now had to tend the fire their desire had ignited, even if those sparks grew into a blazing flame. Both of them were ready to bear the consequences, even if the fire might consume them.

Dasamuka no longer felt the need to ask Rara Ireng if she was happy with Den Mas Suryanata's proposal. He was certain of her answer.

The three of them drove back in the carriage driven by Dasamuka. While, at the start of their trip, Rara Ireng sat on the backseat with Den Ayu Larmi, she now chose to sit in the front seat next to Dasamuka. Both of them silently contemplated the future of their relationship.

Once they arrived at Puri Wibawa, Dasamuka whispered, "Please wear that jarit, tonight. I'll come and knock on your window."

Rara Ireng answered him with a smile that she quickly covered with her palm; her grandfather and mother stood by the door waiting for her.

<hr />

Later that night, Dasamuka returned to Puri Wibawa. Sneaking across the stone path along the loji walls, he followed the directions Den Ayu Larmi had given him and managed to find Rara Ireng's room. He tapped on the window, softly.

A white-feathered owl, perched in a nearby cananga tree, noisily flew away.

Startled, Dasamuka pressed himself against the wall and froze. His heart skipped a beat when the window opened with a thin squeak and a shaft of light tumbled onto the dark pathway.

Dasamuka quickly looked to his left and right. Although the guards of Puri Wibawa were already gone at this hour, several female abdis might still be working in the kitchen and catch sight of him standing near the window.

"I thought you wouldn't come." Rara Ireng's whispers folded into the rustles of mango tree leaves blowing in the wind.

"It would be my loss if I missed the opportunity to meet the princess whose beautiful eyes fill my dreams," Dasamuka whispered and, grabbing the windowsill with one hand, gently pushed against the shutter until the opening only fit Rara Ireng's slender frame.

"Great-aunt Larmi has told me many stories about you."

"Ah, is that so? Well, your great-aunt is also my aunt. We're still related to each other."

"And we share a similar kind of fate. We both lost our fathers to revolution and war. Luckily, my grandfather and mother took care of me, while it seems that you had to fend for yourself."

"Aunt must have spoken too highly of me. A self-taught man? I don't think that's an accurate description. I just don't want to be a burden to anyone. That's all."

"You speak too low of yourself. Great-aunt told me that you've reached a level in life that other young men of your age only dream about."

"I don't deserve the credit you're giving me, but I'm taking the courage to offer you a position in life that is better than what Den Mas Suryanata has to offer. A man's wealth and power does not matter if he only makes you his concubine. You deserve to be someone's *garwa padmi*, a wife. And it's what I'm offering you right now."

"I'm sure you know that's every girl's dream."

"And you'll be living in your dream house as well."

"I no longer think about my dream house."

"Rumah Gajah, your father's mansion in Srondol, will be yours again."

Dasamuka had only learned about the story behind the house the day before. He had never seen the house that had been a subject of conversation among the royalties for its splendor.

Rara Ireng remained quiet.

The whistling wind and flapping wings, accompanied by an owl's mournful hoot, were the only sounds that broke the silence.

After a while, Dasamuka said, "I'm asking you to run away with me. We don't have much time." Dasamuka tightened his grip on the window frame.

"You must know why my grandfather accepted Den Mas Suryanata's proposal," Rara Ireng said quietly. "He wants to restore the glory of Puri Wibawa, and I want to repay his kindness." She broke into tears.

Dasamuka pressed himself closer against the wall and leaned into the room.

"I don't want him to suffer during his final years," the girl wept.

Dasamuka reached for her hand. "I'll be back tomorrow. Prepare yourself. We'll run away together before the end of this month. You agree, right?"

Rara Ireng nodded.

"Is there anything more you'd want to tell me?" Dasamuka squeezed her hand, softly.

Rara Ireng shook her head. She brought her free hand to her chest and moved the heel of her palm across her heart as if trying to calm its rapid pounding.

Dasamuka felt Rara Ireng's fingers tremble in his grip. He gritted his teeth. Mustering up every ounce of self-restraint, he let go of Rara Ireng's hand and slipped into the cool darkness of the night. The lonely call of the owl escorted him out of Puri Wibawa.

———•———

That night, Rara Ireng could not fall asleep. Dasamuka's mention of Rumah Gajah reminded her of the times her father had taken her for a walk in their large back yard. The mention of Rumah Gajah also reminded her of the day her father carried her as they fled from the house where she had been born. During that time, she did not understand what was going on, but sensed the presence of peril, looming over her parents' heads.

For Den Mas Wibawa, the trouble that had befallen his son-in-law was the most complicated matter he had ever faced in his life. His daughter's sighs and his granddaughter's tears forced him to spend large sums of money. The cost of their discreet prison visits, and the well-being of his son-in-law during his captivity, had depleted his coffers very quickly.

He had to sell houses, rice fields, teakwood plantations, and so much more for the sake of his beloved family members. When the Dutch overruled the British in 1816, his son-in-law's whereabouts became even more uncertain.

Bankrupt was the correct word to describe the present condition of Puri Wibawa. Its owner had borrowed money from several places just to maintain the lifestyle of an aristocrat, though nowhere near the opulence he had formerly enjoyed.

After Den Ayu Larmi had convinced him of the advantages his association with a nobleman like Den Mas Suryanata would have, Den Mas Wibawa accepted the latter's proposal on behalf of his granddaughter.

Den Mas Suryanata then sweetened the pot even more. He not only promised to erase all Den Mas Wibawa's debts—he knew well his creditors—but he also promised to assist with the restoration of his mansion, so it would return to its splendor of the golden days.

During their nightly meetings, the discussions between Dasamuka and Rara Ireng narrowed down to some important matters. One was the amount of money Dasamuka had to come up with before Rara Ireng could leave Puri Wibawa. It was critical because, once Den Mas Suryanata realized his plan to marry Rara Ireng had failed, there was no doubt he would immediately collect Den Wibawa's debts and even use brute force in the process.

Rara Ireng asked Dasamuka to supply enough money to pay off her grandfather's debts, which Dasamuka was more than willing and able to do.

They planned to leave the money purses and a letter on the round teakwood table, where Den Wibawa routinely started his morning with a cup of tea while listening to the chirping of his pet turtledoves.

For Dasamuka, who relied on skills gained by living in the streets, getting the required money to pay off Den Wibawa's debts was easy. However, he needed more time to return Rumah Gajah to Rara Ireng. One of his acquaintances, a government official in Semarang, had informed him that the luxurious house was worth as much as three grand princedom estates in Yogyakarta. If he were to be honest with himself, Dasamuka knew it was beyond his means to purchase such an expensive mansion for Rara Ireng. Still, he had promised to do so. Dasamuka's promises were always able to persuade anyone, including Rara Ireng.

Hence, a day before the entourage of Den Mas Suryanata was scheduled to arrive at Puri Wibawa, Dasamuka and Rara

Ireng ran away. Just before midnight, soon after the *isya* prayer call, they boarded a curtained coach and drove off into the night. They left behind a large amount of money, a letter, and a mountain of problems, which the next day Den Mas Wibawa had to face all by himself.

The disappearance of the bride scandalized the household of Puri Wibawa. However, the uproar did not last long. Just a week after Rara Ireng eloped with Dasamuka, life at Puri Wibawa returned to its normal routine. Secretly, many people, especially their close neighbors, hated the idea of a pretty, young girl being violated by Den Mas Suryanata, the infamous lecher. They thought the girl deserved to pursue her own happiness with a man of her choice.

That was the love story of Dasamuka and Rara Ireng. The story had not ended yet. According to Branjang, Dasamuka still lived within the vicinity of the Yogyakarta Sultanate, but moved like the wind: He was around but never seen.

>———◆———

I was now convinced that Dr. Leyden wanted me to write about bronjong and not branjang. However, somehow I could not help but feel that my meeting with Branjang was not merely a coincidence. I was also curious about the connection between Dasamuka and Prince Diponegoro II. How I wished I could talk about this with Kiai Kasan.

The very next time Branjang came to check on me, I asked, "Earlier, you said that there was a link between Dasamuka and your master. Can you tell me more about that?"

Branjang hesitated before he answered. "Nowadays, my master's younger half-brother, Sultan Hamengkubuwono IV, spends a big chunk of his time collecting beautiful women and visiting beautiful places. Other than that, he recently took up a strange new habit.

"For entertainment, he rides his chariot at full speed on the streets near the Keraton, with little consideration for people around him. Many accidents have occurred due to his recklessness. My master tried to talk to him.

"As an older brother, Pangeran Diponegoro II asked Sultan Hamengkubuwono IV to come to his mansion. During their meeting, my master told his younger half-brother a story from the holy book of *Nasihat-al-muluk, The Counseling King*, by Al-Ghazali, a Persian philosopher who lived in the mid 1100s.

"In his book, Al-Ghazali tells about a king who met his downfall due to his own indecency, instead of by the attack of foreign enemies. Thus, the prince addressed state affairs as if they were merely a subject of conversation between brothers.

"Afterward, Prince Diponegoro II walked the sultan to his carriage.

"Dasamuka was among the sultan's entourage. His ability to provide the Sultan of Yogyakarta with the best horses that could be found in the territories of the Yogyakarta and Surakarta sultanates had placed him in the sultan's favor.

"The prince patted Dasamuka's shoulder and said, 'Use your good relationship with Sultan to convince him not to waste his time with the mere pursuit of his indulgence.'

"Dasamuka only nodded his head in reverence."

Branjang's story had given me a glimpse into Dasamuka's complicated life. I needed time to digest the information. "That was quite a story," I told him, as an end to our conversation. "Thank you."

On the third day, I felt much better. The nausea and headache that had plagued me for the past few days had vanished, and I decided to bid my host farewell and return home. Unexpectedly, Branjang's employer, Prince Diponegoro II, paid me another visit.

"Do you feel better now, sir?" Prince Diponegoro II asked gently.

"Yes, I do. Thank you for everything."

"I'm a good acquaintance of your superior, Resident Crawfurd. Please convey my regards to him."

"I will."

"I hope you won't hesitate to visit us again. Our door will always be open for you, sir." For a moment, Prince Diponegoro II held me in his calm gaze, then he turned and walked away.

It was difficult to convince Branjang that I was healthy enough to make the journey home by myself. He was still worried about my health and wanted to accompany me.

Assuming that my disappearance for the past three days had worried my office colleagues and the people at the Rejawinangun loji, I stopped by both places before I went home. I told everyone what happened, but withheld the story of Dasamuka from the much-celebrated Hindu epic, which I still wasn't sure what to make of.

My days were soon filled with assisting Resident Crawfurd with the completion of his manuscript, *History of the East Indian Archipelago*. The work erased any doubt I might have had that he was a determined scientist and also an organized administrator. My colleagues told me that the differences in

Resident Crawfurd's and Governor Raffles' personality traits and habits were the source of conflict between them.

The most interesting thing about Resident Crawfurd were his close ties with the royalties and aristocrats of the Yogyakarta Keraton. Aside from being a capable academic, he was also a great humanist who had an appreciation of the culture around him.

He knew how to adapt to the customs and norms of the Javanese aristocracy. His willingness and capability in doing so did not merely derive from the job requirements of a government official, but was also based on his philosophy as a humanist. I thought his knowledge of Javanese culture equaled that of colonial government officials who had been working with the Keraton for more than fifty years.

"Are you going to join me and return to our homeland, Willem?" Resident Crawford asked shortly after the London Convention, which was signed on August 13, 1814. His appointment as Resident was ending in September, and he was planning to make the journey home soon.

"Actually, I would still like to assist you with writing about this beautiful island, sir."

"Ah, I forgot. You must be thinking about Daisy, right? Understandably, you'd rather wait here for her instead of in the cold weather of Edinburgh or London." Resident Crawfurd smiled. The way he raised his eyebrows reminded me of Uncle Harvey.

"I discussed the matter at length with Harvey Thomson before deciding to extend my stay in Java—more precisely, in Rejawinangun."

"I suggest you keep your job with the government. Rejawinangun will still be within your reach." Resident Crawfurd paused. "Your safety will be ensured if you're a government official instead of merely an independent writer. I can write a letter of recommendation for you."

"Thank you, sir. I will definitely consider your advice."

Resident Crawfurd leaned toward me and whispered, "And, just for your own information, the British government still needs you." He threw me a meaningful smile.

I figured that my bronjong article had impacted the empire's foreign affairs policies. It had apparently raised an awareness among the British for the need to support the struggle of those who wanted to build their countries by exercising common sense and a clear conscience. The Tegalrejo group led by Prince Diponegoro II was undeniable the best place to start. Through my association with Den Wahyana, I would connect them to the British government. Of course, this matter was always to be kept confidential.

In the interest of my own safety and Uncle Harvey's, as well as to ensure a smooth communication between the Tegalrejo group and the British government, I decided to follow Resident Crawfurd's suggestion and remained a government employee under the Dutch.

My position as an administrator under the Dutch colonial government didn't fill my days. I spent most of my time writing articles for the Edinburgh Club and *London Times*.

My job only served to further endorse my disdain for the Dutch. During the course of our work affiliation, I often witnessed the way a Dutch government official, including Resident Crawfurd himself, were instrumental in Sultan Hamengkubuwono IV's physical as well as moral destruction.

It was unfortunate that the young sultan was too vulnerable to the temptation of food and drink, especially imported from The Netherlands. The dairy-rich foods and alcoholic beverages were not only offered to him at the parties often held by Dutch officials in the Karesidenan, but were also served at his dining table in the Keraton. The Dutch officials saw to it that the household staff of the sultan's palace were provided with such luxury items.

Slowly, but surely, the young sultan began to enjoy drinking *jenever* more than *legen*, the Javanese traditional drink made from the lontar tree's fruit. He also enjoyed eating pastries more than native desserts made of rice flour and coconut milk.

The damage done was most visible through the changes in his physical appearance. Those close to him noticed his ballooning body that his clothes could no longer hide. Though the sultan was only a teenager, dangerous illnesses had started to nestle in his body and soon began to gnaw at his health.

If the physical destruction was not enough, the gluttony also destroyed the sultan's morals by blinding his conscience. He couldn't care less what means were used by the Keraton to provide him with such excessive luxury. He should have known—or someone could have told him—that the funds he squandered carelessly were generated by unfair and cruel taxes levied on his citizens.

The nature of those taxes were strange and irrational. Taxation of the number of doors in a house, or the number of children carried by a mother to the market, were only a few of the costs that started to suffocate his people. The sultan was neglecting his duties regarding his people's prosperity and dignity.

There were also uproars caused by affairs between the Dutch officers and the wives of the Javanese nobilities; something he could have prevented, but instead was simply ignored.

The latest incident involved one of Den Mas Suryanata's concubines. She was secretly involved with one of my supervisors in the Karesidenan, a Europesche ambtenaar who was just as old as the highly esteemed nobleman.

I was convinced that Den Mas Suryanata was aware of the affair between his concubine, who could have been his daughter, and the Dutch officer. However, rather than showing his anger, he cunningly used the situation to tighten his collusion with the Karesidenan in regards to his share in the tax collection and opium trade.

Sultan Hamengkubuwono IV's careless squandering of tax collections, his apathy toward the adulteries happening around him, and the way he treated women merely as objects, caused him to lose the sympathy of his people.

At times, I seriously considered quitting my job.

———•◦•———

I was reading my mail from the Edinburgh Club and the *London Times* on my front porch when Den Wahyana came to visit. I had not seen him during the past month.

I invited him to sit down and, very unlike the Javanese norm, he opened our conversation with a question. "Has Dasamuka been here?"

"No, he hasn't."

"Hmm...."

"Is there something going on with him?"

"There's always something going on with him."

I remembered Branjang's story and prodded, "Can you tell me about it?"

"You must still remember Semi." Den Wahyana paused to throw me a scrutinizing look. "She told me that she came to look for you here, yesterday, but you weren't around."

"These days, I spend more time in Rejawinangun." I worried that Den Wahyana had noticed the jolt I experienced when he mentioned Semi. The memory of her beautiful face still brought me pleasure, and her Javanese beauty helped keep the presence of Ailsa from my mind.

"Why would she want to meet me?"

"She thinks that Ngusman, her husband, is in great danger."

"What kind of danger? Isn't he one of the sultan's guards now? Who would dare to bother him?"

"The threat comes from Sultan Hamengkubuwono IV himself."

"I don't understand."

"Ngusman has been assigned to ride in front of the sultan's chariot. He will be trampled and either instantly killed or seriously injured when the sultan's chariot overtakes him."

"Why is Semi looking for me? What does it have to do with me?"

"She thinks you're among a handful of people who are able to give an order to Dasamuka. Semi is asking for your help to have Dasamuka change Ngusman's position to one at the back of the sultan's chariot, which is pulled by eight Persian horses."

"All right, I'll go see him. Can you show me where I can find him? Many people say that he's disappeared as if the earth has swallowed him."

"Absolutely. Let me take you to him."

I rose and was following Den Wahyana when I noticed a Javanese woman standing outside. The woman must have come after Den Wahyana. She could not have been there too long.

"I've been looking for you day and night, and here you are in this Dutch heathen's nest," the woman yelled. She was visibly upset.

Den Wahyana did not answer. He looked back and glanced at me nervously.

Hostility filled the air. I walked into the living room and took a seat, to give them some privacy.

"Now, I'm even more convinced that you're no longer fighting the Dutch," the woman shouted. "Instead, you've sided with them and are their lackey."

Through the loosely closed door, I could hear her yelling.

When Den Wahyana remained silent, she prodded impatiently, "Why are you not saying anything?"

Den Wahyana's stoic silence caused another outburst.

"Well then, I can play your game as well. If you can't turn up Ganjar in three days, it means you're the kidnapper. And just so you know, I can't live like this anymore."

A breeze of fresh air came through as the door opened and Den Wahyana stumbled backward trying to catch himself.

I rose from my chair and, standing behind Den Wahyana, watched the woman walk briskly to a waiting, curtained carriage.

The wheels creaked as the carriage moved away from my house.

"Who is she?" I asked.

"My wife," Den Wahyana responded quietly.

I did not feel right to ask more, and we walked to the stable without conversation.

As we rode through the Yogyakarta Sultanate, I noticed many new crossroads. This indicated that the construction of new streets was underway. According to a rumor, the young sultan had ordered these developments. He enjoyed racing through the roads of his territory and became bored when he had to use the same routes every day.

We soon entered a Keraton area I recognized as the residence of Gusti Ratu Kencana, the mother of Sultan Hamengkubuwono

IV. I thought it was rather strange to look for Dasamuka in this *kaputren*, the enclosed quarters of the princesses in the palace.

"The loji over there, the one with the wooden fence," Den Wahyana pointed, "is where Dasamuka lives now."

"Aren't you coming with me?" I sensed that he was going to leave.

"You're fluent enough in the Javanese language now. All you need to say is that you want to see Dasamuka or Danar."

"Dasamuka or…?"

"Danar. That's his real name. I apologize; I can't accompany you, sir."

"Why?"

"I dislike the mistress of this house. Nyi Wersi is currently Dasamuka's patroness. I'm sorry."

I didn't quite understand why Den Wahyana could not accompany me—I suspected the sudden appearance of his wife and her demand to find someone named Ganjar had more to do with it than his dislike of Nyi Wersi.

Den Wahyana said, "It would be easier if you ask for Nyi Wersi first, sir."

After he left, I stood for a while looking at the shingle-roofed loji behind the wooden fence he had pointed out. I guessed that Ganjar was Den Wahyana's son. I wondered what was happening with him.

Chapter 8

SULTAN HAMENGKUBUWONO IV

I had accepted the fact that I had to look for Dasamuka by myself. My horse was about to move towards Dasamuka's loji when I heard a thundering sound approaching. Instinctively, I pulled the reins to halt my horse. The terrifying sound reminded me of a preacher's sermon about God striking a valley of sinners with thunder.

The roar was getting closer and clearer. There were shouts ordering people to move aside. I quickly dismounted my horse, as the story I had heard from the government officials in the Karesidenan became a reality.

From my left, hundreds of cavalry soldiers, dressed in brightly colored uniforms, spurred their horses as fast as they could. The thick cloud of dust from the beating hooves was unable to hide the golden chariot that thundered behind them. Suddenly, one of the riders was thrown from his saddle. Before I could wrap my head around what was happening, I saw several other riders tossed by their mounts as the chariot gained on the front riders and spooked their horses.

The soldiers were immediately crushed under the weight of the chariot's wheels. As the golden chariot disappeared into the distance, limbs lay on the pavement, crushed body parts and blood scattered in the dust. It was a horrific scene.

I prayed under my breath that none of the bloodied bodies was Ngusman. I did not want Semi's nightmare to turn into a reality. I had to find Dasamuka quickly.

I hurriedly approached Nyi Wersi's loji. As soon as I entered the gates, an agitated group of uniformed, armed guards surrounded me. They resembled a pack of mad watchdogs, snarling and growling while baring their teeth. I told them I wanted to see Nyi Wersi. Despite my identification tag, they bodily searched me and demanded I surrender my gun before they led me to the loji's verandah.

The most arrogant of the boisterous group was Reja, who I recognized as Ki Sena's stepson. My long wait was slightly relieved by the beautiful design of the loji, a mixture of Dutch and Javanese architecture. The elegance of the European house blended well with the refinement of the Jepara carvings. While I was absorbed in my admiration of the building, a middle-aged woman, who walked with a limp, entered the room and introduced herself as Nyi Wersi.

Without further ado, I asked, "Nyi, may I see Dasamuka now?"

"Dasamuka? Aren't you looking for him in the wrong place, sir?"

"Den Mas Wahyana said I would find him here."

Nyi Wersi gave me a silent, scrutinizing look, then asked, "Why are you looking for Danar?"

"A business matter," I answered. I did not want to divulge my intent.

"I need some funds to bring him here." Nyi Wersi was trying to turn the situation into an opportunity to make money.

"Doesn't he live here?"

"I need something to lure him out of his room." It was as clear as day that Nyi Wersi was asking for money.

I gave her a few coins, and her face brightened. She waved at the wooden, carved chairs, told me to take a seat, and left.

While waiting for the second time, I once again heard the terrifying, thunderous sound of an approaching herd of horses in full gallop.

Since Nyi Wersi had not called for their help, Reja and the guards figured it was safe to leave me and walked toward the road. One of them politely returned my gun before joining his friends. Only one guard remained at the gate.

It was quiet for a moment. Then the faint sound of a *gambang*, a xylophone-like instrument, accompanying a soft, lilting female voice, drifted across the compound. Immediately following a very tense situation, the sound was enchanting.

I rose and started walking in the direction of the melodious sounds. The music came from behind a tall wooden fence. Because I was much taller than the average Javanese, I was able to look over the fence easily.

The sight was stunning. Everything in the fenced-in area was the opposite of what was on the outside. It was a different reality, as different as the flaming red lava of Mount Merapi and the calming blue waves of the Indian Ocean.

Several young girls sat around a lake with a fountain. Some of them dipped their legs, calf high, into the water and splashed around. Others leaned against the trees with closed eyes and enjoyed the gentle breeze caressing their waist-long hair. I wondered if this is what heaven looked like.

The music that had lured me came from two girls. One calmly played the gambang while the other sang, cheerfully.

The garden around the lake was obviously created by experts. It looked similar to the Keraton's garden. The only slight disturbance of tranquility was caused by the *mbok emban*, the ladies-in-waiting for female royalty, who walked back and forth carrying silver trays filled with plates of fresh fruit and drinks, while fluttering birds pecked at spilled crumbs of food scattered on the neatly laid pavers.

I noticed a group of girls surrounding someone who was practicing a dance. In a section of the lake I had seen earlier, girls—dressed only in their bustiers—were bathing. The beautiful young women, ripe fruits, garden, and crystal-clear lake were all features of heaven as often described and lauded by the preachers.

I stared at the garden until my hands clutching the fence started to feel stiff, and the soles of my feet ached from standing. These pains brought a thought that made me cringe: according to rumors, Gusti Ratu had gathered these girls to satisfy the lust of her son, Sultan Hamengkubuwono IV.

"In case you're interested, I can help you, sir." The voice was gentle but still it jolted me. I whirled around and was met by the wide smile on Dasamuka's face.

"I know the ones who are no longer of use to the sultan," he said.

Dealing with someone like Dasamuka required the ability to adjust quickly. "Not now," I told him. "Right now, I need you, Danar."

"Whoever calls me Danar must know me well. I won't dare to fail someone who knows me that well." His smile was still as wide as before. "Is there anything I can help you with, sir?"

"I came here to find you because I need to save my friend's life." I caught myself as the words left my mouth. The friend I wanted to help was Semi, not Ngusman.

"Someone's life? Well, I'd need a lot of money if it concerns someone's life," he said, businesslike.

"I heard you're a rich man now. Why would you need more money?"

He burst out laughing. That was the first time I heard him laugh out loud. His wide-open mouth showed a neat row of white teeth. Danar was a handsome young man. No wonder Rara Ireng had been immediately attracted to him. I remembered Branjang's story about them and wondered if he were clever or cunning.

"What's your friend's name, sir?"

"You must've heard of him. He's Ngusman, one of Sultan Hamengkubuwono IV's cavalry soldiers."

"Oh, in that case, I won't charge anything."

"It's unusual for Danar not to charge a fee for his service. I'm sure there will be other consequences."

"I feel that I'm going to require your assistance in the near future." Danar looked sincere.

"Me, helping you?"

"Correct. Besides, Ngusman's wife is my aunt." Danar lowered his voice and, leaning toward me, whispered, "I hope you can keep this secret."

This made me curious. "Why does this have to be kept secret?"

Danar did not respond.

"Now, can you tell me what kind of danger Ngusman is in?"

I told him about the danger that threatened Ngusman's life, and how he had already lost almost a dozen friends in tragic accidents involving the sultan's chariot. His friends had been thrown out of their saddles, trampled under the hooves, and ultimately crushed under the chariot wheels. Each of them died a futile death while on duty.

I wanted him to help Ngusman by placing him somewhere other than at the front of the sultan's golden chariot.

After listening to my story, Danar nodded. "That's easy. I can assure you that by this afternoon, or tomorrow morning at the latest, Ngusman will be placed at the back of the entourage."

"Apparently, other than being a rich man, you're also in power now." I tried to find out more about Danar's current position. "Are you working as a government official now?"

Danar did not respond to my question. Instead, he said, "Thanks to Semi's effort, Ngusman entered into the service of the sultan. That's what I heard. I don't remember giving him a weak horse." Danar was trying to avoid my question by explaining what he had done instead.

"Actually," he added, "the most important thing isn't the location of the soldier. It doesn't matter if he rides in front or at the back. What matters is his horse. If he rides a weak horse and is placed in front of the chariot, he won't be able to keep up with the chariot horses. He'll be overrun, trampled, and, later, buried. If he rides a weak horse and is placed at the back of the carriage, he will be left behind and, after receiving his punishment, get fired. It's certainly better to be fired from the job than to be buried."

"Why don't you provide all the soldiers with good horses?"

For the second time, Danar burst out laughing.

I noticed he looked straight at me while he laughed; apparently, that was his way to avoid answering questions.

I tried to guess why Danar wanted to hide the fact that Semi was his aunt. Perhaps he wanted to prevent being involved with any mishap that could befall Semi. The sort of intrigue that characterized life in the Keraton should be handled strategically. If not, Semi would not have been able to work as a member of the royal household. She was, after all, the sister of the rebel Ki Sena. Such precarious relationships should never be revealed in a place like the Keraton. I assumed that was why Semi had come to me and not asked her nephew directly.

———•—•———

I was able to take care of my business regarding Ngusman properly, and the time I was waiting for most finally came. Semi came to my house to express her gratitude. The short visit did not last more than half an hour, yet brought me much pleasure. A strange feeling filled my chest when we faced each other. Unable to describe the feeling, I decided that not everything was meant to be analyzed.

If I were to look at Semi's appearance carefully and compare it to the appearance of European women, I would find the latter stiffer and disproportioned. Their necks were too long, and they were big-boned.

Compared to Semi, the faces of the European women lacked elegance. Their square features lacked softness. And we had yet to talk about the suppleness of her skin. Alas, my opinion was very subjective.

After taking care of Ngusman's safety, I went back to doing a small amount of office work and my routine of writing and sending articles to the Edinburgh Club and the *London Times*. It had been almost ten years now, and I felt very comfortable in my job writing and submitting scientific articles.

On the other hand, after John Crawfurd was replaced by Hubert G. Nahuys in August of 1816, my dealings with the government officials at the Resident's office became increasingly stressful. After my previous working experiences with Dr.

Leyden and Resident Crawfurd, it was extremely difficult to deal with individuals who were only interested in filling their stomachs and satisfying their lusts. To compare Hubert Nahuys, with such great figures as Leyden and Crawfurd was like comparing the fearsome crater of Mount Merapi with the serene Sarangan Lake.

My visits to loji Rejawinangun no longer relieved my anxieties, as they had in the past. Whenever Daisy and I had a conversation, she often talked about her father's plan to return to Edinburgh. It was not that he no longer liked living at Rejawinangun, but the situation was not as peaceful as before; it was no longer safe. It was apparent that reigning fools had been creating problems everywhere.

Uncle Harvey could not be faulted for his heightened sense of security. He had heard about the recent lootings of plantations. Many plantation owners had doubled the number of their guards. Some had even armed their workers. Storing gunpowder had become a necessity, just as important as storing fertilizer. Despite the widely reported increase of crime, however, the plantations at Rejawinangun remained relatively safe from such harm. The workers at the loji had yet to arm themselves with spears and guns.

I wondered why the robbers now seemed able to roam freely, looting plantations, and figured that the cause lay with the sultan's and Resident's behavior. The sultan's focus was on his concubines and outings, and the Resident only thought about ways to satisfy his gluttony and lust. While neither seemed to care about the fate of the commoners, a small group of aristocrats did—discreetly.

The princes met regularly at Puri Tegalrejo. According to Den Wahyana, Prince Diponegoro II was the only remaining hope for the commoners.

When Den Wahyana came to visit me in late August, I immediately told him about my meeting with Danar. A pensive look spread across his face when I mentioned Danar's current wealth and power. After a while, he said quietly, "I'm sure Danar will soon fall out of Sultan Jarot's favor." Den Wahyana used the more familiar form of address for the sultan, favored by the Javanese.

"Is that so? I heard that he's one of Sultan Hamengkubuwono IV's favorites."

"For the past month, Danar has been distancing himself from the sultan. I'm even afraid he'll rebel against him."

"Why would he do that?" My curiosity was piqued again. I had been intrigued by the story of Danar, better known as Dasamuka, ever since Branjang told me about him.

"It's a long story, sir. If you're busy now, I can tell you about it next time."

"As you can see, I have nothing to do right now. Please tell me the story."

Working with the ogres of the Karesidenan office had placed me under mental duress, and I needed a good distraction.

Den Wahyana's story was a continuation of what Branjang had told me. It started as a curtained coach was galloping away from Puri Wibawa with the runaway pair, Dasamuka and Rara Ireng.

The carriage moved swiftly through the empty streets of the Yogyakarta Sultanate. Dasamuka, who was the coachman, gradually slowed the carriage horse when they approached the servants' quarters of Gusti Ratu Kencana, the sultan's mother.

From his experience in associating with the nobility, criminals, and preachers, Dasamuka knew that the safest hiding place was not in a remote gorge at the slope of Mount Merapi, or an isolated treetop in the Menoreh forest. The safest place for a fugitive like himself was in proximity to the sultan's presence.

The most important thing was to determine the proximity. The term itself did not always refer to a physical distance. Instead, it could have something to do with a relationship.

Dasamuka had decided to hide in an area that was ruled by the sultan's mother. Or, more precisely, he would take refuge in a loji where a confidante of the sultan's mother would welcome him. The woman was in charge of the kaputren.

Dasamuka steered his coach to the side of the road and parked it in an inconspicuous spot. He fed and watered his horse, so it would remain calm even though it would be left alone for quite some time. After that, he helped Rara Ireng, his bride, step out of the carriage.

Rara Ireng seemed tired and looked slightly pale.

They walked hand in hand to a house that had a shingled roof and was surrounded by a wooden fence.

Dasamuka nodded and waved at several people whom he seemed to know quite well. They were the guards who were getting ready to go home after their night shift. Reja, his stepbrother, was amongst them, but just like he had hidden his relationship with Semi and Ngusman, Dasamuka now hid his true relationship with Reja and did not acknowledge the youth.

Dasamuka had known Nyi Wersi, the owner of the house, for quite some time. Both of them were like ghosts who liked to dwell among humankind.

Nyi Wersi needed the sultan's mother's protection because her husband, who was one of Raden Rangga's followers, had been persecuted by the government. Dasamuka needed Nyi Wersi's protection because he was now a fugitive of the Suryanata family and their mercenaries.

Nyi Wersi could live comfortably in a loji close to the kaputren, because her service was greatly needed by the sultan's mother. Gusti Ratu Kencana really wished to see her son mature. Unfortunately, that wish was not accompanied with wisdom and knowledge. Instead of inviting intelligent tutors with noble manners, or wise and sage-like men of letters, she brought in beautiful, coquettish, teenage girls to satisfy her son's desires. Nyi Wersi was the best person to get that job done.

Still holding her hand tightly, Dasamuka led Rara Ireng to the entrance of Nyi Wersi's loji. The caretaker of the loji, whom Dasamuka knew well, allowed them to come in. Those who were of the same kind would always find a way to find each other in times of need.

The lovers did not have to wait long. A woman emerged from the house and walked, swaying, toward them. The sunlight in her back made it hard to see her face. As the woman moved closer, Rara Ireng gripped Dasamuka's arm tightly. To anyone seeing it for the first time, Nyi Wersi's grinning, spooky face was terrifying.

"What brings you here, early in the morning? I thought you'd rather roam at night." Nyi Wersi looked like a ghost, and her hoarse voice made her sound like one, too.

Rara Ireng tightened her grip on Dasamuka's arm.

"I have to get married to Rara Ireng immediately, Nyi." Dasamuka answered her straightforwardly. He put his arm around Rara Ireng and moved her gently toward Nyi Wersi.

"Getting married? Ah, right, you're no longer a child. How old are you now? I heard that you're a rich man now, Danar. Who's your master?" Nyi Wersi always addressed Dasamuka with his real name, Danar.

"It's unimportant who I'm working for, because your master will definitely rank higher than mine. Aren't you working for the sultan's mother now?" As always, Dasamuka sugarcoated his words when he wanted to get his way.

"Do you think that serving Gusti Ratu Kencana pays a lot? It's not that simple." Nyi Wersi's voice filled with pride. "It's true, I have more power now. And with the kind of power I have, I can earn some money. It's too bad I'm not as cunning as you are."

"Power. Ah, yes, power. I'm now asking you to use the power you possess to help us. You don't have to worry about the money."

"Well, well. I think I just got a whiff of your cunningness. What can I do for you and this beautiful young lady?" Nyi Wersi glanced at Rara Ireng who, without letting go of Dasamuka's arm, moved slightly behind him.

"First, help us to become a husband and wife, legally. You can call any clergyman to officiate the marriage. Second, allow us to live here for a month or two. Third, protect us by keeping our presence a secret."

"I don't know why I never can deny your requests. Maybe it's because you look just like your father, Ki Sena. I'm sure you don't know that I once had an eye on your father. Don't laugh! Where's he now?" Nyi Wersi had a habit of pacing while she talked. She was also known for asking rhetorical questions. Hence, Danar did not feel the need to reveal his father's whereabouts.

"You have a place to stay for us tonight, right?"

"Sure thing, Danar. For the meantime, this beautiful lady can sleep with my children in the back room. You can sleep there." Nyi Wersi pointed at a room separated only by a curtain. With nothing more than a piece of cloth protecting him from the outside, Danar would not be able to sleep peacefully. Anyone could enter the room and kill him.

Danar simply nodded. He then whispered something into Rara Ireng's ear that made her let go of his arm.

Nyi Wersi only needed three days to prepare a small wedding ceremony for Danar and Rara Ireng. There were not many guests, but Rara Ireng's mother was amongst the handful who attended the wedding. Danar had managed to bring his mother-in-law into the secret wedding venue. The wedding ceremony was kept simple, not because of the lack of funds, but for safety reasons.

Something at his wedding made an impression on Danar. Other than the priest and Rara Ireng's mother, the invited guests were all beautiful teenage girls. It made him wonder what exactly Nyi Wersi's current job entailed.

After the wedding, Danar and Rara Ireng, now a lawful husband and wife, stayed in a room in the back of the loji. However, during the first day of their stay there, a problem occurred.

"Why are those beautiful guests still here?" Rara Ireng asked with a sour face. She seemed to object to her husband's continued friendly exchanges with the talkative, coquettish girls. They boldly touched her husband without considering her feelings.

"I already asked Nyi Wersi about those guests. They actually live next to us, in the big house with the beautiful garden. We share a common courtyard with them," Danar tried to explain.

"Do you know who they are?" Rara Ireng still seemed disgruntled.

"Why do you keep bothering yourself with them? Just pay attention to your husband, who is right here." Danar looked at his wife tenderly. "You can do a *kerokan* to me, right? I'm afraid I'm coming down with a cold." Danar's question didn't need an answer, as he had already taken Rara Ireng's hand and led her to their bedroom.

In the bedroom—which, instead of a mere cloth, had a real wooden door that could be tightly closed—the kerokan, a traditional healing method of scraping the skin using a coin and oil, did not last too long.

Someone blew out the light from the coconut-oil lamp. Creaking sounds from the rocking divan, accompanied by sighs and moans, soon filled the night and the nights that followed.

Despite the fact that they were fugitives, the newlyweds seemed to be very happy during the first week of their stay with Nyi Wersi. It turned out that the scary old woman was a lovely hostess. Not only did she allow Rara Ireng to use her kitchen, she did not hesitate to offer Rara Ireng her daughters' face powders and body scrubs. Nyi Wersi even offered her homemade *jamu sari rapat*, a medicinal brew of various herbs drunk by women to strengthen their reproductive system.

During the second week of their stay with Nyi Wersi, another problem occurred.

The sultan's mother made her routine visit to Nyi Wersi's *loji* to check on her girls. As usual, she ordered Nyi Wersi to carry out several tasks. When she noticed Rara Ireng, she said, "I've never seen her around before. When did she start living here?"

"She has been here for only a week, Gusti Ratu," Nyi Wersi answered respectfully.

The sultan's mother threw another look at Rara Ireng, whose beauty set her apart from the rest of the girls.

"You must have brought that girl for my son." Gusti Ratu Kencana's gaze was still fixed on Rara Ireng.

Dressed only in her wet bustier, the young woman was hanging her husband's clothes out to dry in the back yard.

Nyi Wersi became flustered and was only capable of responding with an empty stare.

"Why don't you say anything? Is that girl not for my son?" Gusti Ratu Kencana raised her voice, something she seldom did.

Nyi Wersi trembled. She bowed until her forehead almost touched the ground.

"Of course, she is for your son, Gusti Ratu," Nyi Wersi's voice cracked.

"You did not speak the truth when you answered my question. I heard no sincerity in your voice when you granted my wish." Gusti Ratu Kencana, who knew Nyi Wersi well, was suspicious of her abdi's behavior. "Tell me the truth. Who's that beautiful girl?"

"Her name is Rara Ireng, Gusti Ratu. She's the wife of my nephew, Danar." There was a shiver in Nyi Wersi's voice.

"Well, then. I want you to be honest. Were my gifts to you not adequate?"

"They certainly were, Gusti Ratu. You've been very generous."

"Really? Then, you won't have any difficulty to discuss the matter with… what's his name? Ah, yes, Danar. Tell him to present his wife to the Sultan of Yogyakarta. It's a big honor, isn't it, Nyi Wersi?"

"Certainly, Gusti Ratu. It would be a tremendous honor for Danar. Please give me three days to discuss the matter with him." Nyi Wersi's voice sounded normal again.

"Meet me in four days in the garden pavilion of the kaputren. I will be waiting for you, Nyi Wersi," Gusti Ratu Kencana warned while walking out of the loji. Her ladies-in-waiting, who followed her like a shadow, joined her quickly.

After Gusti Ratu Kencana left, Nyi Wersi remained seated on her pandan mat from the noon to the evening prayers. Thoughts tumbled through her mind. *Would the request destroy her life? Or would it bring her fortune?* She finally concluded that whether it was going to be a disaster or a blessing depended on Danar's decision.

It was not until the third day that Nyi Wersi found the courage to meet with the newlyweds and discuss the matter with them. She opened the conversation carefully. "I'd like to talk to both of you, Danar and Rara Ireng. This pertains to your fate and also mine." Nyi Wersi was well aware that Danar was no longer an innocent child. He was an adult who controlled many affairs in the sultanate area. His transactions always had something to do with money.

"As you wish, Nyi." Glancing at Nyi Wersi's face, Danar easily sensed something bad had happened. "I'm ready to hear the worst news."

"It is about my promise and your promise." Nyi Wersi tried her best to find the appropriate words to convey her message. "My promise is to give you protection in this loji, and your promise is to make your wife happy."

"Regarding your promise, we understand. We're ready to leave anytime. You've housed us long enough. Now, as I told you before, fulfilling the promise I made to my wife is my own responsibility." Danar turned to his wife, who was sitting next to him with her head bowed. Danar had told Nyi Wersi about his plan to return Rumah Gajah, Rara Ireng's father's villa in Srondol, to her as soon as possible.

"If you do not mind, I'd like to offer you some help with realizing your dream, which is your wife's dream as well. How much money do you have now? Please forgive me for asking such an intrusive question. Think of it as an aunt's concern for her nephew."

"Honestly, I'm not ashamed to admit that I only have a fifth of the required amount."

"So, then, when would you be able to realize your plan?" Nyi Wersi turned to Rara Ireng. "Young lady, you're still dreaming of living in the house your father built, aren't you?"

"Of course, Nyi. My most beautiful memories… my childhood memories were made there. Am I wrong for longing to return to where I spent the happiest time of my life?" Rara Ireng answered quietly, her voice filled with doubt.

"Of course not. You're not wrong at all." Nyi Wersi turned back to Danar. "There—you just heard your wife's wish. What will you do to make it come true?"

"I have yet to figure it out." Danar had no idea how to acquire the luxurious villa. Deep inside, he knew it was impossible to fulfill his promise during the next two or three years. However, he would never admit this openly to Rara Ireng or Nyi Wersi.

Everyone turned quiet. In the thick silence that filled the air, the giggles coming from the kaputren could be heard clearly. Most likely the laughter came from the ladies-in-waiting, because girls living on the Keraton's premises were not allowed to laugh that freely. In the tense silence, even the rustle of a falling dry leaf of the breadnut tree as it made its way to the ground was startling.

"I know what you could do about it, Danar." Nyi Wersi broke the silence. Her voice was soft, but it still jolted the newly-weds.

"Please tell us what you have in mind, Nyi."

Rara Ireng only muttered in agreement with her husband.

"Danar, are you willing to make sacrifices for your wife's happiness?" Nyi Wersi asked.

Danar quickly nodded.

"Rara Ireng, are you willing to make sacrifices to enable your husband?"

Rara Ireng also nodded.

Nyi Wersi let out a deep breath and remained silent for a moment. She needed the couple to be calm when she proposed her plan. Shifting her gaze between Danar and Rara Ireng, Nyi Wersi decided to address the young woman.

"Gusti Ratu Kencana, the sultan's mother, was very impressed by your beauty, Rara Ireng. She wanted you to serve her." Nyi Wersi kept a keen eye on Rara Ireng.

"Is it serving Gusti Ratu Kencana—or serving her son?" Danar cut straight through the matter by articulating what Nyi Wersi had been meaning to tell them. He could guess where the conversation was leading.

"Yes, Gusti Ratu Kencana is asking for your wife to serve the sultan." Nyi Wersi avoided looking at Danar's face. Instead, she gazed into the distance where a sawo kecik tree swayed in the blowing wind. "It's such an honor, Danar, isn't it?"

Danar tensed and clenched his jaws.

Rara Ireng was unsure about the whole situation, but sensed something dangerous was about to occur. "What do you mean by serving the sultan, Nyi? Can you please explain it?" It was in her interest to know what it exactly meant.

"The young sultan is fond of beautiful things. Beautiful voices, beautiful dances, and surely, the beautiful faces and slender bodies that are the center of all that."

For Rara Ireng, a young woman who had only been married for less than a month, the explanation was not clear enough.

On the other hand, the explanation was more than sufficient for Danar. It was clear that his wife was being asked to become the sultan's courtesan. She wouldn't be a concubine and definitely not his consort. *Where would that place her dignity?*

Danar was in touch with the poets and clergymen of the Korps Suranatan who worked in the Keraton area. He knew the scholars and holy men did not approve of what Gusti Ratu Kencana was doing.

The sultan's mother thought that by providing her son with as many beautiful girls as she could, she would be able to accelerate the process of the young sultan's maturity. Now his wife would be one of the women used to achieve Gusti Ratu Kencana's quest.

Danar rose as if the pandan mat he had been seated on had suddenly turned to coals. Without a word, he quickly walked towards the door.

Nyi Wersi ran after him, trying to calm him down, but Danar walked too fast for her to keep up.

Even though she had yet to fully understand the problem, Rara Ireng followed suit.

Danar headed the small procession. Nyi Wersi hobbled behind him, with Rara Ireng closely following. The three of them scurried across the porch and cut through the yard.

Nyi Wersi's howling attracted the attention of the gardeners and some guards. Some of them automatically followed the threesome headed for the main path of the loji's yard.

No one could catch up with Danar, who walked with a tense face and high chest. He would have kept walking if it were not for a disturbance that was as fierce as the turmoil in his heart. The sudden disruption halted him abruptly.

The thundering sound of galloping horses was followed by a thick cloud of dust rolling in from a distance. A hundred soldiers rode in front of the golden chariot, drawn by eight strong Persian horses. Another hundred soldiers followed behind.

The horses and the carriage dashed across the road. Whoever encountered the entourage was left standing, flabbergasted. Some people, mostly women and children, had to hold onto each other to steady themselves on the shaking ground and slow their racing hearts.

Danar stood glued to the sidewalk. His eyes fixed at the chaos in front of him; he did not notice that Nyi Wersi had managed to catch up and now stood right behind him.

Rara Ireng and a few gardeners stumbled towards them.

"That's Sultan Jarot, Danar," Nyi Wersi blurted out. "If you let your wife go to the kaputren to serve him, you, Danar…," Nyi Wersi stopped to take a breath before she quickly continued, "You'd be the one assigned to take care of all of sultan's needs. The sultan is really fond of riding in his chariot." Nyi Wersi had noticed Danar's astonishment as he witnessed the fierce incident and made a great effort to finish conveying her message. This was the right place and time to do so.

"Sultan Jarot…," Danar muttered. His insides were in upheaval.

"Serving him. Yes. If you allow Rara Ireng to serve him, you'll not only be able to buy Rumah Gajah in Srondol, you'd be able to buy anything you want. You'll be powerful and wealthy," Nyi Wersi whispered into Danar's ear.

The noise started to move away. Only a yellow shimmer in a thick cloud of dust remained and blurred the people's view.

"Sultan Hamengkubuwono… Sultan Jarot…." Danar's heart filled with uncertainty.

"Trust me, the sultan won't ask for your wife's service for very long. Many girls in the kaputren are waiting for a wave of his hand. I predict that, in less than a month, Rara Ireng will be able to return to your arms.

"Upon her return, she'll bring you a golden opportunity to achieve something you've dreamed about all along: becoming rich and powerful. Haven't you been working hard for this? Didn't you once tell me that you want to be a king without a crown and a merchant without merchandise? Gusti Ratu Kencana has promised to make you both."

"Sultan Hamengkubuwono…," Danar lisped.

"Kakang, let's go home. People are watching us." Rara Ireng had caught up with her husband and now stood next to him.

"Aren't we hiding in Nyi Wersi's loji to avoid people's attention?" She looked around her nervously.

Danar slowly turned to Rara Ireng. His lips no longer moved to spell the name of the ruler of the Yogyakarta Keraton. As he looked at his beloved wife, his shattered heart slowly gathered itself.

For a moment, the couple stood facing each other. In the cloud of dust that still hung in the air, husband and wife clung to each other in a tight embrace. Silence overtook the crowd. A sob was heard. It could have come from either Rara Ireng or Danar—or, perhaps, from both. They whispered something to each other. People around them were not able to hear what they said. Neither was Nyi Wersi, who had moved close and leaned toward them to eavesdrop.

To be powerful and wealthy—Danar thought it was the best option for both of them. It was much better than receiving the death sentence or becoming a lifetime fugitive. If he disobeyed Gusti Ratu Kencana's order, he would wind up in one situation or the other. He could not seek protection in Nyi Wersi's loji forever to avoid sudden attacks from Puri Wibawa. Nor could he keep lying to his wife about buying the Rumah Gajah for her in the near future. He had worked hard all his life, and it had always been his desire to be rich and powerful. He now forced himself to let his wife serve Sultan Jarot, the young and handsome sultan—a lad who was barely eighteen years old. Danar forced himself to let her go.

─────•◦•─────

Danar's decision quickly changed his life. Only two days after he succeeded in convincing his wife to follow Gusti Ratu Kencana to her kaputren, a confidant of Patih Danureja contacted him.

The old duke clearly stated that he was willing to pass on his current position to Danar.

Thereafter, Danar was in charge of taking care of the sultan's recreational needs. On top of the list of his daily pleasures were outings in his golden chariot.

Whether the sultan went for a leisurely drive through his territory or spurred his horses to thunder with a maddening speed across the sultanate's roads, he required two hundred escort horses and eight Persian horses to pull the chariot. Because Danar was responsible for the purchase of the horses, the horse breeders and traders bowed low upon hearing his footsteps, hung on his every word, and welcomed his hand, the palm of which was lined with gold coins.

Whenever Sultan Hamengkubuwono IV became bored of passing the same routes several times, he ordered Danar to quickly prepare new routes. When issuing the order to build new roads, the sultan never considered the amount of money needed for the construction of the new streets, nor did he give any thought to the landowners who had to give up their land.

People who were not willing to surrender their lands would go see Danar, who had the full authority to determine which way a road would run. They did not care about the amount of money Danar charged for his assistance to save their land. For the Javanese, inheritance of land and houses were considered *pusaka*, something sacred.

Danar's last source of extra income came from the cavalry soldiers. There were too many soldiers losing their lives by being thrown out of the saddle and then trampled by the horses or crushed by the chariot's wheels. Soldiers would come to Danar requesting to be placed behind the chariot, which was clearly safer.

Danar cleverly took advantage of the situation. The money he received from the soldiers was not that much, but flowed steadily into his pocket. He enjoyed his new job so much that he lost track of time. While satisfying his long-harbored desire for power and wealth, he failed to realize that a month had passed since his wife had been forced to service the sultan.

Danar's enemies, especially the Suryanata family, were now forced to cease their animosity toward him. To attack Danar would be considered a disruption of the sultan's pleasure, and their heads would be the price of their treachery.

Despite the power his current employment provided, Danar still held on to the business he had cultivated for many years. He still frequented the princedoms in the Yogyakarta jurisdiction, where his integrity in matters of wealth, thrones, and women, was still highly in demand. He also did not forget to tend to his business in Salatiga, his hometown.

Danar was known for his ability to easily manage several jobs at the same time. His friends often said that his nickname, Dasamuka—meaning ten faces—was inappropriate; he clearly needed only one head to take care of several matters.

⊢——•——⊣

The story of Danar's extravagant lifestyle did not last long, however. His life was disrupted when Ngusman quietly handed him a secret letter Semi had passed him.

When Danar opened the letter, the sender turned out to be his wife, Rara Ireng. And even though the letter was very short, it caused Danar to fall off the carved mahogany chair where he was seated. Lying on the ground, he read the letter again: *Kakang Danar, I can't possibly remain alive at the kaputren. Your wife, Rara Ireng."*

━━•◦•━━

In the days after he received the letter, Danar felt gloomy. The sky over the Keraton seemed always cloudy. Even the clean floor tiles of the palace looked dull and sooty. However, the cloud and soot were merely in his mind. And to him, Sultan Hamengkubuwono IV, whom people called Sultan Jarot and praised as the most handsome descendant of the Mataram kings, was in fact a horrifying figure: a combination of Dasamuka, Kumbhakarna, and Shurpanakha; a pulsating blood clot with big ears and sharp nails.

Danar had been able to help a wife who wanted to see her husband who was being held in an Ambarawa prison, to help a father who wanted to free his daughter from the claws of Nyi Wersi's accomplices. He could order criminals to do the dirty jobs of kidnapping and killing people. However, he was unable to even see his own wife, let alone help her escape from the palace. Was he really that powerful and wealthy now? Perhaps he was rich enough, but he was definitely not that powerful.

Den Wahyana ended his story of Dasamuka by repeating his earlier statement: *There will be an uprising against Sultan Hamengkubuwono IV.*

━━•◦•━━

Each day I grew more restless about having to work under government officials who cared only about increasing their retirement savings. I was sure this had been causing the constant nausea I was experiencing. I vomited several times after I caught sight of the new Resident. My colleagues told me I had caught a cold, but I was convinced my illness was caused by emotional stress.

For unscrupulous people, like my superiors in the Karesidenan, money only served to satisfy their indulgences; it was nothing more or less than that. This conviction caused me to despise myself for staying amidst people who were the source of deceit. Hence, I often visited Loji Rejawinangun.

I had started to think about colonialism and imperialism. The British built colonies to improve the inhabitants' prosperity and civilization. Once they were able to govern themselves independently, those colonies would join the British Commonwealth.

The Dutch, on the other hand, were what I would call true colonialists. At least, this applied to the Dutch I encountered at my workplace, the office of Resident Nahuys.

My positive opinion regarding imperialism, however, was at odds with the looting and robbery incident of the Yogyakarta Keraton treasures, a tragedy I had seen with my own eyes. The cruelty and disregard I witnessed that day would stay with me forever.

Observing Uncle Harvey's passion for his plantations and Daisy's dedication to the plants that Dr. Reinwardt had entrusted her with, as well as her involvement with women's rights issues, had been able to lift my spirits. Spending time with them distracted me from the shallowness of my superiors' minds and hearts, especially that of Hubert Nahuys, the new Resident. However, Uncle Harvey was now plagued by an anxiety that had infected Daisy and ended up affecting me as well. I tried to keep busy. I also tried to reflect on what I had been doing on this island for the past ten years.

Time had passed very quickly since I set foot on Java in August of 1811. It felt as if I had just fought with the British in Batavia, chasing away the Dutch soldiers who ran for their lives from the cannonballs.

I often spent my nights at Rejawinangun, but recent robberies around the plantation made staying there a different experience. The peace and the tranquility I used to enjoy was disappearing.

While my visits to Rejawinangun were not driven by any romantic or erotic motives, the public had its own opinion. I was often referred to as Uncle Harvey's son-in-law, Daisy's husband. Once, when I attended a wedding of a Keraton family member by myself, I was even asked about my "wife." I did not have the heart to tell them that Daisy was not my wife. I merely smiled. I wondered if Daisy had encountered such a situation and how she reacted if people asked her about her husband.

———•••———

Den Wahyana was right. Danar came to see me early one morning. With bloodshot eyes, bluing lips, and clothes in disarray, he appeared exhausted and disheveled. Before I had a chance to ask him what was going on, he stammered that, after locking himself in his room for a whole day, he decided to come to see me.

I was curious why he had decided to turn to me with his problem. Even though I had lived among the Javanese for a good decade, I was still a foreigner. Given the overall turbulent situation, I wondered if Danar, known as a man of many trades, had gotten himself in trouble with the law.

A typical Javanese, Danar did not address his problem during the visit. Instead, he delivered a monologue about his condition and then left abruptly. I was certain this would not be the end of the story.

Danar was waiting for me when I came home from the office that afternoon. He still looked the same; the only difference was that he had changed his clothes.

"I need your help, sir," Danar said quietly.

"If Danar, Dasamuka, lord of the underworld, the invisible one, needs help, the task to meet his need would be enormous," I replied, using the same phrases Den Wahyana used when telling stories about the most mysterious man I'd ever met.

Danar chose not to respond to my joke, which might not have been appropriate under the circumstances. "Please allow me to explain my situation."

"Go ahead, I'm listening."

"My problem involves Sultan Hamengkubuwono IV, the sovereign of the Yogyakarta Sultanate. My wife was ordered to serve the ruler of Java," Danar explained with a trembling voice. It was the first time he had showed desperation.

"Why did you allow such a thing to happen?" I already knew the answer, but I wanted to hear him say it.

Danar remained silent. After a while, he muttered, "My wife was forced to serve the sultan, and I was forced to let her go. We were forced to do so, sir. The King of Java can easily behead someone for refusing to obey his orders."

Danar turned silent again. Only after letting out several sighs, he complained, "According to Nyi Wersi, Sultan Jarot usually dismisses his courtesans in less than a month and forgets about them immediately. However, as it turns out, my wife has been servicing him for more than a month now—a month and two weeks to be exact—and the sultan has still not released her."

"Have you made any attempts to take her out of the palace?"

"When I asked Nyi Wersi about it, her answer was, 'Sultan still needs her.' When, after a few days, I asked her the same question, she replied, 'Rara Ireng is Sultan's favorite; he won't let go of her in the near future.'"

"Are you still staying at Nyi Wersi's loji?"

"Not at the moment. I left after having a heated disagreement with Nyi Wersi. When I told her that I wanted to take my wife back, she said I was a foolish husband. No one has ever dared to call me a fool before. I lost my temper and slapped Nyi Wersi, hard. She fell, and I don't know whether she died or was merely unconscious. I don't care. I'm homeless now.

"In addition to being hunted by the thugs from Puri Suryanata, now Nyi Wersi's accomplices are also after me. Soon, the soldiers from the Keraton will join the chase."

"Are you planning to run away with your wife?"

"Yes, I'm going to kidnap her. That's why I'm here. I need your help, sir."

"Are you expecting me to kidnap Rara Ireng?"

"Of course not. I need Ngusman, Semi, and Den Wahyana to help me. They will only listen to you. My money doesn't have any power over them." Danar looked absolutely miserable.

Had my move to Java not been initiated by my desire to commit suicide in Edinburgh to avoid running into Ailsa and the people who would mock my downfall, I would have surely rejected Danar's request. However, my wish to die and be buried on Java was still present. The phrase, *It's better to die in honor than to live in infamy* continued to echo in my mind.

The problem was that I was still trying to form an opinion about Sultan Hamengkubuwono IV. I wondered if he really was an evil person and if opposing him would bring me the kind of honor I wanted. Or was he merely a spoiled child, victimized by the poisonous act of pampering?

"I will help you under one condition," I finally said, trying to change the sad look on Danar's face.

Danar did not say anything. When he raised his head, his eyes were swollen.

I had not yet thought about the prerequisite I was going to attach to my help. At first, I wanted to ask him for money, which I later could use to pay those whose help we would need.

However, after seeing his face, I changed my mind. I said, "You have to convince me that your wife really suffers at the hands of the sultan."

"Fine." Danar covered his face with both hands, the same way I had seen people do when praying. "Tomorrow, I will ask Semi to tell us how my wife is doing at the kaputren. As an abdi dalem, a member of the Keraton's household staff, she is able to move freely in that restricted area."

My meeting with Danar was concluded with an agreement to involve Semi.

I wondered why Danar had chosen Semi to report on his wife's situation. I felt uneasy, thinking that Danar possibly knew about my feelings toward her. After all, Semi was still married to Ngusman. To protect myself from unwanted things that could happen, I asked Daisy to attend the meeting with Semi. At least I could let Danar know that I was not motivated by the desire to be alone with Semi. It was important he knew that.

Chapter 9

SEMI

Daisy and I waited for Semi's visit to my house for almost half a day. The servant who usually came to do daily chores was absent that day and hence there were only the two of us. Daisy seemed uncomfortable with the situation and started to clean and straighten my place. I was unable to stop her. She not only cleaned the kitchen, but also everything in my living room.

I had the strong urge to wipe her perspiring forehead with my handkerchief, but quickly dismissed the thought.

"Is that the Semi we're waiting for?" Daisy pointed at a woman who stood awkwardly in front of the house.

"Yes, she is." Daisy's question had caught me off guard.

"So, this is what my competitor in winning your heart looks like," Daisy teased, and

I blushed. Seeing my face reddening, Daisy laughed.

I did not want Daisy to continue laughing and asked her to open the door for Semi. Anyone watching us would know that there were three of us. Many Javanese people believed that if a man and a woman spend time alone in a quiet place, the devil would soon join them. For some unknown reason, I somehow felt to be surrounded by ten of Danar's heads, and each of the twenty eyes from those heads was upon us.

"Are you alone? Where's your husband?" I asked Semi in *ngoko* Javanese, a dialect used among Javanese to address close friends or a person of lower status.

"Yes, sir, I came alone because my husband is escorting the sultan on an outing." Semi answered in krama Javanese, the dialect used to address someone of higher status.

Daisy watched Semi intently.

Even though she was no longer young, Semi was still as charming as when I met her for the first time. Javanese beauty was indeed entirely different from European beauty. I quickly dismissed such inappropriate admiration.

"Did you see Rara Ireng?"

"Yes, sir, about a week ago."

"How was she doing?"

"She was very thin, and her eyes were swollen from crying. I've told Dasamuka this."

"Is it possible to kidnap her from the kaputren?"

"The chance is quite slim. Since she is the sultan's favorite, she's guarded heavily."

"All right, thanks, Semi. You've told me enough for now. You can go home. And, oh, we've something for you to take home from Rejawinangun." I turned to Daisy who rose and walked to the table.

Daisy picked up a small package that contained a loaf of bread she had baked from sweet potatoes and Java almonds. After handing Semi the package, Daisy gave her a big hug.

Semi was surprised and, moving awkwardly, dropped the gift.

Daisy and Semi both hurried to pick it up and inevitably collided. Laughing, Daisy rubbed her forehead while Semi grimaced shyly. She was clearly uncomfortable and, after excusing herself quickly, walked out of the house with her head lowered.

"This Javanese woman is surely capable of making you forget the one in Edinburgh," Daisy smiled. She was clearly teasing me.

"I never forget Daisy when I'm with Semi," I answered. I tried not to take Daisy seriously.

"Am I the Edinburgh girl? I don't think so. I'm quite sure that I'm not the one who lives in your heart." Daisy now flashed a thin smile.

Both of us then fell into silence. Neither of us could benefit from continuing the banter.

I began to scrutinize my own feelings. I wondered if my attraction to that Javanese woman was to keep Ailsa away. I still could not figure it out. There were too many questions still unanswered, including my involvement in Rara Ireng's predicament. *What good would it do me?* I was British, born and bred, not one of the ruling Dutch. By helping Danar, I would be considered an enemy of the sultan. I hoped my behavior was not still motivated by an unconscious desire to commit suicide.

———•••———

A week later, I managed to gather Den Wahyana, Semi, and Ngusman in my house for a meeting. I had chosen a time and day when there were not too many people wandering around the Karesidenan complex.

The meeting was short. I told them that, while none of us would gain anything from our involvement, there would be a big problem if we refused to help Danar. He could be blinded by rage and act carelessly.

His current position gave him the opportunity to be near the sultan at will. This could be dangerous, as they could end up in a deadly duel.

I told them we needed to solve this problem without casualties, and turned to Den Wahyana. "What's your opinion, Den Wahyana? You're knowledgeable in the Keraton affairs."

Den Wahyana was seated next to Ngusman with his back leaning against the wall. He looked tired and had dark shadows around his eyes.

"You're right," he said. "I agreed to get involved because I'm afraid that Danar will act irrationally. He's the kind of person who's capable of committing horrible crimes, including murdering the sultan."

"What if we send Semi to help Rara Ireng escape?" I suggested. "With Ngusman's help of course."

"We won't send Semi to rescue Rara Ireng, but to convince her to run away according to a plan we will devise," Den Wahyana said. "Considering the heavy surveillance she is placed under, Rara Ireng needs to run away to rescue herself. We then will pick her up at an agreed-upon spot and guide her to a place where she will be safe."

"She's suffering right now, and I'm sure she dreams of escaping from the palace," Ngusman weighed in.

"Even though Rara Ireng is suffering, I'm not sure she's thinking about escaping. And even if she thought about it, she won't know how to go about it." Den Wahyana sighed and continued, "We first have to convince her that it is not only possible to escape, but there's a big chance she'll succeed. It will be Semi's task to relay this message to Rara Ireng."

"So, after we manage to convince her, and she has gathered the courage to run away, all we need to do is to wait for her somewhere on the fringes of the kaputren and help her reach her destination. Am I right?"

Den Wahyana then took a pen and a piece of paper from my desk and drew a map of the kaputren complex, showing buildings and pathways.

"If Rara Ireng can reach this place at one o'clock in the morning," Den Wahyana pointed at a spot on his map, "we'll be able to sneak her out of the Keraton long before two."

"But it means she has to pass at least five guard posts," Ngusman said anxiously.

"We'll ask her to walk through the gardens instead of using the pathways," Den Wahyana explained. "She's been living there for more than a month; she should be familiar with the intricacies of the complex by now.

"And the guards would never expect someone wanting to escape from the kaputren. They think that Rara Ireng is one of Nyi Wersi's girls—they're convinced that Nyi Wersi's girls are happy to live in luxury."

"Oh, now I understand." Ngusman sounded relieved.

"Then, let's decide now to send Semi right away." Den Wahyana turned to Semi. "You hold the key to the success of this plan."

When everyone in the room looked at Semi, she nodded; she understood and agreed.

I was not sure why Semi and Ngusman were willing to help Danar. The couple currently lived well. It could be that they were just unable to refuse my request—having helped their family several times. Or perhaps they empathized with Rara Ireng's plight. It was also possible that family ties moved them to help. Though they hid the fact, Danar was Semi's nephew.

Whether they realized it or not, both Ngusman and Semi had just plunged themselves into something very dangerous, a plan to abduct the sultan's favorite consort.

It wouldn't be until much later that I heard the full report of what happened and was able to weave together into one story what Den Wahyana, Semi, and Ngusman told me. That tale started when Semi—who, as an abdi dalem, was free to wander around the kaputren—managed to speak with Rara Ireng soon after the meeting at my house.

"I'm sent by your husband, Den Ayu," Semi whispered, once she made sure there was no one around them. "Den Danar asked me to find out about your condition."

"Did you give him my letter? I don't need to explain my condition any further." Rara Ireng sighed. After staring at Semi for a while, she murmured, "Both of us are women, Semi. Take a look at me now."

"Yes, Den Ayu. Your thin body and gloomy expression are proof of what you are enduring here." Semi sighed. She had noticed how Rara Ireng, one of the kaputren's most beautiful flowers, was wilting and dying.

"Please forgive your husband for only sending me now." Semi chose her words carefully, so she would not create the impression that Danar had forsaken his wife in exchange for power and wealth. "There was a slight doubt in Den Danar's heart."

"What was it that he doubted?"

"Aren't you currently serving someone who is desired by many women out there? He's young, handsome, and powerful. He doesn't lack anything. Are you sure you still want to return to Den Danar, who's a mere commoner?"

"Sultan Hamengkubuwono IV is wealthy and handsome—but anyone who claims him to be powerful is wrong. He is nothing but a spoiled and childish teenager, far from being a king. His mother makes all his decisions. Any woman with integrity would never admire such a king."

"Doesn't Den Danar have weaknesses, too?" Semi wanted to make sure that Rara Ireng would be easy to work with once their plan unfolded.

"It's true Kakang Danar also has his weaknesses. His shortcomings are a result of the fact that he was forced to fend for himself at a very young age, and he had to teach himself many things. He reminds me of my father. Both of them are adventurers. I always admire those who survive despite being surrounded by obvious dangers. Neither my father nor my husband relied on other people's help."

"If tomorrow Den Danar comes and asks you to leave with him, are you willing to follow him without Sultan's permission?"

"I'm ready to go now. All I need is the clothing I'm wearing. I will leave all the gifts I received from Sultan. I don't want to carry these bad memories for the rest of my life."

"Very well, let's go for a long walk outside. Please act as if everything is normal, Den Ayu," Semi said, and started to lead Rara Ireng to the place within the kaputren that Den Wahyana had marked on the map.

Acting as if they were taking a leisurely walk, Semi and Rara Ireng looked at the calming greenery and beautiful flowers. They passed by several guard posts without difficulty. Sometimes, Semi purposely laughed, loudly. Finally, they reached the furthest point from the center of the kaputren.

"I have to ask you to refrain from sleeping tomorrow night, Den Ayu. Please wear dark clothes and come to this place soon after isya prayers. Please don't use the pathway we used today, come a different way. You'll need to find a path that's hidden by shrubbery, even if you have to cross ditches. Then, please sit on that rock so we can see you from a distance. We'll be on the lookout for you after midnight." Semi whispered to make sure no one could overhear her. "And you were correct when you said you won't bring anything. Den Danar has prepared everything you'll need."

They meandered back to the main building of the kaputren, where Rara Ireng was housed. Before she left, Semi whispered to Rara Ireng once again. "Please remember, Den Ayu, tomorrow...."

———•—•———

I anxiously paced the floor of my house while waiting for Semi and Ngusman to finish loading supplies in the carriage. I was also waiting for Den Wahyana. He still had to reveal his choice of a temporary hiding place for Rara Ireng after she managed to sneak out of the kaputren. Overcome by impatience, I saddled my horse and rode to his house.

"I've prepared the places for their temporary hideout," Den Wahyana said when I arrived at his place in Tegalrejo.

"That's the news I've been waiting for." I was relieved.

The small house with bamboo-plait walls and straw roof was very quiet that afternoon. The silence reminded me of the incident in front of my house, when the enraged woman attacked Den Wahyana with sharp and cruel words.

"I never met your wife and children. Where are they?" I asked. Then I bit my lip. I should never have asked something personal like that, but I could not retract my words.

"They are living inside the Keraton walls now," Den Wahyana replied and looked away. "I may not be able to see them again."

I had never seen Den Wahyana so sad. All of a sudden, he rose and walked toward the window. It seemed that facing me made him uncomfortable. Or was he, perhaps, hiding something?

Not wanting to add to his grief, I did not ask. I regretted nosing into his family affairs.

I had sensed a change in my friend's behavior ever since the incident with his wife in front of my house. He rarely engaged in long conversations anymore, and he only spoke when being asked something, and even then, his answers were short. I also noticed a change in his appearance. He no longer shaved his moustache and trimmed his beard. His hair was unkempt and his clothes were in disarray.

I joined Den Wahyana, who stood looking out of the window, and tapped him on the shoulder. "I'm sorry if my question disturbed you," I said. "I'll leave now. Later this evening, we'll meet at my house. Please get some rest. We will need to stay alert through tomorrow evening."

—•—

The time had come to make the last-minute preparations for Rara Ireng's escape. The escape route from the Keraton to the first destination had been checked. The familiarity of the Keraton guards with Semi's job as an abdi dalem, Ngusman as a guard, and Den Wahyana as a language interpreter, were beneficial for our plan. My presence would create the illusion that our actions were authorized by the government. The guards never took notice of the fact that I was British, not Dutch; a fair-skinned man dressed in a Europesche ambtenaar uniform was enough to deter them.

On the night the escape was planned, Den Wahyana arrived at my house on horseback, while Ngusman and Semi came with Danar, who drove the carriage. I quickly saddled my horse, and we headed for the place Den Wahyana had chosen as a pick-up point for Rara Ireng and the start of the actual escape.

It didn't take us long to arrive at the secluded bend in the back road near the Keraton complex. Den Wahyana had chosen a spot just outside the Keraton boundaries near a back entry that was seldom used and often skipped by the guards when they made their rounds.

After Den Wahyana and I tethered our horses to a tree off the road, he climbed one of the taller trees. Rara Ireng was seated on the rock Semi had shown her at the edge of the kaputren garden. Den Wahyana heaved a sigh of relief and hurried down. Turning to Semi, he whispered, "She's waiting. Hurry, go fetch her. Remember, your safety depends on the paths you choose."

Semi merely nodded and soon disappeared into the dense foliage.

Keeping his eyes on the spot where Semi had disappeared, Den Wahyana instructed, "Danar, leave as soon as Rara Ireng has boarded the carriage."

Danar did not respond. He merely nodded emphatically and clutched the reins.

I walked my horse toward the road and readied myself to ride ahead once Semi and Rara Ireng appeared.

There was a rustle of brush followed by muffled, excited voices.

Den Wahyana opened the carriage door and Semi almost pushed Rara Ireng into the coach.

I jumped onto my saddle and spurred my horse. With a quick look over my shoulder, I made sure the carriage and Den Wahyana followed. According to the plan, Ngusman and Semi were to go home.

We still had to travel some ten miles before reaching Sleman, where we were to go directly to a hut that belonged to one of Den Wahyana's underground connections. We hoped to arrive by two in the morning.

Even though this was the very first time Danar and Rara Ireng had seen each other after being separated for more than a month, they only exchanged glances. Having to drive a carriage at high speed through the dark night across a winding road demanded Danar's undivided attention.

When the carriage slowed and rolled onto a graveled area, Rara Ireng carefully parted the curtains to peek outside.

Someone carrying an oil lamp ran toward them.

Den Wahyana and I dismounted, while Danar brought the carriage to a halt at the edge of a coconut tree grove. He jumped out of the carriage and quickly opened the door to help Rara Ireng step out of the coach. They briefly clung to each other before joining the group.

"Kang Bewok, this is Mr. Willem." Den Wahyana bowed in my direction, then, pointing with his thumb at the other two, he continued, "These are my friends I've told you about earlier, Rara Ireng and Danar. Please accompany them while Mr. Willem and I hide the carriage and take care of the horses." Den Wahyana started to walk his horse to a cluster of banana trees at the end of a path through the coconut grove.

After we took care of the horses and hid the carriage between the banana trees, I turned to Den Wahyana. "Since there's no reason I should join you to Magelang, I'll return to the Karesidenan. A smaller group will attract less attention. Besides, this way I can also circumvent questions about my absence."

Den Wahyana went along with my decision. Later, Den Wahyana and Danar filled me in on what happened to the runaway couple after I left.

———◆———

Kang Bewok was a heavily built man who moved with great agility. "I'm very pleased you all arrived safely. Come." He headed toward a thick grove of tall castor bean trees that flowed into a dense patch of cassava. From afar, no one would have guessed there was a hut concealed in the greenery.

Walking behind Kang Bewok, Danar and Rara Ireng held each other's hand tightly. Every so often, Rara Ireng turned her head to throw Danar a quizzical look, which he responded by squeezing her hand and pressing it tightly against his chest. Still overwhelmed by the enormity of having escaped from Gusti Ratu Kencana's grip, neither was able to speak.

"Mangga, pinarak, please come in," Kang Bewok said, and opened the door to a small hut almost covered by the growth of cassava trees.

A single oil lamp lit the entire hut, but even dim light was unable to hide the fatigue on Rara Ireng's and Danar's tense faces.

Kang Bewok showed the couple to the only room in the hut with a door. He placed another oil lamp alongside a bamboo cot lined only with a pandan mat. A clay water jug with two enamel cups sat on a small table in one of the corners.

Danar checked on the wooden latch of the closed window.

"Thank you, kakang...." Rara Ireng said softly, while leaning against the closed door.

"This is all I can do for you, *diajeng.*" Danar took Rara Ireng's hand and pressed it against his chest. He usually had a hard time verbalizing his feelings; this was the first time he had called her darling.

Rara Ireng lowered her head. A teardrop fell on the back of Danar's hand.

"Please rest, diajeng. I will be back soon." Danar stroked Rara Ireng's forehead, then left the room to join Kang Bewok and Den Wahyana, who were in the front room where the window and door were tightly shut.

The three of them took a seat on the *tikar*, a woven mat of pandan leaves.

"How long will we stay here, Den?" Danar asked Den Wahyana.

"I suggest we move towards Semarang as quickly as possible." Den Wahyana looked at Kang Bewok, who nodded.

"We will head to Magelang first, because it will take too long to travel to Semarang directly," Den Wahyana continued.

Danar and Rara Ireng planned to settle in Semarang with fake documents. Danar, skilled in obtaining these papers, was confident that he could execute his plan smoothly.

"Tomorrow afternoon, a friend of mine will come to report on the situation outside," Den Wahyana said.

"Very well. Thank you for everything." Danar rose, excused himself, and headed for the bedroom.

At the door, he seemed suddenly overcome by a mixture of emotions, and his knuckles whitened as he gripped the door handle. He felt longing for his wife, jealousy when he imagined what the sultan had demanded of her, and shame at not having acted earlier. When Danar finally turned the handle and slowly pushed the door open, Rara Ireng was seated on the edge of the bamboo cot.

She rose immediately and embraced him.

For a moment they held each other in silence, each of them curious about their time apart, but so exhausted they only could hold each other tightly and, every so often, move apart to look at each other.

When, after a while, Rara Ireng walked to the cot and lay down, Danar followed her. Lying silently next to each other, Danar's chest heaved as he reached for Rara Ireng's hand.

She sighed, then dropped off to sleep.

Danar remained wide awake. He turned carefully on his side and smiled, looking at Rara Ireng's face. Danar loved to watch his wife's face when she was asleep. Rara Ireng never snored. Not even the slightest sound escaped from her soft, closed lips. When she was asleep, Rara Ireng looked like she could be meditating instead of merely sleeping.

A rooster crowed, and thin rays of sunlight crept through the slits in the bamboo-plaited walls.

Danar rose slowly, taking care not to wake Rara Ireng. He tiptoed toward the window and opened it cautiously, filling his lungs with the fresh morning air while taking in his surroundings. The simple hut, surrounded by a thicket of cassava plants and castor bean trees at the edge of a coconut plantation, was a perfect hideaway.

"Kakang?" Rara Ireng's voice was still coated with sleep.

"Yes, diajeng." Danar quickly closed the window and helped Rara Ireng up.

For a moment, the couple sat on the cot that creaked every time they moved closer to each other. Danar gently put an arm around his wife's shoulder.

"When will we be able to be alone and talk, just the two of us, kakang?" Rara Ireng scanned her husband's face.

"After we find a safe place to live, diajeng." Danar kissed his wife's cheek.

The sunlight now penetrated the slits in the bamboo-plaited walls.

When Den Wahyana called them, they walked to the other room holding hands.

There was boiled cassava on a *tampah*, and next to the big platter made from woven bamboo stood a clay water jug and some enamel cups.

"Where is Kang Bewok?" Danar asked.

"He left early this morning. He wanted to check on the safety of the roads we will use to go to Semarang." Den Wahyana rose. He opened the window just ajar and observed the situation outside. "There he is," and quickly walked towards the door to remove the cross bar.

Soon, the four of them were seated on the mat.

"Kang, how safe are the roads to Semarang?" Danar impatiently asked Kang Bewok,

"I didn't see anyone checking on the passing carriages, so there's nothing to worry about. We can leave tomorrow." Kang Bewok's answer was well received by Danar and Rara Ireng.

"Our friends in Semarang will need at least two days to find a safe house for you." Kang Bewok helped himself to a piece of the boiled cassava and filled his cup with water from the clay water jug. "It is not easy to find a place in an area that's controlled by the Dutch."

"Danar and Rara Ireng will need at least a week to take care of all the documents to be able to stay legally in Dutch territory; they will need the help of a corrupt officer," Den Wahyana added.

Rara Ireng spoke infrequently. Most of the time, she only listened to the conversation.

Meanwhile, Den Wahyana continued to ask Kang Bewok about the situation of the roads around Sleman. They planned to use country roads to Magelang and stop there before going to Semarang.

Later that afternoon, a man dressed in black knocked on the back door. He was a messenger sent by Den Wahyana's underground friends in Semarang. They discussed their plans until dusk. With the arrival of the informant from Semarang, their escape route became clearer and more detailed.

"Our people have acquired a house in the coastal area of northern Semarang," the informant said after he had poured himself a glass of water from the clay water jug.

"This means that tomorrow we will have to leave before dawn," Danar said.

Den Wahyana and the man from Semarang did not say anything. They seemed to have something on their minds.

"Den, we'll be leaving tomorrow, right?" Danar turned to Den Wahyana as if asking for his approval.

"Kang Bewok still has to check out the area near the banks of the Elo River. However, we can start preparing for the trip now. Yes, we'll leave before dawn." Den Wahyana rose and headed for the back door.

The bamboo door creaked when Den Wahyana opened it to go check on the carriage and the horses that were hidden between the banana trees. The carriage's roof was covered with *kelaras*. The dried banana leaves hid the carriage well.

Before dawn, around four in the morning, while the roads were still empty and wrapped in darkness, Rara Ireng and Danar, along with Den Wahyana, Kang Bewok, and the informant from Semarang, started for Magelang.

Kang Bewok, acting as a scout, rode ahead of the group, while Den Wahyana stayed closer to the carriage, which Danar drove.

Inside the carriage, Rara Ireng sat surrounded by piles of banana leaves normally used to wrap food items. She had been told to hide under the leaves in the event they encountered a roadblock.

They rode over dirt roads through several coconut groves.

To keep Den Wahyana apprised of the road condition ahead, Kang Bewok moved back and forth between Den Wahyana and his position as lead rider.

Just before they reached the bank of the Elo River, Kang Bewok dismounted and waved at Den Wahyana to catch up to him.

"What happened, Kang?" Den Wahyana trotted his horse closer to Kang Bewok.

"I suggest we postpone our journey to Semarang." Kang Bewok nodded in the direction of the approaching carriage. "A lot of informants are wandering around the border area; there are also guards at the bank of the Elo River."

"All right, let's turn around. It's better if we retreat in the direction of the Keraton. We can stay in Cebongan. Can you notify our people in Cebongan, Kang?"

Kang Bewok nodded in response.

The informant from Semarang, who now joined them, also agreed with the idea. "Yes, it's better if we hide," he said. "They won't expect us to still be in the vicinity of the Keraton. After the border patrols between Yogyakarta and Magelang loosen up, we can try to resume our journey."

When the carriage arrived at the place where the three men were planning their retreat, Danar climbed out and joined his friends.

Inside the carriage, Rara Ireng listened to their conversation.

Apparently, the Keraton had figured that the runaways would move toward Semarang, which fell under Dutch jurisdiction and where the Keraton had no authority.

Danar agreed to Den Wahyana's and his friends' suggestion to retreat. He knew that Den Wahyana had a tight and reliable underground network.

The sun began to warm the faces of the horseback riders.

Kang Bewok spurred his horse, leaving the group behind. He wanted to arrive at the house where Danar and Rara Ireng were supposed to stay as soon as possible.

The group arrived in Cebongan around ten in the morning. The house was slightly different from the place in Sleman, because no one had been living there, and it took almost an hour to wipe off the dust and get rid of spider webs. This house was more spacious than the one in Sleman and was part of a neighborhood that had more empty houses than occupied ones. Kang Bewok said that many Cebongan residents had moved away to avoid the new high taxes being imposed on them.

Unfortunately, Cebongan gave them only a day of relief. On the second day, just before the sun started to sink into the western horizon, Den Wahyana and Danar noticed someone from the Keraton hanging around their hideout. It was easy for them to distinguish a palace associate from a commoner.

The group quickly decided to move to Gamping, an area even closer to the Keraton. Later that day, however, Kang Bewok reported that the Keraton guards had begun to search all the carriages leaving town and to escort suspicious individuals to checkpoints for further investigation. The group decided to leave for Gamping close to midnight, after Kang Bewok confirmed that the road was safe.

As usual, Kang Bewok headed the group. Accompanied by the light of a crescent moon and the friendly hooting of a barn owl, they traveled to Gamping and arrived about an hour later at a small, empty house tucked between the rice fields.

Danar knew Gamping quite well. Before he worked for the Keraton, he had often come here to check out the area. He knew all the streets and alleys—and hiding spots that the Keraton people would not be able to detect.

"Danar, I think you'll be safe here for a while. I have to leave. I have to take care of some business in Tegalrejo," Den Wahyana said as soon as Danar brought the carriage to a halt.

"All right, Den. I will get a hold of you if I need anything," Danar said, helping Rara Ireng out of the carriage.

Kang Bewok and the informant from Semarang immediately took up a post to guard the house from the roadside.

"When will we be able to stay permanently at one place, kakang?" The constant moving had begun to exhaust Rara Ireng. They had moved three times since she left the kaputren, four days prior.

"We have to keep moving until we have gathered all the required documents needed to reside permanently in government territory. I've told an *ambtenaar* to take care of it." Danar was tired, but his eyes sparkled. That night, the sky above the straw roof of the small hut was lit by starlight.

"Are we going to stay in Gamping for a while? I mean, we don't have to leave again early in the morning, do we?" Rara Ireng felt safe in this particular house.

"Maybe we won't have to leave tomorrow, but definitely in the next two or three days. The spies of the Keraton are still combing the Cebongan area, so we have to stay alert."

"Then I will tell you a story tonight."

"A story? I'd like that."

Rara Ireng gathered her thoughts while waiting for quiet to settle between them. In the silence, the rustle of the jackfruit tree leaves suddenly seemed loud.

Rara Ireng folded her hands in her lap and, looking down on them, said, "Kakang, I'm still like Sita."

"You've always been as beautiful as Sita." Danar smiled and kissed her on the forehead.

"That's not what I meant." Rara Ireng looked up. She took a deep breath and, looking straight at Danar, said, "The sultan has not touched me."

Danar was stunned.

The two of them held each other's eyes. There was a lack of understanding that had to be bridged with words.

"Haven't you lived in the kaputren for a month?" Danar asked.

"The sultan was more interested in my stories than my body," Rara Ireng said proudly. "Every time he summoned me, I told him a story that was more entertaining. I said that even animals could enjoy intercourse, but only highly educated humans were able to enjoy a story."

"Did he believe you?"

"I told him I had Indian ancestors. India is where the *wayang* stories come from. The stories of the puppets are not only enjoyed by the Javanese, but have been imbued into their daily life. Don't the Javanese believe that they're the descendants of Parikshit, the grandson of Arjuna?"

"I still don't understand."

"There are many differences between the wayang stories of India and Java, and that was what drew his interest. In India, many people believe that Dasamuka is not a bad person. Just because he was not from the reigning clan when the story was written, he was depicted as such. Dasamuka was unwilling to violate Sita, Rama's wife, even though he had captured her. He wanted to have Sita's love, not just her body."

"You managed to distract Sultan by telling him stories that would interest him and eventually drew him away from his initial intention of sleeping with you?" Danar smiled.

"You're right. I told him that Rama is not really a sympathetic character. He refused to believe his wife's faithfulness to him after she returns home from her capture by Dasamuka. Even the flame that could not touch her pure soul was unable to convince him. He rather believed his own prejudice," Rara Ireng said smugly.

"Therefore, the only good character in the epic of *Ramayana* is Sita," Danar rebutted.

"You're entitled to your own opinion, but I think Sita is not without fault either. She doubted Lakshmana's intention to protect her while Rama went in the jungle to hunt the golden deer. She thought Lakshmana would take advantage of her and dismissed him with harsh words." Rara Ireng felt a tinge of jealousy when Danar sided so completely with Sita. She continued, "Lakshmana was so hurt by Sita's accusation that he vowed to remain unmarried forever."

Dasamuka smiled. "No wonder the sultan was very interested in your stories; I am, too. Do you have other stories to tell?"

"There are plenty of them. According to my father, the Pandava brothers are actually one individual instead of five, and the Kauravas, the one hundred siblings, actually, are nonexistent."

"I don't understand."

"Initially, neither did the sultan, but he wanted to. So I told him about my father's opinion about the philosophy of the epic of *Mahabharata*. Since the Pandava brothers are actually only one person, they have one common wife, Draupadi.

"The twins, Nakula and Sahadeva, symbolize the early childhood stage of the Pandava; Arjuna the adolescent years; Bheema adulthood; and Yudhistira represents his senior years."

"Are the names of the five Pandava brothers then actually the symbols of character?"

"Yes, you're correct. And the Kauravas are not one hundreds siblings who were born from Gandhari's womb. The word 'hundred' points to the numerous obstacles that a Pandava faces in his life. A purposeful life will be filled with obstacles and struggles, indeed."

"I must admit that I'm not a good man, but I admire Pandava. I want to be like Pandava."

"Remember, kakang, Pandava is actually one person. He has only one wife. Are you willing to remain with one wife for the rest of your life?"

"I already told you that I want to be like Pandava, like the man in your father's stories. And, of course, I will only have one wife, you, diajeng."

"You won't remarry, should I die one day?"

"I told you already: As long as I live, I will only have one wife."

"Is this your vow, kakang?"

"Yes, this is my vow. You must remind me should I forget."

They looked at each other for a while, holding hands. A deep sense of relief and pride flooded their hearts and filled their beings with warmth.

Overcome by emotions, Danar took Rara Ireng in his arms. "I'll never, ever, let you go away from my side again," he murmured in her hair.

"You do understand now why the sultan has not touched me, right?" Rara Ireng pulled away from Danar to look him in his eyes.

"Yes. I made no mistake when I decided to pursue you with all my heart. I'll never regret any effort it will take to keep you by my side. I'll even risk my life for it."

Danar and Rara Ireng gazed at each other again. This was the first time they'd had the opportunity to be alone after Rara Ireng's escape from the kaputren. They remained silent for a long time.

When Danar pulled Rara Ireng toward him, she entered into the fold of his arms eagerly. They lay down on the cot lined with a mat of bamboo pulp. Their passion, suppressed by forced separation, flared into a roaring fire and soon consumed them. They fell asleep in each other's arms until sunlight spread across the eastern sky.

———•———

Even though Danar and Rara Ireng had been on the run for nearly a week, their dream of a peaceful life kept crawling away from them.

Danar worried that his presence in the Keraton area had been discovered and decided that Gamping would be their last hideaway before heading for Semarang. He started to plan a new route with a detour through Salatiga. When, early in the morning, on the fourth day in Gamping, the informant from Semarang reported a search operation in the area near Rejawinangun, he advised Danar to evacuate before the hideout was found.

"Is it the Suryanata group again?" Danar peeked out of the window.

"No, this one is far more dangerous. They're probably sent by the Keraton."

"Then, I'll head to Salatiga today. Please get a carriage with four horses ready."

"The carriage will be ready in the afternoon."

"Please wait a moment. I'd like you to take a letter to Den Wahyana."

In his letter, Danar asked Den Wahyana to come to Gamping as soon as possible. He needed the company of someone he could rely on. Taking on the guards of the Keraton would require someone who understood war strategies.

He was barely finished writing when the door flung open and Den Wahyana entered, out of breath. Placing several packs on the floor, he exclaimed, "Oh my God, am I happy to find you here."

"Who's after me this time, Den?" Danar walked to the open window and closed it after canvassing the yard.

"I'm afraid that they're the special force of the Keraton Guards. I caught sight of them near Rejawinangun. I didn't take the time to find out who their commander is. I hurried to come here. A soldier friend of mine told me about the preparation of a special operation to be conducted early tomorrow morning."

"How about leaving tonight? I already figured out a new route via Salatiga."

"That sounds like a good idea. I'm very certain they will come to attack us after dawn. There's no protection around here. Their bullets will destroy this hut in no time."

"You'll come with us to Salatiga, wouldn't you? I don't feel safe traveling alone with Rara Ireng."

"That's why I came. I brought a bulletproof carriage and a span of horses. It's already loaded with everything we'll need. I'll help you as much as I can. If you're captured, it will endanger Mr. Willem, Semi, and Ngusman."

Overwhelmed, Danar looked at the packs on the floor. "You seem to carry a lot of things. What's in those packs?"

"I brought four firearms for both of us. The guns are loaded and ready to be used when needed. If we run out of ammunition, we won't have time to reload. If the rumor I heard is true, our pursuers are the best soldiers the Keraton has."

Gunshots and a terrifying howl outside the hut interrupted their conversation.

Danar quickly peered through a peephole in the hut's wall. Near the entrance, Kang Bewok held someone at gunpoint. A few feet away from them, another man and the informant from Semarang were lying in a pool of blood.

Danar rushed outside, carrying his rifle. By the time he reached Kang Bewok, the man had already fired. "He was looking for money in the wrong place," he told Danar.

"We must leave now. The gunshots could have attracted the attention of those who want to kill you!" Den Wahyana shouted anxiously. "Tell your wife to hurry. We must leave immediately."

Rara Ireng was becoming accustomed to her new life as a fugitive. She was already dressed in her best clothes and wearing the bracelet and necklace Danar had given her. For Rara Ireng, the journey to Salatiga meant she would meet her husband's family for the first time. Her dazzling beauty was a stark contrast to the situation around her.

Passing the bloody scene in the front yard, Rara Ireng shivered. Shaking, she climbed into the carriage driven by Kang Bewok, and they quickly left their hideout.

Danar and Den Wahyana, seated in the back, carried loaded rifles and kept their eyes on the road behind them.

That afternoon, white, spear-shaped clouds floated across a blue sky. After the carriage had traveled about ten miles, Danar and Den Wahyana felt they could relax their vigilance for a moment. They shifted their sight to other directions, instead of constantly watching the road behind them, until two dots appeared in the distance.

Den Wahyana tightened the grip on his rifle.

As the two black dots drew closer, they turned into the figures of two horsemen, their galloping mounts creating a yellowish dust cloud. Soon, other horse riders followed the first two, and it looked like there was an entire battalion of cavalry soldiers approaching.

Den Wahyana tapped Danar on the shoulder. "We will soon begin today's game. It could very well be the most exciting one."

"Yes, Den. I'm ready." Danar turned to his wife. "Diajeng, please kneel down. Spread the jarits on the carriage floor so the road bumps won't hurt your knees. We have some business to take care of."

The lead rider moved closer to the carriage, but Kang Bewok, under instruction of Den Wahyana, did not increase speed. Den

Wahyana knew it would be useless to race the powerful horses of the Keraton Cavalry.

"Don't shoot unless they start," Den Wahyana warned.

"It looks like they're ready to shoot us anytime."

"Once they open fire, we'll shoot back. I'll take the ones coming from the left; the right ones are yours."

Soon, the lead rider fired his first shot. The explosion made the carriage horses lose the rhythm of their gait. However, a well-aimed shot from Den Wahyana toppled the attacker, who had not expected his target to react that quickly. The second rider immediately slowed his horse, not wanting to share his friend's fate, and ordered the approaching riders to disperse.

Danar tried counting the fierce horses facing them. There were twenty men—five of them approaching from his left and five others coming from his right. The rest maintained their distance.

Den Wahyana and Danar looked at each other. They had agreed to kill rather than be killed. They targeted the riders, who now closed in on the carriage. Four of them soon fell from their horses. One man grabbed on to the top of the carriage, and Danar beat him with the butt of his rifle until the man vomited blood. Before the man crashed to the ground, Danar saw the necklace he was wearing, which identified him as a member of the special forces of the Keraton. The other five riders slowed down their horses. Slowly retracting, they still flanked the carriage on the left and the right.

The remaining fifteen riders now took aim at the carriage, and bullets whistled around them. It seemed the attackers wanted to capture the fugitives, and it no longer mattered if they were alive or dead when they were taken.

DASAMUKA

Den Wahyana unloaded his rifle, firing a spray of bullets at his hunters. Three more riders fell from their horses, and their bodies rolled in the dust.

Twelve men continued to pursue the carriage and kept firing.

Den Wahyana and Danar began to run out of ammunition. When Danar reloaded his rifle, he heard a painful moan.

Rara Ireng, kneeling down in the carriage with her head lowered, let out a quiet groan.

Danar quickly climbed down to the floor of the carriage and embraced her shaking body. When he noticed blood on his hand, he carefully laid her on the carriage seats and yelled for Kang Bewok.

There was no answer from the coachman, and Danar watched as Kang Bewok's body fell sideways, blood gushing from a shot wound in his ribcage, one of his hands still holding the reins.

By the time Den Wahyana managed to shoot down three more of their pursuers, Kang Bewok's body had rolled down to the carriage floor.

Now, nine riders chased them like a pack of wild animals, and Danar climbed up to the coachman's seat, trying to grab the horses' reins.

With no time to reload his gun, Den Wahyana pulled out a set of small spears.

Danar, who was now driving the carriage, understood Den Wahyana's strategy immediately. He slowed down and shouted a watchword to Den Wahyana before he pulled to the left side of the road. When all nine of his hunters were forced to the right side of his carriage, Danar made a sudden sharp turn and crossed over to the yellowing rice field on his right.

A violent crash between carriage and pursuers was unavoidable. The horsemen were thrown out of their saddles. The carriage ran over two of them and the wheels pushed the bodies into the soggy soil of the rice field. The creaking carriage came to a jolting halt when one of its wheels fell off.

Den Wahyana, who had anticipated Danar's move, immediately jumped out of the carriage and stabbed the two men nearest to him with the small spears he had prepared. They dropped, groaning, to the ground, blood seeping from their abdomens. Three men managed to get up and attempted to run for their lives, while two others struggled to pull themselves out of the mud from the wet rice field.

Danar jumped out of the carriage. He emptied his gun on two of the men who tried running away. While he chased the other one, Danar heard shots behind him and knew Den Wahyana had taken care of the two men he had left struggling. The man he was chasing used his remaining strength to run as fast as he could. Armed with a spear, Danar kept after him. The man soon collapsed with his face to the ground.

"Who sent you here?" Danar shouted.

When there was no answer, Danar, using his foot, turned the body over.

"Uncle Mangli! Uncle! Is that you?" Danar stared at the man whose body was almost completely covered in mud and blood.

"Kill me, Danar," Mangli groaned and extended his two hands toward Danar.

"Who sent you here to kill me, Uncle?" Danar ignored his uncle's plea.

"Kill me, Danar," Mangli's voice was no louder than the rustle of rice stalks blowing in the wind.

"If you refuse to tell me who sent you, I will kill you for sure. Who is paying you? Answer me!"

"Kill… kill me."

The spear in Danar's hand penetrated deep into Den Mas Mangli's heart. Fresh blood splattered Danar's forehead.

A short gurgle escaped from Mangli's throat, and then he was dead.

"Danar! Come help your wife!" Den Wahyana's voice pulled Danar out of his storm of emotions. He had just killed his mother's brother, the uncle who had often taken him riding when he was young.

Danar quickly left his uncle's body and climbed back into the tilted carriage.

The jolt that brought one side of the carriage down when the wheel fell off had caused Rara Ireng to roll off the carriage seat where Danar had left her. Now, her limp body leaned against the sloping wall. The seat, and the fabric of the jarit truntum she wore, were soaked in her blood.

Danar was stunned.

All he could do was kiss his wife's pale forehead. Tears, rolling down his cheeks, fell onto Rara Ireng's face.

"Kakang Danar," Rara Ireng whispered weakly.

Danar was unable to answer her.

"Are you going to remarry when I die?" Rara Ireng was barely audible. Her eyelids fluttered.

Danar still could not utter a word; he could only shake his head.

"Thank you, kakang...." Rara Ireng whispered as her body went limp and she, who had been able to defend her honor as a wife, let go of life.

Danar, a man used to the hard life in the streets and the dirty mud of gutters, burst into uncontrolled sobs. With trembling fingers, he pulled the jarits from under Rara Ireng's limp body. He refolded the crumpled, bloodied cloths, one by one, and lay them on the carriage seat. He then gently picked up Rara Ireng's body and laid her down on her beloved jarits. She looked as beautiful as the nymph Nawangwulan sleeping peacefully in her chamber.

Outside, Den Wahyana slowly walked away from the carriage. He wanted to give Danar privacy to express his grief. He walked toward a bird-watch shelter and watched the heartbreaking scene.

Danar stepped out of the carriage carrying Rara Ireng's wrapped body in his arms. He staggered across the rice field and headed for a tall magnolia tree nearby.

In the shade of the tree's lofty canopy, Danar lay down his wife's body. For a moment, he remained kneeling next to it. Then, he slowly rose and started to walk around Rara Ireng's body.

Den Wahyana startled when Danar lifted his face and, screaming, punched at the air above him with clenched fists.

Den Wahyana was unable to make words out of Danar's screams, the wild howling sounded like the angry cry of a wounded animal.

Meanwhile, scattered, spear-shaped clouds slowly grew into massive, gray bulges.

Rain started to fall. The light drizzle soon turned into a heavy downpour. Thunder rolled, and lightning struck.

Den Wahyana braced himself to cross the rice field in the pouring rain and approach Danar, who now stood statue-like under the magnolia tree with the body of his wife at his feet.

Den Wahyana halted about three feet away from Danar and softly called out to him. The former war commander shivered when their eyes met.

The agony in Danar's eyes was terrifying.

———•—•———

One afternoon, while we were having our coffee on the verandah, Daisy handed me an opened letter. "This is from my aunt, who keeps me abreast of Edinburgh news," she said. "I received it yesterday."

The first line made my heart skip a beat. Ailsa had given birth to another girl, but had been unable to see how beautiful the baby was; a few minutes after giving birth, Ailsa had died.

I could not keep my hand from trembling when I returned the letter to Daisy; she undoubtedly noticed it.

I spent the remainder of that afternoon with Daisy, but without saying a single word. I was engulfed in my own emotions and thoughts, and she was kind enough to let me be.

I hurt—but the pain I felt was no longer caused by Ailsa's betrayal. The thing I worried about now was the possibility that my ill will toward her during the time I was consumed by anger might somehow have contributed to her unfortunate death.

No matter what, I had once loved her very much. I never wished her harm.

The news of Ailsa's death seemed to have weakened the daredevil in me. I lost interest in participating in dangerous adventures that might help me bury my pain but that could also end with my burial. Perhaps it was also hearing the stories of what had happened after Rara Ireng died that made me more cautious.

Chapter 10

NGUSMAN

"Do you know any assassins for hire?" Danar asked Den Wahyana, when visiting him one evening.

"You can go to Ungaran and find a gangster to do the job for you," Den Wahyana replied. He knew there were people called *wong durjana*, outlaws, who would kill for money.

"I went to talk to them already, but no one dared to do it," Danar answered, disgruntled.

"That's strange."

"It's actually reasonable. After I told them who they'd have to murder, all of them, including my own men, feared the curse that would befall them."

"Who is it?"

"Sultan Jarot," Danar whispered. "Remember, not even the ants shall hear about this."

Den Wahyana rose. At hearing Danar's plan, his chest suddenly felt tight, and his stomach knotted. He took a deep breath and straightened his back.

"I know you were one of the commanders of Raden Rangga's rebel group and supposed to be imprisoned in a dark and narrow cell in Ambarawa," Danar said to Den Wahyana. "Only because Pangeran Diponegoro II vouched for you are you able to live as a free man in the sultanate area."

"You seem to know a lot about me," Den Wahyana replied.

"I also know that your ability to speak foreign languages is an advantage to the Tegalrejo group led by Pangeran Diponegoro II."

"And what does this knowledge have to do with your plan to murder the sultan?"

"The thing is," Danar paused before continuing, "you shall never reveal my secret to anyone, just like I will never reveal yours."

"Sure thing. What good will it do me to reveal your secret?"

Danar did not answer. He rose and started to pace.

Tension slowly filled the silence between them.

"Now, you have to bring me to the headman you think is capable of murdering Sultan."

"Frankly, I don't agree with your plan," Den Wahyana replied.

"All burdens will be placed on my shoulders. All curses and sins will only befall me. You won't be involved. You might disagree, but you can't interfere with my plan." Danar threw Den Wahyana a wild, terrifying look.

"Well, that's your own business." Den Wahyana knew he was dealing with a tiger who was ready to kill. He shrugged, "Why don't you look for Ki Bule?"

"You're right. I'll go to find him soon."

But the answer Danar received, when he finally found Ki Bule, was not to his liking.

"I drink water from the springs on the land of Java. I eat what grows in the soil of the island of Java. How could I murder the King of Java? Any man who proclaims himself Javanese, would not dare to murder the Sultan of Yogyakarta," Ki Bule told Danar.

"I can give you a fully furnished house in the city of Yogyakarta, if you're willing to murder him. If you succeed, the rice fields around your house will be yours as well."

"Even if you give me the palace itself, I won't do it. I don't dare. I fear the curse."

"Then, who do you think will be able to carry out an assassination?"

"Someone who's not Javanese."

"Bring me to him."

"It's not easy to find him. I need some money."

Danar nodded. All he could think of was how to take the life of the person he believed had murdered his wife. He was more than willing to lose his wealth to avenge his wife's death and quickly handed Ki Bule a handful of silver coins.

Ki Bule and Danar went to search for the assassin. According to Ki Bule, the man was like the albatross: he could live anywhere and always moved around. When they heard the man was seen in the Lipura area, living next to an abandoned Chinese temple, Danar and Ki Bule immediately rode their horses to that area.

"If you're lucky, you can meet him today. The last time I saw him, he lived there." Ki Bule pointed at a windowless bamboo hut next to the abandoned temple.

Ki Bule threw a handful of small stones at the bamboo wall three times, a secret code of the underworld people for whenever they wanted to offer each other a business deal.

The creaking door of the house slowly opened, but no one appeared in the doorway. Apparently, the man had only unlocked the door.

"You wait here. Come in when I call you," Ki Bule said.

Danar nodded. He understood how the underworld worked—and this was someone from the darkest part of that world. He tried to adjust himself to the situation as quickly as possible, and observed the area carefully to be able to return later. But he had only managed to glance at the abandoned temple and its surrounding area before Ki Bule called him.

Once he took his first step into the windowless hut, Danar felt as if he was stepping into a haunted cave. The large shack was too dark and too big for an average person to live in. There was not a single piece of furniture around—instead, there were piles of strange-looking items, as though the room was a combination of a mechanic's workshop and witch's house.

"Sit down, young man." A hoarse male voice traveled through the darkness and broke the icy silence in the room.

Danar could not quite understand the man. He spoke the language but was obviously not Javanese.

"Thank you," Danar replied quietly.

"Turn this way," the same voice spoke again. Danar realized he was facing too much to the right side; he had a hard time adjusting his eyes to the darkness. He turned to face the direction the voice came from, but quickly jumped backward. Even though Danar could barely see him, the grinning man looked frightening. Danar thought he was seeing a ghost.

Once his eyesight adjusted to the dimness of the room, Danar saw the person who had almost scared him to death.

The man's face was terribly scarred. His nose and ears were merely holes. His right hand had a thumb and pinky, while his right foot was nothing but a jagged stump at the instep.

Danar could not keep from staring at him.

"Are you scared of me, young man?" The man did not seem offended by Danar's reaction. He continued in a somewhat louder tone, "It's important you know that I'm proud of my condition. I earned each of these scars the same way a general earns his stars."

"Just tell Mr. Pieter what you need from him," Ki Bule said. He was seated on his haunches, slightly behind the man he referred to as Mr. Pieter.

"I want you to murder Sultan Jarot," Danar replied straightforwardly.

"Do you know any palace insiders?"

"I do. I can call on them any time."

"How much money do you have?" Pieter asked without looking at Danar.

"I will give you all five of the most wanted gifts coveted by royalty and nobility—a house, horses, pet birds, a kris, and—of course—women. Each gift will be in accordance to the taste of Javanese royalties." Danar tried to emphasize the quality of the gifts.

"I'm not Javanese," Pieter scoffed, before flashing a wide grin that made him look even more terrifying.

"I can replace the gifts with gulden," Danar said quickly.

"It'll be more than enough to return to Amsterdam, Mr. Pieter," Ki Bule whispered.

A gecko called out from the ceiling. In the silence of the dank room, the call sounded loud enough to pierce their eardrums.

"I do hate this country. And also its kings," Pieter grumbled.

"It sounds like Mr. Pieter has agreed to help you with murdering the sultan." Ki Bule tried to draw their meeting to a conclusion.

"Take this as a token that we have an agreement," Danar said, while handing Pieter a money crock. When he placed the heavy earthenware crock on the ground, there was a sound of rattling coins.

"Give me a week. Then, come in the afternoon and bring two carriages with you." Pieter ended their secret meeting in the dark and stuffy room.

On their trip home, Danar asked Ki Bule what kind of help Pieter had talked about earlier. Danar was certain that the disfigured man would not go to the palace himself to murder the sultan.

Ki Bule did not answer him straight away.

"You'll see for yourself next week. What you need to do now is to contact your connections at the palace. Tell them now about the task they're expected to perform."

Heeding Ki Bule's advice, Danar immediately contacted Semi and Ngusman. They were willing to help as long as Den Wahyana and I agreed with the plan.

Hence, I was dragged into the most dangerous situation I had ever encountered during my stay on the island of Java: a plot to murder the sultan! And just like when we planned Rara Ireng's escape, my house once again became a secret meeting place for all conspirators.

"I advise you to reconsider your plan. It's very dangerous," I tried to remind Danar.

"Mr. Willem is right, Danar. You need to understand one thing: According to my source, the soldiers who chased us before were not the official guards of the palace. They were sent by the sultan's mother," Den Wahyana said.

"They were from the palace; I know who they were. Their leader was my own uncle, Den Mas Mangli."

"You're correct—however, they tried to kill us for money, *not* to defend the honor of the sultanate. These are two different things, Danar."

"It's all the same to me. My decision is firm. Sultan must die. He must."

The meeting ended without an agreement.

I asked Danar to reconsider his plan.

Den Wahyana asked Danar to abandon it altogether.

Meanwhile, Danar asked Den Wahyana and me to come with him to meet Pieter.

I refused immediately, as I was sure that we were dealing with the same Pieter we had left to die in the Menoreh jungle.

Den Wahyana strongly disagreed with Danar; he believed that the mastermind of Rara Ireng's murder was not the sultan, but his mother, Gusti Ratu Kencana.

Meanwhile, Ngusman and Semi did not say a word. It was difficult to guess what was going on in their minds.

———•••———

"He works for me, Mr. Pieter." Danar pointed at his coachman, who stood a short distance away from the house. Ki Bule had refused to come along after receiving his payment, and Pieter did not want the coachman to come in.

"Well, then. The reason I invited you to come this evening is because I want to show you how the device I invented works." Limping, with a crutch slipped under an armpit, Pieter took Danar to a far corner of the room.

In the darkening light of dusk, Danar saw two boxes the color of teakwood leaning against a wall near the door. Each box was about eighteen inches long, sixteen inches wide, and six inches deep. A split wooden log, as big as a man's thigh, was placed next to the boxes.

Pieter explained, "Place this box in Sultan's chariot and secure it tightly to the bottom of Sultan's seat. A jolt caused by the chariot's movements, along with the right pressure, will ignite the gunpowder and flare up to burn the target right away. In less than half a minute, the person will turn into ashes."

Danar quietly listened. The word "minute" was related to a length of time—he didn't hear the word very often. He wondered how long half a minute actually was. He threw Pieter a quizzical look, then shifted his gaze. Through the open door he saw the coachman seated in his carriage.

"I don't expect anyone to believe me. That's why I made two boxes. One to convince the buyer, the other to execute the actual murder plan." Even though Pieter's Javanese was not perfect, Danar understood him.

"Come." Pieter grabbed a gun hanging off a hook near the doorway and slung the weapon across his free shoulder. He then bent, with great difficulty, to pick up one of the boxes. "It needs to be held upright. Like this. Don't lay it flat." Pieter carried the brown box very carefully. He signaled Danar to follow him and limped to an old carriage parked in front of his house.

After he ordered Danar to dust off the carriage beneath the passenger seat, Pieter peeled off the outer side of the box and carefully attached the strange-looking thing to the carriage.

"Young man, fetch one of the wooden logs we left in the hut and lay it across the road, over there." Pieter gestured at a pathway that ran through a bamboo grove.

"Call your coachman," Pieter said after Danar returned to the carriage. "Tell him to harness one of your horses and drive this old carriage over that pathway at a normal speed."

Danar quickly followed Pieter's instruction.

Darkness began to wrap around Pieter's hut, the abandoned temple, and the surrounding trees. The coachman lit the carriage lanterns and, spurring the horse, put the vehicle in motion.

A moment later, an explosion filled the quiet evening. Soaring blue flames soon became a yellow and red blaze, sparks like fireworks flew into all directions.

Danar ran towards the still-burning carriage, amidst the swaying bamboo, and watched the old vehicle reduced to ashes.

Pieter caught up with him and fired his gun. At Danar's feet now lay the coachman, dead. Without a word, Pieter moved to the sprawling carriage horse and shot it in the head.

Although Danar had been a part of the underworld for a very long time, the incident left him speechless and shaking.

"That's how my box works. It took me years to create this device. I'm sure one day people will come looking for me. They might be motivated to fight for power, or merely need to defend themselves," Pieter spoke calmly.

Danar was too stunned to say anything.

Pieter continued talking. "My invention is based on the bronjong-branjang concept, and inspired by the behavior of a caged bird. I made this wire bird and built the cage out of rod iron. Just like a real bird flutters in its cage, my wire bird, when no longer fastened by this latch, will bounce in its cage when transported across road bumps. At a certain speed, the wire bird will hit the iron enclosure fiercely. The sparks resulting from that friction will ignite the pack of gunpowder wrapped around the iron cage. For your own safety, make sure this latch remains fastened until you're ready for the box to explode."

"I'm telling you all of this because I'm the only one in this whole world who knows how to build the bronjong and branjang. I'm not worried about imitators."

On his way home, driving his carriage with only one horse, Danar was preoccupied with his own thoughts. If it had been Den Wahyana who had come with him instead of the poor coachman, the former commander would now be a charred corpse with a hole in his head.

How long had the coachman worked for him? What would happen to his wife and children now that they had no breadwinner?

Danar promised himself never to deal with Pieter again. This would be the first and last time.

———•—•———

"I need Ngusman's help to place this box in the golden chariot that will be used for the sultan's trip tomorrow," Danar told Den Wahyana, whom he had invited to his hideout early in the morning. "And I want to ask you to supervise his work and help Ngusman when he faces difficulties."

When Den Wahyana remained silent, Danar continued. "Surely, you don't want to hide all your life, do you? You're only able to breathe fresh air in the sultanate area thanks to Pangeran Diponegoro II's protection. I can return to you the house in Salatiga you loved so much but the government confiscated. You want it back, don't you?"

Den Wahyana sighed. "Frankly speaking, I disagree with your murder plan. That being said, I also objected to Sultan Jarot ascending to the throne. I agree with Resident Crawfurd that the only suitable heir would have been Pangeran Diponegoro II, not that spoiled boy. Still, once again, I must tell you that I strongly disagree with your plan."

"If the sultan dies, your protector, the Lord of Puri Tegalrejo, will ascend the throne and can make those cursed officials, the corrupt counselor, and immoral Resident vanish in no time. You know that would mean your freedom."

"I still can't do it," Den Wahyana said firmly. "I am asking to be excused from this case; I don't want to be involved." He quickly left and walked, without looking back, to the horse he had tethered to the fence. For a moment, the warrior stood pensively by his horse. He then jumped into the saddle and rode to Puri Tegalrejo.

Danar contemplated Den Wahyana's words for a short while, then clapped his hands. Two of his men appeared in response to his call, and the three of them began a serious discussion.

———•—•———

Danar was extremely busy on the morning of December 6, 1822. He had to take care of every detail in the plan he had been preparing for days. When he was done, he walked Ngusman and Semi to the carriage he had prepared at his hideout.

"The success or failure of this plan will depend on your performance." Danar said. He had delegated all the responsibilities that were originally to be borne by Den Wahyana to Ngusman.

"I have to tell you, honestly, I'm really scared," Ngusman said in a low voice.

Danar had been worried about this.

"Why are you scared? You must remember how your father was put into the bronjong to fight a tiger. Who would pit a man against a tiger? The corrupt government. We will fight against tyranny. There shall be no fear in fighting evil. We will fight them with our own ways," Danar encouraged, whispering.

"Like I told you earlier, I need Semi's help."

"As you wish. The most important thing is to have the box in place before ten o'clock in the morning. Think of your father's death and the wealth I promised you. Now, go."

———•·•———

The sun had barely broken through the eastern horizon when Ngusman scurried along the path leading to the kaputren with a large package in his arms. He was a familiar figure within the palace walls, and his presence didn't attract attention. However, the package did arouse the curiosity of one young guard, who approached Ngusman.

"What is that, Kang?"

"It's a mirror for the kaputren," Ngusman answered calmly. He had prepared for questions like this.

"A mirror? Can I borrow it? Just to take a quick look at myself. It won't be long."

"Don't! You'll be cursed, and your face will become uglier." Ngusman was annoyed by the guard's behavior and quickly walked away.

As planned, Ngusman carefully placed the package on the porch of the kaputren and found a spot to hide in the shade of nearby mangosteen trees to watch over his charge.

Semi was supposed to take the package to the carriage house next to the kaputren and install Pieter's device in the sultan's golden chariot.

Meanwhile, Ngusman was supposed to stand guard and be ready to protect her from people who might endanger their mission. There was a big chance that a guard or mbok emban would catch Semi red-handed. If that happened, Ngusman would deal with the matter.

Semi soon appeared. She threw a quick glance at the mangosteen grove. When she saw Ngusman come out of the shadows, she walked up the steps to the kaputren porch. With Ngusman following her at a safe distance, Semi carried the large package to the carriage house.

"What are you carrying, miss?" an abdi who crossed her path asked Semi in passing.

"It's a mirror for the golden chariot. I'm sorry, I'm in a hurry." Semi continued to walk. Ngusman had told her to avoid lengthy conversations with anyone.

In the dimly-lit carriage house, Semi carefully placed the package in a far corner. Ngusman told her the surface of the chariot had to be as clean as possible—to make sure the device would adhere—so she squatted near the chariot to clean the surface under the floor with her scarf. Suddenly, an unexpected voice startled her

"Even if you can't hold it—don't urinate near the sultan's chariot. You'll be cursed."

Semi jerked up and hit her head against the back of the chariot. For a moment, she saw stars.

"Reja?" Semi stuttered, when she finally saw who was standing at the door. She hadn't seen her nephew in a long time. *Was he still working as a guard for the kaputren?* She thought he had run away with Nyi Wersi a while back.

"I've been stalking you, *Wong Ayu*. I really miss you, beautiful." Reja moved slowly toward Semi, who was pulling herself up.

"Do you want to talk to me? Just wait outside. I'm on duty to clean this chariot. The sultan will use it for his trip today." Semi tried to hide her fear by making light of Reja's sudden appearance.

"It won't be safe to make love outside. This is a better place. Isn't this a good opportunity?"

"I'm not young anymore, Reja. I have a husband and children. You know that."

Reja took a few steps toward Semi. "To me, you're still the same—beautiful and pleasantly plump. You're much more attractive than any of the sultan's courtesans."

"Don't come near me or I'll scream."

"Go ahead, scream. I'll be happy to get fired after having enjoyed the warmth of your body."

Reja had suppressed this desire for a long time. Now he spread his hands and, bending his knees, moved toward Semi like a wild animal ready to pounce.

Semi was aware she could not scream—her mission would fail if anyone came to the carriage house. All she could do was anchor herself and hope that Ngusman was still standing guard.

As Reja moved closer, Semi grew more nervous. She inched away from the chariot, eyeing the door.

Reja, noticing Semi's fear, barreled toward her. Covering her mouth with one hand, he forced her to the ground with the other.

Blinded by excitement and passion for the woman he had lusted after for years, Reja dropped his caution. He lowered himself and pulled on Semi's jarit when she tried to get away from him.

It was the moment Ngusman had been waiting for. Not wanting to make a scene that would draw people's attention, he silently moved toward Reja and stomped on his neck. There was a cracking sound as Ngusman leaned into his foot, then Reja slumped away from Semi, his body limp.

Ngusman ordered Semi to resume her task while he dragged Reja's body behind the flowering shrubs of the kaputren, where he stuffed it into one of the open sewers as if it were garbage.

In the carriage house, Semi carefully picked up the explosive device. When she peeled off the top of one of its sides, the shiny residue of the adhesive substance appeared. With trembling hands, she secured the device to the chariot floor.

Despite the cool morning, Semi was drenched in perspiration. While gathering her loose jarit and fixing her hair, she hurriedly left the carriage house.

Ngusman watched her from afar. He needed to join the other guards as soon as possible and walked away in a different direction.

———•———

On the day the sultan was to visit Karangbolong Beach, Ngusman contacted Danar in his hideout, to notify him of the event.

Given the frequency of the sultan's excursions, the Keraton's security in regards to the route and road conditions of the outing was no longer as tight as it had been. Danar knew the downhill, curvy trail well. While Pieter's box could very well explode when the carriage drove over rocks or through potholes, Danar would not leave matters to chance. He ordered two of his men to place Pieter's wooden log across the road where it sharply curved at the bottom of a steep hill.

Later that day, the sultan's entourage assembled at the Keraton gates. The ruckus that went along with the pompous event no longer attracted people's attention. As usual, the sultan's golden chariot was rolled out of the carriage house, a span of eight Persian horses were hitched to the chariot, and the entire cavalry of the sultanate prepared to escort the sultan on his outing.

Ngusman was one of the riders who rode behind the chariot. He was the most nervous soldier that day.

Other than strangely delighting in the death of his own soldiers, the sultan loved to watch the harvesting of swallow nests from the sheer cliffs on the beaches of Karangbolong. He was intrigued by the life-threatening occupation. Whenever an unfortunate climber slipped and crashed on the sharp rocks beneath him, the sultan jumped up and screamed in delight. The scene that would horrify most people gave him enormous pleasure.

Once he left the palace complex, the sultan increased the chariot's speed and, as usual, there were casualties of soldiers thrown from their saddles and trampled to death.

Ngusman hated the sultan for his disregard of other people's lives. He often had to console his colleagues' wives and children who came to him sobbing uncontrollably after losing their breadwinner.

Semi's feelings toward the sultan were no different from her husband's. She was sick of the sultan's habit of treating women as if they were flowers he could discard when they were no longer deemed attractive. She was especially upset by the latest tragedy she had witnessed, the futile death of Rara Ireng. Semi pitied the beautiful young woman.

Even though she kept it secret, Semi had a blood tie with Dasamuka, her nephew. Perhaps she took part in the plot to protect her and Ngusman's jobs at the palace, or perhaps it was because of another secret family tie: that Ki Sena, the prisoner, was her brother.

After a three-hour ride, the sultan's procession stopped at a small clearing near Gombong. Nestled in the bend of a stream that skirted along the tree line, the turnout was surrounded by shade trees. They usually rested here on their way to Karangbolong Beach, where there was no shade and it was too hot to have lunch.

With an attendant holding a golden umbrella over him, and accompanied by several ladies-in-waiting, the sultan walked gracefully to a luxurious tent that had quickly been erected.

Delicious food and refreshing drinks were prepared for the sultan. Surrounded by his closest aides, the sultan enjoyed a drink of coconut water.

At a glance, Ngusman saw that Pieter's device was still firmly in place.

Soon, everyone was satiated. Someone suppressed a burp. Rested and content, the ladies-in-waiting and nobilities in the entourage started to return to their carriages. The gong was struck three times to indicate departure. Everyone, except for the sultan, seemed to be ready to travel the last eighteen miles to Karangbolong, the beach area of the Indian Ocean near Parangtritis.

After enjoying the food and beverages, the sultan had become lethargic and, turning pale, he dropped his head onto the table. The abdis thought he had been overcome by fatigue and fallen asleep.

When, after quite some time, their sultan remained asleep, the abdis grew restless. Since they did not dare wake him up, they decided to call his trusted counselor, Patih Danureja.

The counselor climbed down from his carriage and hurried to the sultan's tent. He tried to wake the sultan by whispering to him. When he didn't receive any response, he gently rubbed his sultan's feet. With rising anxiety, Patih Danureja rubbed the sultan's arms and his back, when he noticed foam at the corners of Sultan's mouth. He quickly checked his pulse, then, with the help of some guards, he carefully picked the sultan up and carried him across the tent to lie him on a red velvet rug prepared for his rest.

Counselor Danureja placed his palm on the sultan's forehead, then moved his hand to the sultan's neck. Both felt cold, but at the same time soaked in perspiration. The nobleman stood stupefied.

Then he ordered a handmaid to call the palace medicine man, who always came along on the sultan's excursions.

With everyone in the tent looking on anxiously, the medicine man rubbed herbal oils infused with ginger and lemongrass on the sultan's feet and carefully massaged the sultan's head around the ears. The sultan's chest began to rise and fall rapidly.

Patih Danureja checked the sultan's pulse again. Shaking his head, he walked out of the tent with the abdis at his heels. He ordered the gong sounded again, to call the attention of everyone in the party. Then he made a somber announcement that the sultan had become seriously ill and the party was going to return home as soon as possible.

Suddenly, more than two hundred people pushed and shoved, trying to get a peek at their sultan. Lying on the red carpet, the sultan's face and hands appeared waxen. His heaving chest was the only sign he was still alive.

Counselor Danureja instructed a soldier to return to the palace ahead of the party's departure, to deliver a letter notifying Gusti Ratu Kencana that her son had suddenly become ill.

As chaotic as the scene was, it could not surpass the turmoil in Ngusman's mind and heart. Bewildered, he stared at the abandoned golden chariot. The deadly box underneath the carriage had to be removed as quickly as possible.

Ngusman squatted beside the chariot's wheel. He wanted to be certain that no one would be able to see him when he struggled to remove the box.

After watching the situation for a while, Ngusman decided that the time was ripe to act. People were still crowding around the sultan's tent, which was to the right of the chariot.

Ngusman eyed the nearby stream. Gunpowder could not explode when it was wet.

He carried the rolls of tent and carpets that had been packed by the guards to be taken to the beach and stacked them on the side of the chariot, to conceal his actions. Then he took a knife out of his pocket and ran his thumb across the edge of the blade. When he was sure it was sharp enough to do the job properly, he crawled under the carriage. Lying on his back, he tried to pry the box loose. He quickly realized the box was fused to the carriage's wooden surface—the only way to remove it without causing dangerous friction was to cut it off.

Ngusman was drenched in sweat by the time he managed to pry the bomb from the carriage bottom. Holding the dangerous box carefully with both hands, he slid on his back from underneath the carriage. He rose gingerly, then hurried toward the stream, and quickly removed enough stones and soil to bury the box. The royal entourage was still in such a commotion that no one seemed to notice.

Before he returned to his squad, Ngusman looked back at the river. A small branch had floated down the stream and now concealed the spot where the box was buried. Relieved, Ngusman sighed and left the river.

He nonchalantly joined the other soldiers' whispered speculations regarding what might have happened to the sultan. They were interrupted by a nobleman, who instructed Ngusman to drive the sultan's chariot to the palace.

Ngusman thanked God he had succeeded in removing Pieter's deadly device. The life he saved would now be his own.

While driving the sultan's chariot, Ngusman started to formulate a series of plans in his mind. He had to be prepared lest Reja's death would lead him into trouble. Sooner or later, the body would be discovered.

Gusti Ratu Kencana stood waiting at the palace entrance when the entourage arrived. She immediately ascended the carriage to see her beloved son.

Counselor Danureja was unable to persuade her to leave her son's side and allow the soldiers to move the sultan.

The sultan's weight, combined with his mother clinging to him, made it very difficult to move him from the carriage into the palace.

Ngusman and other cavaliers stood waiting for further instructions in the palace yard. No one had dismissed them, and they didn't dare leave. Some of the soldiers, tired of waiting, started to make themselves comfortable on the terrace steps and the big rocks under the shade trees when, suddenly, the air filled with screams and crying.

Everyone fell silent and rose to their feet. All eyes were on the open bedroom windows of the palace where the sound was coming from. The screaming now turned into long howls. There was no doubt it was Gusti Ratu Kencana. All soldiers bowed their head deeply.

A nobleman came running from inside the palace and approached the stupefied soldiers.

"Sultan Jarot passed away just now. You may leave," he said shortly.

Ngusman and his friends lingered around the palace, reluctant to go home. They were curious what had caused the sultan's death. Ngusman heard a nobleman ordering a soldier to ride to Tegalrejo to inform the sultan's elder brother, Prince Diponegoro II.

◦————•————◦

Meanwhile, Den Wahyana was preparing for his journey to Semarang via Magelang. Prince Diponegoro II of Puri Tegalrejo had sent him on a secret mission to meet with a British agent. England was building their new colony in Singapore, and Den Wahyana was to discuss possible cooperation from the British regarding the provision of ammunition and weapons in case Governor General van der Capellen ordered an attack on Tegalrejo.

Pangeran Diponegoro II was convinced that, sooner or later, the Keraton government would attack him. With the backing of the Dutch army, Patih Danureja was capable of doing anything he wanted.

Den Wahyana quickly prepared the weapons and horses he needed. He had not been able to sleep the previous night. He had spent all night thinking about the conversation he had with his son, Ganjar, who had come to visit him, unexpectedly, that afternoon.

Their short conversation had a deep impact on Den Wahyana.

"Mother doesn't know I'm here," Ganjar said, after Den Wahyana invited him to sit down.

"Next time, you need to get your mother's permission." Den Wahyana took a seat across from Ganjar on the bamboo mat.

"She wouldn't have allowed me to come here."

"Then, don't come."

Den Wahyana sent Ganjar a piercing look while the youth chose to rest his eyes on the small holes in the bamboo plait wall. Their respective loneliness filled the still air.

"I'm sorry, Father."

"Of course, I forgive you. Just don't do it again."

"It's not the first time I've run away from home. I don't like it there."

"Your behavior has brought me problems. Your mother once came after me because you had gone missing for days."

"Yes, I know—and I apologize for that. But today I need to see you, with or without permission."

Once again father and son locked eyes, silently.

"Yesterday, Dasamuka came to see Uncle Dibya," Ganjar paused then continued, "I overheard their conversation. He asked Uncle Dibya to kill you."

"Why are you telling me this?"

"I want you to be able to save yourself. Uncle Dibya and his friends plan to kill you, tomorrow."

"Apparently, you can't bear to see me die at the hand of your father and his friends."

"Uncle Dibya is *not* my father."

"Doesn't he love you like his own son? He also treats your mother well."

Ganjar became teary-eyed. He finally stammered, "I can't believe you're working for the Dutch now."

"I don't hate the Dutch people—I'm opposing their behavior. What they are currently doing to us is unbearable. You should know that hatred is not enough to support our struggle. We need ammunition and weapons. Remember, we can't fabricate such weapons yet. That's why I'm often seen around the Karesidenan."

The teenager rose. Tears burned behind his eyes, and he was unable to keep them from rolling down his cheeks. He brusquely turned and quickly walked out of the house.

From afar, Den Wahyana watched his only son mount his horse, then turn to glance at him before riding away.

Long after the dust of horse hooves had settled, Den Wahyana stood gazing down the quiet, empty road.

Even without Ganjar's information, Den Wahyana had prepared himself well. His intuition as a former soldier warned him to be alert. His knew his disagreement with Danar would have dangerous consequences. For his journey to Semarang, he had chosen to ride a horse over traveling in a carriage. He also had armed himself with knives and rifles.

The bright morning did not bring Den Wahyana relief. Ganjar was correct. He sensed something unusual in the air. The night before, he had not heard a single sound coming from the insects that usually buzzed around his yard. He was sure people were watching him from the thick bushes that surrounded his house.

At daybreak, Den Wahyana saddled his horse and left Tegalrejo, headed for Magelang. His uneasiness made him look back, occasionally. His intuition was correct. Soon, a group of men on horseback appeared behind him. After he made sure that they were indeed tailing him, Den Wahyana turned his horse into the jungle. The wooded trails would provide more protection than the straight, open road.

With a quick glance over his shoulder, he counted ten riders. If he did not try to bring down several of them now, he would definitely be killed.

Den Wahyana turned his horse into the middle of the thick bushes that surrounded a patch of grassland and positioned himself at a strategic corner. Soon his attackers passed by him. *Shameless robbers like these can only be dealt with by attacking them from behind.* And without further thought, he raised his loaded gun and shot them in the back.

He brought down three men without trouble. The remaining men ran frantically to save their lives and position themselves strategically.

Now, Den Wahyana could be attacked from any direction. He had to quickly decide between being mobbed and trying to flee from his hunters.

He spurred his horse and turned it back to the place where he had entered the forest. As soon as he emerged on the open road to Magelang, his hunters reemerged.

There were only seven of them now, but it seemed the loss of their comrades had agitated them. They raised their rifles and came galloping after him like a pack of wild beast being attacked.

Den Wahyana soon realized that his hunters' horses were mighty Persians, the best breed of all horses. He would be caught in no time. Not willing to be brought down like a boar, he made a quick turn back into the woods. Unlike the first time, he did not wait for his hunters. Instead he looped back.

His actions confused his pursuers. Some followed him into the jungle, others stayed behind. Den Wahyana's earlier successful attack had them leery.

Wanting to end his hunt, Den Wahyana jumped off his horse and walked away. He had decided to fight his hunters using his rifle while standing on his own two feet.

One of his followers, obviously lost, blundered into his range. Den Wahyana pulled the trigger and brought the man down.

However, Den Wahyana did not fool all of his hunters.

A shot in his right arm caused Den Wahyana to drop his rifle. Staggering, he tried to find his balance when a second shot shattered one of his ribs and sent him reeling to the ground.

His assailant released a gunshot in the air and was soon joined by other horsemen.

Some of them jumped out of their saddles, laughing and mocking Den Wahyana's helpless state. One of them crowed, "Hey, Wahyana! Start counting the minutes you've left to live."

When someone rode up so close he could have trampled him, Den Wahyana winced. Blinking, he saw Dibya towering over him.

Bent in his saddle, Dibya held the reins tight and spat, "You're nothing compared to Rangga, your damned master."

Someone in the group yelled, "Den Dibya, a gunshot to his head or chest is more than he deserves. It would be too easy a death." Another bent over Den Wahyana and hissed, "You killed four of our friends."

Dibya bellowed, "Tie both of his hands and feet to four horses. Let's see what he'll look like quartered."

Den Wahyana lay helpless in a puddle of his own blood as the men began to tie rope around his hands and feet. He tried not to imagine his body torn in four parts as the horses were spurred in different directions.

Den Wahyana began to lose consciousness when he suddenly heard gunshots, followed by screams. He heard horses whinny excitedly as, one by one, his attackers fell to the ground. In a short time, all six of Dasamuka's mercenaries lay lifeless around him.

"Shall we take Den Wahyana to Puri Tegalrejo, your highness?" he heard one of his rescuers ask.

"Go ahead. I will continue my journey to the palace. I just received news that my brother, the sultan, became ill during his excursion and passed away," Prince Diponegoro II replied. He then turned to a young boy who stood behind him and said, "Ganjar, find Branjang. Tell him to take good care of Den Mas Wahyana."

The lord of Puri Tegalrejo then went to gently rub Den Wahyana's pale forehead before mounting his horse. As he turned in the direction of the palace, the prince's eyes were filled with grief.

<hr />

I missed Den Wahyana. I hadn't seen much of him after we helped Danar and his bride escape. During the thirteen years of my stay on Java, I had always relied on him to answer any question that might come up regarding Javanese society and culture. Along with Semi and Ngusman, he disappeared around the time of the Sultan Jarot's passing.

Afraid that an affiliation with me would endanger them, I refrained from investigating Semi and Ngusman's whereabouts. However, I could not refrain from searching for Den Wahyana.

When I tried visiting him at his house in Tegalrejo, it turned out that he had moved.

Next, I went to see Branjang. Hopefully he knew where Den Wahyana had gone. When I asked Branjang if he knew where I could find Den Wahyana, however, he shook his head and apologized. He did not know.

"When was the last time you saw Den Wahyana?" I prodded.

Branjang stared at the floor and knitted his eyebrows as if trying hard to recall, then said, "It's been a while." He paused and looked into the distance as he ended, "I haven't seen him for more than a month, sir."

I felt that he was lying, but didn't want to burden him more and changed the subject. Hopefully, he wouldn't feel inhibited to share information regarding the situation in the Keraton government. There were rumors that the sultan's death had caused a chaotic situation, triggered by Gusti Ratu Kencana's concern about Prince Diponegoro II ascending as a king, because the next sultan, Hamengkubuwono IV's son, was still a toddler.

"By the way, what's happening now that the sultan has passed away?" I asked casually, rubbing my hands together. "Do you know who'll succeed him?"

"Next week, the coronation of Sultan Hamengkubuwono V will be performed." Branjang was obviously relieved I had dropped the subject of Den Wahyana. "He is the oldest son of Sultan Jarot and his consort. I heard this from some princes who often come to Tegalrejo, sir." Branjang paused a moment before adding proudly, "Pangeran Diponegoro II will be one of the guardians."

"Why will a toddler be installed as a king?" I did not understand how a three-year-old could be given such responsibility.

"It's just to make Gusti Ratu Kencana happy. She was terribly worried that Pangeran Diponegoro II would take her son's position as a king." Branjang's facial expression changed when he uttered the name of Prince Diponegoro II. It reminded me of the look on Den Wahyana's face when he spoke the name of Raden Rangga.

"And there is, of course, Patih Danureja, who will be appointed as the sultan's representative."

I chose not to respond to Branjang's observation. The subject was too sensitive.

What I gleaned from this conversation was that the tension in the political circles had increased significantly—due to Counselor Danureja tightening his grip on governing the sultanate, and the colonial government's anxiety regarding the possibility that Prince Diponegoro II would seize this opportunity to secure the throne for himself.

I never expected to be invited to the coronation of the Javanese king. Much to my surprise, however, our office received an invitation to attend the festivities. Considering Branjang's information, I concluded that the successor of Sultan Jarot would simply be the next puppet king.

I attended Sultan Hamengkubuwono V's coronation with my colleagues and Baron de Salis, the current Resident.

I really was not interested in the noblemen present at the coronation. Instead, I paid attention to the *lurahs*, the village heads, and abdi dalems, who sat solemnly, cross-legged, on mats that were laid out on the verandah, where they were seated due to their lower social status.

Still, they were the people I respected. I fully supported Governor van der Capellen's policy, which, in 1819, granted the lurahs a very important and powerful position as tax collectors.

I also respected the abdi dalem. These people were the real Javanese. They dedicated their lives to the palace, regardless of who the ruling king happened to be. Their devotion truly moved me.

The coronation of Sultan Hamengkubuwono V didn't impress me.

However, when I noticed the lurahs and abdi dalems anxiously stretching to catch a glimpse of the ceremony, I became curious. Seated among the Javanese nobility and Dutch government officials, I had no trouble seeing what they wanted to see.

The child sultan sat nervously on the throne, a large, ornately carved, high-backed armchair. Dressed in a black outfit heavily embroidered with gold thread and wearing a *kuluk*, a fez-like court headdress, the little boy looked lost. His short legs, dangling from the high chair, he kept touching his kuluk. The ornate pieces of gold jewelry made him look like a Christmas ornament.

His grandmother, Gusti Ratu Kencana, sat next to him. I noticed the Resident having a conversation with Counselor Danureja. There were many noblemen I didn't know. There were also several men wearing white turbans and tunics; they were most likely members of the Korps Suranatan, the Islamic clergymen of the Keraton. Compared to the coronations of the kings and queens of Europe, the Javanese coronation ceremony was quite simple. The most important person in this coronation was the Resident, for without his approval, the sultan would not have been able to ascend the throne.

I left the event with a nagging thought: The cheering and laughter came from those who would take advantage of the puppet king, and they were no other than Counselor Danureja and his cronies. For me, the best thing that happened during the event was that, toward the end of the evening, I spotted Den Wahyana among a group of other noblemen I had seen at Tegalrejo.

———•———

The appointment of Resident Smissaert, on February 10, 1823, gave Counselor Danureja and Colonel Wiranegara, another Dutch stooge, additional powers. The threesome were ready to destroy anyone who stood in their way of gaining more power and wealth, and they perceived Puri Tegalrejo as their biggest threat.

Various new taxes made the rift between the government of Yogyakarta and its people even wider. The only purpose for the new taxes was to fatten the wallets of the three conspirators and their accomplices. Sultan Hamengkubuwono V, who was still a toddler, was easily disregarded.

The situation became even more precarious when, on May 6, 1823, Governor General van der Capellen issued a decree stating that Javanese nobilities were no longer allowed to rent their land to foreign businessmen. The regulation had an adverse impact on the renters, as well as the landowners, as foreign businessmen were forced to leave the plantations they had run for years.

The Javanese land barons not only lost their main source of income, they were forced to return the rent that had been paid for the remainder of the lease term. The Javanese royalty, who were not used to working as hard as the Europeans or Chinese, were not suited to taking over plantation management chores.

Uncle Harvey was one of the businessmen greatly affected by the new rule. He was forced to return the plantation he had managed for years to Den Mas Suryanata, the owner.

———•——

Like we often did, Daisy and I enjoyed the balmy hours of the late afternoon on the verandah of Loji Rejawinangun with a tall glass of tea.

"So, Father's wish to retire in Edinburgh instead of Rejawinangun turned out for the best, after all," Daisy said between sips.

"Do you also want to go home?" I asked curiously.

"I actually have grown to feel at home here; the workers are like family to me. I feel grounded in my work here at the plantations, as well as in Buitenzorg with Dr. Reinwardt. I would like to stay and be buried here when I die someday," Daisy said pensively.

Her gaze roamed across the yard, then she sighed, "But how will I be able to live here without Father and the plantation?"

"I can ask the Resident's permission to let us stay in my office housing." I threw her a scrutinizing look. I was touched by her wish to die and be buried on the island of Java; I had similar feelings.

"But… what will people say?" Daisy hung her head.

I found the courage to reach for her hand as it lay on the arm of the chair, and she let me hold it in mine.

A tear fell on my hand as she whispered, "Tell me about Ailsa."

Her words caught me off guard, and my grip on her hand tightened.

Daisy pulled her hand back.

I hurriedly let go. Perhaps, I had unintentionally hurt her.

"There's nothing to tell," I said after I had gathered myself. "I've erased her from my mind, along with her treacherous deed." I took a deep breath. The reality of it rushed through me like a warm stream: I really had let her go. Suddenly, I felt relieved, light. I rose and reached for Daisy's hand again.

"You're not a replacement for her. She's been gone for a long time," I explained.

"I'll never be able to replace her, anyway. She's a lady sheltered by the roofs of universities. I'm just a farmer's daughter who lives among the bushes on the island of Java."

"I can continue to write for the *London Times,* and Mr. Crawfurd is trying to get me a position in which I'll work directly under the Governor General, instead of the Resident, whose behavior is too absurd to understand."

A spotted dove tripped among the jasmine shrubs, busily pecking the ground. Its lively movements chased away the last tension between us.

"Daisy...."

"Yes, Willem?"

"Will you marry me?"

With a quick tug, Daisy pulled her hand out of mine and walked away with decisive, long steps.

"Daisy!" I called after her, without avail.

From the way Daisy walked, I concluded that I had upset her. Driven by an urgency that bordered on panic, I ran after her. One thought reverberated in every step I took: *I can't lose her now.*

Daisy headed for her favorite part of the garden, a large grouping of hibiscus.

I caught up with her and watched as she stood between the shrubs, quietly fingering some of the flaming red flowers.

As usual, she greeted her flowers warmly.

"Hello, my dear hibiscus. I need your opinion." Daisy cocked her head as if she were listening.

The flowers did not respond.

"All right, all right, you told me to ask Willem again to tell me what he feels." Daisy nodded, and her hibiscus nodded along in the light breeze.

"All right, Willem, now tell me about Ailsa." Daisy turned around to face me.

"Didn't I tell you that...." I stammered, leaning against a wooden rack that held various flowering plants.

"You didn't." Daisy interrupted curtly and continued, "If you can't talk about her, then just answer my questions with a 'yes' or 'no.' Okay?"

I was speechless and could only look at her blank face. Her cold expression seemed to hide the thoughts tumbling inside her mind.

"Ailsa talked to you before she decided to marry your father, didn't she?"

"Yes, she did."

"Ailsa was more attracted to your father because you, Willem, are not as handsome as your father, right?"

I didn't respond.

"Every woman has the right to marry the man of her own choice. Now, please listen to me. This is the way I see it.

"Ailsa's decision to leave you doesn't make her a bad woman.

"Your father's decision to marry his own future daughter-in-law doesn't make him a lecherous man.

"You're the master here—the master of your own thoughts; you're the only one who can determine the extent of your misery."

"Please don't judge me, Daisy," I could no longer keep quiet. Daisy had gone too far.

"All right then, if you think that I'm wrong, you have to tell me why you think Ailsa had the heart to leave you, and why your father ended up marrying your fiancée," Daisy retorted.

I was unable to respond. My mouth twitched and my lips quivered, but I remained silent.

Apparently, Daisy wanted to break the growing tension between us. She turned to the hibiscus shrub on her right and said, "He can't answer me. Why do you think Ailsa chose Jeremias over Willem, dear hibiscus?"

The plant responded with a rustle of the leaves in the late afternoon breeze.

"Willem, you've heard what my hibiscus said, haven't you?"

"Yes," I smiled. Grateful for the out she gave me, I was ready to play along.

"Then tell me, what did the hibiscus say?" Daisy threw me a piercing look.

"It said that fate had Ailsa help me decide to go to the island of Java because she wanted me to meet another…," I paused.

Daisy stood looking at me. Her fine eyebrows began to pull together into the beginning of a frown. Questions, almost disbelief, began to replace the sharp look in her eyes.

I suddenly saw how frail she was, despite her sturdy frame. Looking her straight in the eyes, I ended, "a beautiful girl named Daisy Thomson."

For a moment, Daisy stiffened. She gave me a quick once-over, then burst out laughing.

She continued to laugh until tears started rolling down her cheeks, and I was not sure whether she was laughing or actually crying. At times, it was indeed difficult to determine whether tears were shed for joy or sadness.

———•———

We had a very small wedding—there was not even a reception. Yet, the short, solemn ceremony, during which Daisy and I exchanged marriage vows and our union was legalized by the law of our country, was the most meaningful experience I've had in all my life. I was sure it would remain such for all my days to come.

Baron de Salis, the current Resident, officiated the wedding on February 2, 1823. Uncle Harvey and Den Wahyana served as witnesses.

Daisy wore a corsage of red and white hibiscus on her simple linen dress. A fragrant tiara of jasmine crowned her auburn hair, which the sun had tinted with golden highlights. Her hand trembled when I slipped the wide gold band on her ring finger.

The small crowd around us cheered as I took Daisy in my arms and, for a very short but intense moment, we became an island. Overcome by an innate desire, I bent to kiss her, whispering hoarsely, "I want to take care of you. Please let me. I love you."

When Daisy looked up at me, her hazel eyes brimmed with tears.

———•———

During the months following Governor General van der Capellen's cancellation of all land lease agreements between Javanese landowners and foreigners, Uncle Harvey was mostly occupied with preparing the forms required to claim the rent money he was now owed. It took the remainder of the year to accomplish this task.

We had decided to live in my office housing at the Karesidenan, as I still worked for the government, and Daisy would still assist Dr. Reinwardt. Uncle Harvey, who no longer had an official job, spent most of his time reading periodicals on my verandah.

One afternoon, when I came home from work, he greeted me with an observation. "To be honest, I don't agree with the way you describe bronjong in your article." Uncle Harvey had apparently come across a journal that had published my writing.

"I'm sorry. The article just reflects my opinion, which is backed by valid arguments. I apologize if I wrote something that offended you." I didn't feel like engaging in a conversation about the bronjong. To me, it was no longer an important subject.

"It's not about what's right or wrong. It's about the pros and cons. Everyone is entitled to their own opinion, Willem. You don't need to apologize." Uncle Harvey's thick eyebrows furrowed, a sign that I should listen to an opinion that might contradict my own.

"Which part of the article do you disagree with?"

"You stated here that the people in Asia and Africa are facing the bronjong threat from their kings. This is not true for all of them. Perhaps the Siamese are a good example. Their kings are good rulers. Colonization is the last choice as a form of human civilization," Uncle Harvey said, while leafing through a journal published by the Edinburgh Club.

I stayed quiet. I could not be bothered to think about such matters these days. I was too occupied with concerns for my friends in Tegalrejo, who were dealing with conflict between Patih Danureja and Prince Diponegoro II regarding colonial meddling in Keraton affairs, as well as the indifference of Javanese royalty toward the common people.

—•—

"Willem, how will we continue to live here, now that we don't have Rejawinangun anymore?" Daisy asked during our walk after dinner. She kicked at a few small stones on the path that meandered through the Karesidenan compound.

I knew she missed Rejawinangun in many ways. Most of all, she missed her daily intimate exchange with the hibiscus grove she had created and raised from seedlings. I wished I could give her a plot of soil that she could call her own to start a new garden. However, considering the current political climate, chances for that to happen were less than slim.

"One of the reasons we wanted to live here was the plantation. What are we going to do now that's all gone?"

The sadness in Daisy's voice cut straight through me. My attachments to Java were different than Daisy's. I had come for my own reasons; she had come in tow of her father. Still, I shared her anxiety and pain over a loss that was similar, yet different.

Lately, I too, had often been haunted by the question, *What's next?*

I looked at the lush greenery around me. For a moment, I tried to transport myself to a warm summer day in Edinburgh. The thought only filled me with an urgent need to somehow make things right.

I want to take care of you. Please let me. I love you.

With all my heart, I wanted to keep my word to Daisy.

I took her hand. "Yes, you're right. We don't have a good reason to stay here anymore. And I just realized that I've been away from Edinburgh for thirteen years."

"Are you saying that you no longer want to live here, you'd rather go back to Scotland?" Daisy asked with a small voice. She raised her head when a turtledove cooed from a branch of the golden rain tree next to the Karesidenan building.

"It's not like that...." I groped for words and finally said, "I just sense that we're headed for political chaos."

Both of us went silent for quite some time.

"What do you think is going to happen in this sultanate?" Daisy asked in a quiet voice.

"A great war is about to break out." I was surprised at the weight of my words in the balmy air. Someone in the neighborhood sang a Javanese love song. I suddenly thought of the story Den Wahyana told me about Ki Sena serenading Den Ayu Ningsih in a cool spring under a full moon. And through it all, my words seem to echo like a prophecy, "A great war is about to break out."

———•——

On the morning of March 6, 1824, three months after Uncle Harvey received the payoff for the remainder of his lease on Den Suryanata's land, Uncle Harvey, Daisy, and I stood on a dock of the Semarang harbor waiting for our ship to take us to Batavia, en route to Scotland.

I kept checking my pocket watch. A week ago, during our last meeting, Den Wahyana had promised to meet me here, around this time.

"Perhaps your friend forgot his promise." Uncle Harvey, who was now also my father-in-law, appeared impatient.

"He wouldn't," I answered curtly. The friendship that had developed between us over the years was not the only reason Den Wahyana planned to see me off.

Lately, the discussions during the weekly meetings at Tegalrejo skirted around the possibility of soliciting British support in terms of ammunition and weapons in the event that the plans to revolt against the Dutch and Keraton oppression materialized. I had been invited to some of the meetings.

I was supposed to stay in Singapore for a couple of months, before returning to Europe, to set everything up. If Den Wahyana failed to appear today, it might mean that he did not need me anymore. Or, more precisely, Puri Tegalrejo did not need me. If that was the case, I was no longer needed in Singapore.

"Is that Den Wahyana?" My father-in-law pointed to a man who was scurrying in our direction.

The man walked differently than Den Wahyana, and I could not make out his face with the distance between us. "No, he isn't," I said, then noticed the man's attire. "Perhaps he's a messenger from Puri Tegalrejo."

When the man came closer, I immediately recognized him. "Branjang! You look very different in these clothes." I quickly walked toward him holding out my hand. "I didn't recognize you at first."

Dressed like a kiai from a pesantren, Branjang smiled sheepishly. "Den Wahyana sent me to give you this letter." Branjang handed me an envelope, then stepped back and waited patiently for me to finish reading.

I read the letter a couple of times. It was definitely Den Wahyana's handwriting, but I wondered about the contents. He wrote that most of the members of the Tegalrejo group had decided to prepare for a religious war. Thus, he could do nothing else but go along.

He also wrote that a religious war, according to Pangeran Diponegoro II, would advocate that religious rules prevail over any other, and was supported by most of the Islamic religious teachers in both the Yogyakarta and Surakarta sultanates. Therefore, they did not need any help from the British.

I gave Branjang another once-over. Instead of his surjan shirt, he now wore a tunic. His head was no longer covered with a *destar,* he now wore a turban. The change was a reference to the shift in strategy Puri Tegalrejo had taken, according to what Den Wahyana wrote in this letter.

While I understood that the spirit of *jihad* was important to the Javanese, I also knew that all holy wars, in the end, were fought with more practical means than a mere belief in a deity and religious rituals. Gunpowder, weapons, and funds were essential to ensure the success of the Javanese people's fight against Resident Smissaert and his accomplices. I really had wanted to discuss this further with Den Wahyana.

As if reading my mind, Branjang said, "Den Wahyana sends his apologies for not being able to meet you today, sir."

"It's fine. Is Den Wahyana now also wearing a tunic and a turban?" I asked.

"No, sir. He's still wearing his destar and surjan, like before." Branjang seemed reluctant to talk about Den Wahyana. He quickly added, "We're preparing ourselves to enter the bronjong to fight against the tiger. That's why we're dressing in clothes similar to the ones Kiai Kasan wore when he killed the tiger."

"The bronjong punishment has been eradicated. Who would now pit you against a tiger?"

"The Sultanate of Yogyakarta has now turned into a bronjong. Resident Smissaert is the tiger ready to sink his claws into our skulls."

We went silent for a while. I was trying to digest his explanation, but Branjang seemed to take my silence as a sign that he should not burden me with further questions. He fidgeted with the tip of his tunic and asked to be excused.

We could not stay too much longer at the harbor. I extended my hand and said, "Please give my regards to Pangeran Diponegoro II and Den Wahyana, of course."

I watched Branjang walk away and kept my eyes on his back as he gradually disappeared into the crowd. Den Wahyana's message was clear.

I turned and adjusted my hat to keep the midday sun out of my eyes.

If the Tegalrejo group had accepted the British offer to provide them with the needed arms in their war against the Dutch and the Keraton, and Prince Diponegoro II had managed to win, this son of Hamengkubuwono III and one of his concubines would have become the next Sultan of Yogyakarta. If the power struggle could have played out that way, the British would still have a strong foothold on the island of Java without the necessity to treat it as a colony.

It was evident that the Tegalrejo group would not only have to fight the Dutch, but also the Javanese who felt more at ease under the Dutch protection, for which they would have to pay dearly. The thought that Prince Diponegoro II might meet the same fate as Raden Rangga was devastating. The way this was playing out, I felt that my relationship with the island of Java and the Javanese people had already been severed, and I regretted that.

I took one last look at the bustling harbor. Branjang had faded into the crowd. During the years I spent here, I had tried to understand these people and had given my all to impart the Western way of rational thinking to them. Suddenly, an image of Kiai Kasan flitted through my mind. *Narima.*

I slowly turned around and stood for a while looking at the ocean liner I would soon board. Then I scanned the crowd for Daisy and Uncle Harvey. I waved at them, indicating I was to rejoin them. While walking to the waiting ship, I said, "I want to return to Edinburgh as soon as possible, together." I no longer needed to make a stop in Singapore before heading home to Scotland.

> ⊢——•——⊣

EPILOGUE

On July 20, 1825, less than two years after Willem's return to Edinburgh, an uprising led by Prince Diponegoro II erupted. The five-year war, referred to in history as the Diponegoro War—*Perang Jawa* in Indonesian, *Java Oorlog* in Dutch—ended with the capture of Prince Diponegoro II by the Dutch. The battle caused the death of eight thousand Dutch soldiers, seven thousand mercenaries recruited by the Dutch, and two hundred thousand followers of Prince Diponegoro II. The war cost the Dutch government twenty million gulden and reduced the population of Yogyakarta by half.

—•—

NOTES

Chapter 1

Bronjong: In this story a large cage used to execute capital punishment in the form of forcing a human to fight against a wild animal.
Branjangan: A Javanese songbird.
Loji: Traditional western mansion.
Keraton: Javanese royal palace and government.
Puri: Javanese castle.
Gubug: A hovel: usually with a dirt floor, straw roof, and walls made out of woven bamboo mats.
Raden or Den: Used to refer to or address both royal men and women.
Raden Ayu: Used to refer or address married royal women.
Ayu: Javanese for beautiful.
Raden Mas: Used to refer or address royal men.
Mas: Abbreviation of emas, meaning gold.

Chapter 2

Europesche ambtenaar: Western civil service official.
Krama: second most polite form of Javanese language.
Gusti Allah: Javanese for Almighty God.
Jagabaya: A marshal at the court of a sultanate.
Abdi dalam: A member of the royal household staff.
Kris: A double-edged dagger.
Jarit: Batik cloth worn by men and women like a long skirt.
Kakek panembahan: Holy man.
Macapat: Love song
Trucukan: A yellow-vented bulbul.

Chapter 3

Garengpung: A cicada; a amall insect known to make a loud buzzing sound.
Kang: Used to informally address a male.

Chapter 4

Surjan: Traditional Javanese clothing for men.
Kula nuwun, ndara Tuan: Javanese for: Please, excuse me, sir.
Narima ing pandum: Accept what God gives us.
Degan: Young coconut water.

Chapter 5

Karesidenan: Colonial government offices and housing complex.
Pesantren: Islamic boarding school.
Khusnul khotimah: A good ending as a result of doing the right thing.
Hidayah: An enlightenment from God.

Tumpes kelor: An act of revenge that kills the entire family and descendants of the targeted individual.
Lelananging jagat: The Javanese version of the ideal male.
Nawangwulan: A well-known beauty in Javanese folklore.
Inlander: Dutch term for "native."

Chapter 6

Adem-ayem-tentrem: Coolly, blissfully and tranquilly. A term to describe a Javanese way of life.
Urip mung mampir ngombe: A Javanese expression meaning this life is only temporarily.
Ambin: A bamboo cot lined with a woven pandan mat.
Raksasa: A demon with sharp fangs and claw-like fingernails.
Pelupuh: Split and flattened bamboo.
Pisang raja: A certain variety of banana.
Joglo: The biggest building of a traditional Javanese housing complex.
Malima: The five bad habits known to the Javanese as: *main* (gambling), *mabok* (getting drunk), *madon* (prostitution), *madat* (taking drugs), and *maling* (stealing).
Atur pambagya: Welcoming speech by the host of a party.
Nagasari: Indonesian dessert made from a steamed banana, rice flour, and coconut milk.

Chapter 7

Kaputren: Women's quarters of the royal palace.
Kakang: A female's endearing address of a male.

Chapter 8

Gambang: A xylophone-like instrument.
Mbok emban: Handmaid for female royalty.
Kerokan: A traditional healing method of scraping the skin using a coin and oil.
Jamu sari rapat: A potion of various herbs drunk by women to strengthen their reproductive system.

Chapter 9

Mangga, pinarak: Please come in.
Diajeng: A male's endearing address of a female.
Tikar: A woven mat of pandan leaves.
Tampah: A big platter made from woven bamboo.

Chapter 10

Wong durjana: Javanese term for outlaws.
Wong Ayu: Javanese endearing address of a woman such as: Pretty, Beautiful, Sugar.
Lurah: Village chief.
Destar: Traditional Javanese headgear for males.
Jihad: A war undertaken as a sacred, religious duty by Muslims.

ABOUT THE AUTHOR

Junaedi Setiyono was born in Kebumen, Central Java, on December 16, 1965. He has taught in the English Language Education Department of his alma mater, the Muhammadiyah University in Purworejo, Central Java, since 1997.

Setiyono is drawn to historical fiction related to the Java War (1825-1830). His first novel, *Glonggong*, published by Serambi in 2007, won the 2006 Jakarta Arts Council Novel Writing Competition and was one of the finalists of the 2008 Khatulistiwa Literary Award. His second novel, *Arumdalu* (Serambi, 2010), was nominated for the 2010 Khatulistiwa Literary Award. In 2010, the manuscript of his third novel, *Dasamuka*, won the Jakarta Arts Council Novel Writing Competition and was published by Penerbit Ombak in 2017. Setiyono was also awarded a scholarship from Ohio State University as part of his doctorate degree in language education, which he received in 2016 from the Semarang State University.

Setiyono's love for writing originates with the Javanese folk stories his mother told him when he was growing up. Through his writing, Setiyono hopes to share his belief that man should not be separated by ethnic, religious, racial, or intergroup relations.

He also believes that literature can unite human beings around the world.

Aside from working on his next historical novel, which is set in a Javanese kingdom in the twelfth century, Setiyono is currently doing research on how English teaching can be a catalyst to promote Indonesian teaching in Indonesia.

Setiyono lives with his wife, Sari Wahyuni, and his children, Martin Nuh Hanan and Maryam Mufidah, in Purworejo, Central Java. He can be contacted via his email address: junaedi.setiyono@yahoo.co.id

ABOUT THE TRANSLATOR

Maya Denisa Saputra was born on July 30, 1990 in Denpasar, the capital of Bali, and grew up on Indonesia's "island of the gods." She left briefly to finish her education, a bachelor's degree in Accounting and Finance from the UK-based University of Bradford in Singapore. While holding a position in the accounting department of a family business, she pursues her interests in writing, literary translation, and photography.

Maya's writings and translation work have appeared in the Buddhist Fellowship Singapore's newsletter, "Connection," an online platform that gathers writings about physical and mental wellness, "B.Philosophy," and "LitSync," online communities of aspiring fiction writers, and "Intersastra," a literary translation initiative.

She can be reached at: maya.saputra@gmail.com

MORE STORYTELLERS FROM DALANG PUBLISHING

Only a Girl
Lian Gouw

Three generations of Chinese women struggle for identity against the political backdrop of the World Depression, World War II, and the Indonesian Revolution. Nanna, the matriarch of the family, strives to preserve the family's traditional Chinese values while her children are eager to assimilate into Dutch colonial society. Carolien, Nanna's youngest daughter, is fixated on the advantages to be gained by adopting a western lifestyle. But when she raises her own daughter Jenny by colonial standards, it puts the girl at a disadvantage in new, independent Indonesia, where Dutch culture is no longer revered. The unique ways in which Nanna, Carolien, and Jenny face their own challenges reveal the complexity of Chinese society in Indonesia between 1930 and 1952.

Price: $17.95
Paperback: 298 pages
ISBN: 978-0-9836273-7-1

My Name is Mata Hari
Remy Sylado
Translated from the Indonesian by Dewi Anggraeni

My Name is Mata Hari tells the story of Margaretha Geertruida Zelle, a young Dutch woman married to an older military officer assigned to the Dutch East Indies. Claiming her mother's Javanese ancestry, she changed her name to Mata Hari, Malay for "eye of the day."

As Mata Hari, she danced on stages across Europe and the Middle East, and took many high-ranking military and government officials as her lovers. Convicted of espionage during World War I, she said at the end of her tumultuous life, "I am a genuine courtesan. And I am a dancer in the true sense."

Price: $17.95
Paperback: 342 pages
ISBN: 978-0-9836273-0-2

Potions and Paper Cranes
Lan Fang
Translated from the Indonesian by Elisabet Titik Murtisari

In Lan Fang's award-winning novel, Sulis is a young woman selling potions in Surabaya's harbor district. She meets Sujono, a day laborer with dreams of becoming a freedom fighter, and whose passion for Matsumi, a geisha called to Java by a Japanese general, is destined to ruin all of them. Each tells the story of their lives during the Japanese occupation of Java and Indonesia's transition from a Dutch colony to an independent republic.

Price: $17.95
Paperback: 252 pages
ISBN: 978-0-9836273-3-3

Kei
Erni Aladjai
Translated from the Indonesian by Nurhayat Indriyatno Mohamed

At the end of Suharto's New Order, the Kei people hold on to their traditions as they flee the violence that divides Muslim from Christian and destroys the villages. Namira, a Muslim girl, works as a volunteer in a refugee camp when she meets Sala, a young Protestant man. Grounded in the islander's belief of "We drink from the same spring and eat from the same land, the land of Kei," the two fall in love amid the chaos that will soon separate them.

Price: $17.95
Paperback: 228 pages
ISBN: 978-0-9836273-6-4

Daughters of Papua
Anindita Siswanto Thayf
Translated from the Indonesian by Stefanny Irawan

Seven-year-old Leksi lives in modern-day Papua with her grandmother Mabel and her mother, Mace. Her companions are Pum, an old dog of unknown ancestry, and Kwee, a pig. Together they look back at the past, as they face an uncertain future. In *Daughters of Papua,* the present is marked by a contentious election, with the gold company that wants to rob Papuans of their heritage the only winner.

Price: $17.95
Paperback: 204 pages
ISBN: 978-0-9836273-9-5

The Red Bekisar
Ahmad Tohari
Translated from the Indonesian by Nurhayat Indriyatno Mohamed

The *bekisar* is a fine crossbreed between jungle fowl and domestic chicken that adorns the houses of the wealthy. Lasi, whose father was a Japanese soldier, fair skinned and beautiful, is such an acquisition for a rich man in Jakarta. She is born in a village where the main source of income is tapping coconut palms for their rich sap, or nira. Her life takes an unexpected turn when she is betrayed by her husband and flees to Jakarta. She meets Mrs. Lanting, procuress of companions for men in high government and social circles, who sells her to the rich Handarbeni. Lasi enjoys her new splendor as a much-desired ornament, but is alarmed when she discovers the marriage is a sham. When she reconnects with Kanjat, a childhood friend now grown into a man, Lasi and Kanjat rediscover their affection for each other. Their bond is the village, its people and traditions. Together they struggle to free Lasi from a net of power, corruption, and deceit.

Price: $17.95
Paperback: 294 pages
ISBN: 978-0-9836273-2-6

Love, Death and Revolution
Mochtar Lubis
Translated from the Indonesian by Stefanny Irawan

During the early days of their nation's revolution, Indonesians were driven by passion and built a future on dreams. In a world still reeling from World War II, Major Sadeli of the Indonesian Army Intelligence travels to Singapore tasked with establishing naval and air routes to Sumatra and Java as well as securing weapons and radio equipment vital to the revolution. His desire for Indonesia to be prosperously independent, and independently prosperous, forces him to choose between personal happiness and commitment to a higher cause.

Price: $17.95
Paperback: 324 pages
ISBN: 978-0-9836273-5-7

DASAMUKA

Cloves for Kolosia
Hanna Rambe
Translated from the Indonesian by Miagina Amal

Elderly widower Gamati swears to save his family line from extinction when he and his family fall victim to the infamous plunder expeditions of the VOC, the Dutch East India Company. To escape the colonialists' cruelties, he leads his orphaned grandchildren and a small group of fellow villagers to the safety of another, more remote, island north of their current location. The birth of his great-grandson Kolosia during the voyage assures Gamati of his family's ability to sail the Moluccan seas freely for generations to come.

Price: $17.95
Paperback: 350 pages
ISBN: 978-0-9836273-8-8

Blood Moon Over Aceh
Arafat Nur
Translated from the Indonesian by Maya Denisa Saputra

The story is set between 1989 and 2002 in Alue Rambe, an isolated agricultural village south of Lhokseumawe City, in Aceh, Indonesia. Born in 1976, into a farmer's family, Nazir's life becomes a part of Aceh's dark, rebellious history that recounts the injustice the Soeharto government imposed on the Acehnese.

Price: $17.95
Paperback: 354 pages
ISBN: 978-0-9836273-4-0

Junaedi Setiyono

Panji's Quest
Junaedi Setiyono
Translated from the Indonesian by Oni Suryaman

Panji's Quest is a love story set before the reign of King Kameswara of Kadiri
(r. 1135–1185). It is a part of the only original Indonesian stories that have
been widely disseminated for centuries and were later combined into the
Panji Tales. On October 30, 2017, UNESCO included The Tale of Panji in
their "Memory of The World" documentary series.

Price: $17.95
Paperback: 300 pages
ISBN: 978-1-7357210-1-9